Born in 1927 and l_____
countryside in whic_____
A. R. Lloyd later se_____
still using horses and _____
and writing about ar_____
of widely acclaimed _____ history and biography,
he is perhaps best known to countless eager readers for
his popular wildlife stories, among them the trilogy of
country fantasies 'The Kine Saga', and his more
traditional animal novels. Each is not only grippingly
entertaining but a celebration of place and nature. As one
critic wrote of *The Last Otter*, 'Lloyd's compassionate,
memorably lyrical prose evokes the primeval beauty of
terrain and the wonder of every creature found there.'

A. R. LLOYD

Wingfoot

Grafton
An Imprint of HarperCollinsPublishers

Grafton
An Imprint of HarperCollins*Publishers*
77–85 Fulham Palace Road,
Hammersmith, London W6 8JB

A Grafton Original 1993
1 3 5 7 9 8 6 4 2

Copyright © A. R. Lloyd 1993

The Author asserts the moral right to
be identified as the author of this work

A catalogue record for this book is
available from the British Library

ISBN 0 586 21146 2

Set in Sabon

Printed in Great Britain by
HarperCollinsManufacturing Glasgow

CONTENTS

PART ONE

Storm-calf

Autumn, 1950

It rained all day, into night. The rain had swept from the
south, from Donegal and beyond, to the Western Isles of
Scotland. Here, it pock-marked the waves and seethed
on skerries and beaches, the downpour torrential. So
intense was the storm that it removed stones from cliffs
and, in the landslides that followed, the startled sea birds
fled damply.

It rained a black, teeming deluge. So had it rained in
the beginning, when first the earth became cool, its thick
vapours condensing; when first the seas started forming.
Then, the isles had been peaks, the tops of straggling
mountains. Now, like whales in the murk, their humped
backs bore the lashing.

As the rain scoured the cove, the seal hauled from the
surf and flopped onto wet pebbles. Ripe with calf, she
was large, close on eight feet in length, and of the long-
faced grey species. She lay quite still for a while, the
breakers crashing behind her, sluicing seaweed and rocks,
hammering on the shingle. Then she started to blow and
her back arched in labour.

Shadowy, the seal rocked, her contractions spasmodic.
Before much longer, they quickened. There was a low,

keening moan and, where her own tail was dark, appeared a luminous contrast, a little swag of hind-flippers and then a silvery body. Before the next wave could break, the cow had rolled to one side, the thin bonding cord snapped, her new calf on the pebbles. To rinse off blood and placenta, the cow vanished seawards.

Alone, the infant seal twitched. Wind and rain drubbed the cove, and the tide was advancing – as had the first tides advanced, implacably drowning land, extending seas and the oceans. In a hole on the cliffs, a sleepless gull eyed the violence. There would be food from the storm; seal-calves battered and swamped, to be picked in the morning. A frothing breaker surged up, rattled back, and more followed.

Soon, the calf was engulfed. The next rush swung it round; the next left the mite limp. Then the undertow dragged it. There was the ghost of a bleat, short and pitifully feeble. The sound was snuffed by the sea but the bathing cow heard it. Cleansed, she sprang from the dark, splashing back to her newborn.

By now the black waves were high, thundering on the strand, and she nudged her babe landwards. As the rollers creamed in, she gathered it to her breast, her broad flippers protective. Slowly, through the cascade, the adult inched up the beach, her charge soggy but sheltered. It was a perilous trip, for every breaker was huge, pounding in like a train, and the undertow vicious. For half an hour the cow toiled, nudging, slithering, pausing. At last she came to the *mul*, the ridge of stones at high water, the danger transcended.

For a moment she rested, then examined her bundle. It was a sad apparition, soused by storm and womb-fluid, its soft white hair squashed and stained, chivvied

4

as the rain beat it. It had bemused, half-closed eyes and slack skin, its trunk straggly and poor, making the head look too large, as seemed the leglike fore-flippers. In the downpour it cowered and a thin mew came from it.

The sheeting gloom wrapped the crags, drenched sheer rocks, drubbed their faces. Water spumed from their clefts and fled the combers as spindrift. The cow seal 'hoooed' to her calf, a deep and comforting sound, then, stretching out on a flank, quietly suckled the infant.

The seagull screamed, wheeling high. It had the eye of a shark, one leg maimed, the foot gone from the tarsus. Again, the gull screamed and turned. The storm had passed to the north and in a grey but calm dawn the sea's swell was subsiding. The gull could see all the island. It could make out the small port, its stone pier and bleak buildings, the few miles of *machair*, or heathery shell-sand, with crofts in its hummocks.

There were strands and wild dunes; and to the west a steep drop, a grim bulwark of basalt. On that side lay the ocean, a dull immensity of waves. Their pulsing quarter-mile crests, mast-high over the troughs, rolled in clear from Newfoundland. Eastward stretched lesser waters, the mainland forty miles off – Oban and Argyll – several islands much closer.

Beneath the gull shone the cove. It nicked the heel of the isle, precipitous on one flank, a crumbling path down the other. By now the tide had gone out and seaweed littered the beach, the sand glistening and wrinkled. The bird could see the new calf – in fact, by daylight, the calves, for many seals filled the cove and many cows tended nurslings. A few lay up on the *mul* but most were down on the sand, some at rest in the shallows.

Beadily, the bird peered. More seals had flopped on the rocks which, straggling out from the cliff, formed small plateaux and shelves interspersed with sea channels. In these, and dotting the bay, bobbed a fleet of slick faces. The seagull swooped, joining others. Seals were huffing and grunting, youngsters hungrily bleating. There was a pungent fish odour. The breeding haul-out brought smells and many gulls were attracted.

One by one, they slid down, skimmed the herding sea mammals. It was an awesome assembly: massive bulls ten feet long, chubby calves fat on milk, pinnipeds of all sizes; old seals, seals in their prime, docile, fretful, aggressive. Those still damp were slate-grey – the grey that gave them their name – but those dried out had soft colours, some sandy, some blue, others mottled and speckled.

Seals were suckling their young, looking on or just snoozing. Several scratched or gave yawns, youngsters playing and squabbling. Every now and again, one would waggle a flipper.

The storm-calf opened her eyes. They filled at once with the dawn, her first sensation of light, snapping shut straight away. When next the calf took a peep, a beady iris stared back, black and circled with yellow. The gull was perched on one foot, its depleted leg dangling. It did not waste any time. The infant's gape was enough, for it held several small teeth already there at her birth, and the bird flew off screeching.

Soon the calf fed again. Every three hours she sucked, her sleek mother obliging. So full of fat was the milk, at least two-thirds of it solids, that the nursling quickly gained weight, almost visibly swelling. And in between meals she slept, as relaxed as a puppy. Her fur had dried like white silk; her soft snout was long-whiskered.

She slept the sleep of the gorged, oblivious of creation, undisturbed by the herd, by the sun when it shone, by the teeming sand-hoppers. Now and then, she would blink, focusing on near objects, a pearly shell, a smooth stone. She nosed the spine of a fish, sharp and bleached in the sun, and the skeleton pricked her. Her little world had its smells – the cow's smell, salty tangs – and its lays, the wind's soughing.

The cow kept guard at the start but later on would slope off, splashing in for a swim, hiking back when demanded. Once when she was away a shadow fell on the *mul* and a great bull humped forward, ugly scars on his neck and a nose torn in battle. The sight did not please the calf and she wailed for her mother.

'Augh.' The cow came at once. 'Augh,' she spat at the male and, by showing her fangs, left him no room to doubt that his call was too early.

Later, things would be different, the female receptive, but meanwhile life went its way, with milk and sleep between tides, a lethargic calf fattening. Within three weeks of her birth she had trebled in weight, her thirty pounds up to ninety. She was beginning to moult, to lose her first velvet coat; she had grown pudgy, a barrel.

And now the cow became tense, her gaze wandering seawards. As lactation tailed off, her oestrus impending, she felt the conflict of instincts, those of motherly care and a quickening libido. At last, one evening at dusk, glancing back with reluctance, she slipped away to the swell and joined the battle-scarred male where the skerries formed channels. For a time the pair sparred, darkening shapes in the flow, then with scarcely a swirl sank from vision united.

That night the little seal cried.

Copious, her tears streamed, pouring out of large eyes as young seals weep when fraught, flooding down her round face. They were no make-do for milk nor did bawling bring comfort. When morning came the calf whined. Alone, she crawled down the beach, but the sea drove her back, for she was still awed by waves – waves which prowled and then pounced; waves which, stalking her birth, had once attempted to drown her.

'Maa-aaa,' she wailed, the gulls screaming.

Now the wild flowers are gone – the kingcups, ragged robin – and the songbirds are silent, just the ringed plovers feeding, making short darting runs. Oh well, pondered the girl, summer can't last for ever, the seals must leave on their travels. But not just yet – not just yet. She set the bike at the path, speeding downwards, freewheeling.

It was a heavy machine of the type used for errands. It dwarfed her slight, sweatered form, and the hair flying from it; made the brown legs look spindly. She squeezed the brakes as she reached the croft and left the bike on its stand, the groceries in its pannier.

She could make out the old man. He was scraping his boat, its hull dry on the shingle, and metal squeaked against wood. Round the bay the seals sang as she set off towards them. There was no hurry for him, his rotting boat would go nowhere, it was not fit for the bight let alone for seal travels, to wind the isles of the epics, plough the seas of the heroes.

Those were the haunts of *her* people, the flippered folk of the sea. She liked to think of them that way, with their haunting storm-voices: Cuchulainn the great bull, the

8

aged female Bragela. She called them after the legends, the first a chieftain of Skye and Bragela his consort. The girl could see the pair now on their crags. And ancient Cellach the Abbot, who lay apart, meditating.

A clutch of moulters lay nearer, their mothers departed. Among her favourites was Oisin, a son of Finn the beachmaster, and Niamh of the Golden Head, sired in myth by a lord, King of the Land of Young People.

As she ranged down the *mul* a few cows ran to water; the juveniles watched her. One in moult caught her eye and she stopped to admire it. The creature lay on its side, staring back with distrust. The mouth gaped but was mute, several chubby chins creasing. On the blubbery trunk were two half-concealed dimples, the cups of small inverted nipples.

'Bonnie girl,' said the child, and the storm-calf spat at her.

'Just you mind,' called the man, 'those young sealies bite children.'

'Ach, get on, they know me. Have you seen this one, Willie?'

The man said, 'Captain Macrae. I'm no' back at your school. I'm no' one of your chums.'

She beckoned him to come over. 'See that coat, will you look? It's silver, Captain Macrae; coming through purest silver.' He was no captain, of course, but did at least know the islands. She granted that to the man for he had fished all his life, knew the seas of the sagas. 'You've never seen one like that, she's a wee princess, Willie.'

He joined her now. 'A wee Satan.'

The fool was empty of feeling, as old as Cellach, she thought, as dry as last winter's jetsam. He had no time for the seals, only time for his boat, if you could call the

9

wreck that. 'You're hopeless, Willie Macrae, this one's fairer than Niamh.'

'Names,' he said with a grunt. 'You've a skull full of names.'

'We'll need a name for the bairn.'

'Your mam's more sense,' the man mused, 'she's a head full of figures. There's sense in figures, shopkeeping.'

'We'll call her Wingfoot, how's that? Don't you think it sounds special? Wingfoot of the Wingfooted.' The girl regarded him smugly. 'The *Pinnipedia* – the Wingfooted. Wait till she's grown, she'll shine, Willie.' Like the moon, she reflected, her arms decisively crossed, the thick sweater hugged to her. Like the moon on the tide, a princess of the water.

'Stores,' the old man was saying. 'You've brought my whisky, eh, Aggie?'

Next day the calves got together – the one the girl called Niamh and the now-christened Wingfoot. No longer bound by the cows, the pair teamed up with Oisin. Then, using flippers as aids, they bounced and humped to the crags, levering with their bodies, and flopped into a rock-pool. Unlike the rumbling waves it held no fears, and they wallowed.

Blowing bubbles they floated, later sinking together. They were at home underwater. There, their heartbeats grew slower, conserving oxygen. They had stayed down for some minutes when Wingfoot's head broke the surface, a little crab in her mouth. It seemed to her a fine plaything. Living now off her fat, she was not needy of food and all she did was toy with it. At length, however, she munched, experimentally gulping.

By the pool a waif watched her. The luckless orphan

was starved; its small eyes glimmered feebly. The handsome poolmates ignored it, robustly indifferent. Sleek and dark, Oisin gleamed; Niamh strong, golden-headed. The lustrous Wingfoot was comely. They formed an enviable group, the runt woeful beside them.

At play, the male liked to brawl, swift to nip in a tussle. More than once when they romped Oisin's teeth hurt the others. While Niamh never complained, easy-going and gentle, Wingfoot quickly snapped back; she did not suffer meekly. Soon she plunged for fresh loot, the sand-crab to her liking. But finding nothing to catch, she joined Niamh, paddling round until bored, idly snapping at seaweed. Tired of bursting its pods, she just lazed, snoring quietly like Cellach.

Presently the tide turned and the three sought the shingle. At close of day the sea rose and they huddled together. Again the wind howled and moaned. Along the beach at the croft the man was drinking alone; outside, the angry waves glowed, their wild plumes phosphor-escent. Somewhere Cuchulainn hissed and a fretful Finn answered. Then, far off, a cow howled, old Bragela's dirge drifting. At last, the breakers drowned all, a rhythmic beat on the rocks, a fierce threshing on pebbles. Wingfoot stirred and felt Niamh. Comforted, she drowsed off, their place safe from the pounding.

She roused again at first light and took stock. The wind had dropped, the swell slight, merely slapping the point, bucketing on the skerries. The little rock-pool was full, its dark seaweed replenished. Something lay at the edge, partly draped in the water: the runt's wasted body. It might have been a wet rag.

The lame seagull knew better.

* * *

11

Engine idling, the *Goosander* rocked slightly, fenders touching the quay where trapped water was sloshing. The girl stood on the stone steps, looking down at the vessel. A stubby mast swayed nearby and she could see into the wheelhouse, a small rectangular turret from which a bearded face scowled, its hair sandy.

Crowding in from behind, the gable-ends of the buildings – her mother's shop, the squat chapel – were as grey as the pier, of the same sombre granite. The effect was depressing. At times she thought of the place as a collection of tombs, as dull as slabs in a churchyard, as her own father's headstone. She had not known the gaunt man, save in an unsmiling photograph.

It was a place of the dead: at least, she thought, the half-living, one foot in their graves, for, all too often, the young, stumped for work, left the island. Its farms were small, the life hard, a living from the sea harder. She wished more young folk would stay, and had been mightily pleased when Donnie joined the *Goosander*.

In his new knitted hat he looked the part on the deck, a real crewman, thought Aggie. She gabbled on in the damp: 'I've not told anyone else, you're the first I've told, Donnie, apart from Willie Macrae, and he doesn't count, does he? I wanted you to know first; I had to let you know, Donnie. You never saw a seal like her.'

The drizzle washed the boy's cheeks. They had an apple-pink bloom, in part a blush of annoyance. 'Is that so?' he replied. At school the two had got on, sharing interests in common, but he had left at term's end, now sixteen and a seaman. He was past chatting with schoolgirls.

'Purest silver,' said Aggie.

'Is that a fact?' Donnie shrugged. Was she twelve or

thirteen? In either case she was small and embarrassed him deeply.

'I'm telling you.'

'I can hear.'

'What's up, Donnie MacDonald?'

'Ach, nothing,' he mumbled.

'Then will you no' show some interest? I'm saying that she's unique; she's a real dazzler, Donnie.'

He slipped a glance up the deck to where Calum was standing, a weathered man, perhaps thirty, good-naturedly smirking. 'Look,' said Donnie, 'not now. They don't think much of seals here.'

'Nor does Willie Macrae. Willie reckons they smell. He should talk,' the girl laughed. 'Have you whiffed the booze on him?'

The youth's voice fell. 'They take fish.'

'Of course they do, don't be daft. They've taken fish since Year Dot. What they take makes no difference.'

'It's not like that when we're out. You wouldn't know,' the boy muttered. 'It's all against you out there.'

Aggie smiled, full of trust. 'You've always cared for the seals; they've a friend in you, Donnie.'

The skipper bawled, his beard bristling. 'Is that brew ready, lad? Make it lively, we're leaving.' Then he withdrew to the wheel and the man Calum added, 'Aye, wee fellow, come on. Make it sweet, he needs sweetening.' He raised his eyes to the girl. They were the blue of sea-holly. 'There'll be another time, Aggie.'

'When you return,' she agreed, her gaze on Donnie MacDonald. She had always admired him and now he seemed doubly fine, sailing off like a hero, a voyager of the myths – another Maeldun the Gael – to the realm of the sea people. Her smile increased in its warmth. 'I'll be waiting,' she promised. 'We'll cycle out to the cove and I'll show you the moulters.'

He turned away looking sullen. The child was going to persist if he said nothing to stop her. 'It's different now,' he began, but it was lost in the noise, the engine suddenly louder. The devil take her, he moaned, he would be teased, made to suffer.

Unabashed, the girl waved.

'When you get back again, Donnie.' She watched the craft move astern, easing out from the quay, turning slowly. 'See you, Donnie!' she shrilled, and ran up-pier, an arm flapping. The vessel's bows rose and slewed. As her prow met the swell the gulls soared from her gunwale. 'See you, Donnie! Be careful!'

She felt the damp on her neck. Her hair was moist from the mist, dripping onto her collar, and she retired to the shop, sheltering in the doorway. She could still see *Goosander*, faintly now in the drizzle, clawing for the horizon.

On board, the boy swayed and staggered. He had begun to feel queasy when, not a stone's throw abeam, a grey seal broke the surface. It clutched a fish to its chest, a large and thorny-tailed skate, scarcely heeding the boat, too engrossed with its victim. The mammal fed like a wolf. Tearing flesh with its teeth, it left the maimed fish to wallow. Then the seal pounced again.

As the butchered skate threshed, a fresh steak was ripped from it. Again, it beat in the water. At last, the carnage complete, the seal flippered and vanished.

Donnie felt his guts heave. From the wheelhouse came swearing.

* * *

The calves had finished their moult, fully-fledged second-coaters, the silver seal a month old. For many days she had fasted and was no longer so plump, a slimmer, hungrier calf of exceptional beauty. In some lights she looked white, her metallic sheen brilliant. It made a bright magpie contrast with the blue-black of Oisin and set off Niamh's soft fawn, which had warm golden patches.

Fewer seals now remained, the dispersal in progress. Many cows had moved off and, though Finn still patrolled, the beachmaster was weak, drained by the chores of his rut and his own need of victuals. The cove looked bare and untidy. Non-tidal pools had grown stagnant, grisly heaps lay around, the stripped bones of dead calves, a few mummified corpses.

In patchy growth near the cliffs the salt-sprayed grasses were thin and the sea-bugloss withered. A clump of briar wept red hips. An empty bottle, washed up, lay with broken-off spars and torn portions of netting, a tawdry line on the stones, these of tide-burnished quartz, shiny felspar and hornblende.

In small and dwindling groups the second-coaters grew restless. Each day more took the plunge, urged to sea by their stomachs. The three young friends viewed the waves, drawing nearer the foam, watching older calves sport. It looked fine from the strand. Several chased in the shallows, playing catch-as-catch-can, and at last Oisin acted. With a resolute snort, he dashed in and was swimming.

Emboldened, Niamh went too. Only Wingfoot held back, calling up extra pluck, and just then a wave hit her. It struck her full in the face, lifting her off her flippers. Suddenly she was blind, wrapped in frothing cascades as she had been at her birth, and in terror she

15

fled, struggling to the shingle. There she turned in dismay, shedding tears of frustration.

She could not see her companions. Beyond the breakers heads bobbed but each looked much like the rest, save for Finn's, which was monstrous. Wingfoot pined on the stones. She lay stretched out, her head flat, and her round eyes were tragic.

There she stayed for some while, slumped in supine dejection.

Then, as the tide left the rocks and swimming seals couched upon them, she heard their hooting and whined. She heard Bragela's sea music, the trembling descant of yearlings. Cuchulainn had slipped off, already bound for the ocean, and many plateaux were vacant. Second-coaters claimed some but they were quiet, soon asleep. The silver calf lay awake. There was no call from Niamh and young Oisin was silent. At length the sun pierced the mist and its warmth made her drowsy.

She napped for maybe an hour until hunger pangs roused her. She was alone on the *mul*. Below her, down on the sand, two young seals had hauled out, a pretty pebble-marked beast and a grey-pelt, both females. Aggie, knowing them well, had named them Pebble and Treshnish, the Treshnish Isles to the north being favourite seal havens. Wingfoot gave them a glance then slouched affably forward.

Above her, herring gulls wheeled, lazing upwards on thermals. They rose on motionless wings, their heads cocked to peer downwards. Two or three black-backs soared, a lone fulmar beneath them, lichen bright where they planed on the brow of the rock-face.

As Wingfoot joined the two females the nearest spat and lashed out: the creature Aggie called Treshnish. She was a querulous brute and, when the storm-calf snapped back, made a spiteful rush, snarling. The charge took Wingfoot aback and she withdrew in disgust, flouncing off round the cove. Drawing close to the cottage, she was teased by its odours.

Macrae's hovel was bleak, swept by a century of winds, as neglected as he was. Its hearth-fire never went out, a twist of smoke always present. This had kippered the roof, which was low and soot-blackened, and at aberrant hours reeked of primitive cooking. Through the dwelling's thick walls a dark interior scowled, grimacing from two holes: an unwelcoming door and a dungeon-sized window.

Wingfoot flopped up the *mul*, gained a path and inhaled. A smell of fish stirred her pangs, quickening obdurate cravings. Elevating her neck, the young seal waddled closer.

There was a judder of brakes and a bike skidded wildly. 'Jesus,' Aggie profaned, 'could you no' give a warning?'

The startled animal stared.

'It's not you, not up here? Lord, it is,' the child marvelled. 'You almost had me thrown off. Poor wee Wingfoot, you're starved.' She calmed the calf, her voice softening. 'You need a bite, you poor thing. Let's see what I can find you.'

The old man stomped from his home. 'You can't bring that brute here.'

'She's famished, Willie, poor beast.'

'Then she'd best get to sea.'

'A feed of something would help.'

Macrae viewed her askance, gesturing at the seal-calf. 'Are you mad, Aggie Fraser? Do you know what you're saying? You gi' that sealie a feed and she'll be with me for Christmas; aye, and Hogmanay after. The crowlin' devil, she'll live. She'll swim as soon as she must; she'll no' starve while the sea laps.'

'I hope you're right,' Aggie told him, 'for if she does, you're to blame. I'll fetch you out no more stores and you can starve here yourself. Stone-cold sober,' she threatened.

Wingfoot humped down the beach. She turned her head by the boat and gazed balefully at them.

'To the water, ye monster, all the way; and keep going.' The 'captain' clapped his hands loudly. 'You'll get no fish from Macrae.'

Across the waves, as they boomed, the girl could hear the seals singing. She held her breath for the calf, willing her to the tide and the food she now needed. 'I think she's going in, Willie.' The silver shape had advanced, poised this time on the brink. Again the shiny head turned as if about to renege, then swung back to the water. Next thing, Wingfoot had gone, swallowed by the green surge, and the surf filled her drag-marks.

'She's in, she's in,' cried the child.

'And good riddance,' the man said.

Beyond the breakers she had feared, Wingfoot came to calm water. It was clear and capacious, a pool of stunning proportions in which she quickly relaxed, its gentle rock-a-bye lilt half-remembered from womb days. It was caressing and awesome, of infinite promise. As far as she could make out – and she saw well when submerged, her eyes like those of all seals shaped for submarine vision – the sea world stretched without end, marbled, green and translucent.

The calf could not help but marvel. Where the head-land plunged down, teeming rocks sank in shelves, in terraced cliffs to the sand, an amazing drowned desert in which lay gravelly beds and great solitary stones like Neptunian follies. The tides had made shifting dunes, shallow hollows and coombes, nurturing rich plan-tations, rippling seaweed oases that danced in the cur-rents. There were olive-hued plants and plants of bright peacock-green, some with broad, glossy leaves, some with fronds tightly crinkled.

Farther off rose blue hills, the steep flanks of the sker-ries. Wingfoot saw their tops gleaming, countless bubbles ablaze as the surface boiled round them. Strands of wrack floated by. They cast long shadows below, mauve on limpet-scabbed rocks while, above the calf's head, the sun webbed the sea's ceiling. It was a dazzling scene and, as she peered through the depths, other seals dived and glided.

They had a thrilling new grace. On land her kind had been clumsy, their fastest pace less than swift. The girl had often jogged faster, racing them down the beach. Now the seals were transformed, like great birds under-water, soaring, plunging and banking, the cool brine a playground. With easy strokes of webbed limbs, they seemed to fly without effort. At speed they swept back their wings and swam with strong body movements, their rear flippers snapping. Then with smooth, snaking thrusts they would zoom through the depths, skim along the sea's bed, climb to break the bright surface.

When merely idling or floating, all four flippers were used, sometimes treading the water to hold a sleek head above it – or more, head and shoulders. Thus, one seal would gaze round, its hands slapping the swell; another, flop with a splash, turtling or crash-diving.

Every ten or so minutes the seals would rise to recharge, breathing deeply and quickly. Then, with oxygen stored, held in tissue and fluid, down again they would plunge. To lose the buoyancy in them, the beasts breathed out before diving, the process so automatic that they could do it while snoozing, floating up in their sleep, drifting down without waking. A lot of time was spent resting and many drowsed on the bottom, now rocking and swaying.

Wingfoot watched a cow hunting, the creature prowl-ing the sea-bed. She used her snout in the quest, for though seals dived with closed nostrils they had, like dogs, clammy noses alert to wafting scent atoms. And now she homed on a signal, whiskers sweeping the floor until the sand plumed abruptly, a small flounder bolting. With a snap the seal pounced, immolating her victim.

Reminded of her own hunger, Wingfoot foraged in turn. The first rewards were not handsome: a cuttlefish shelled and swallowed, a little crab caught in flight, reminding her of the rock-pool. Later, flushing a dab, she was slow off the mark and it gained a safe refuge. Annoyed, she made for the seaweed. Suddenly, to her front, a shoal of fry caught the light, its anonymity foiled as each flank turned fluorescent. Then, as she dashed at the throng, it exploded and scattered, a single morsel immured, slithering down her gullet.

With modest triumph she surfaced, beaming self-satisfaction. Against the arc of the sky she could see the cove's cliffs, the sun's glow on the *mul* and the jut of the headland. It was a novel perspective and one she studied with interest, taking in the land's form, its high shoulders, deep throat, the *machair*'s grassy mantle: erstwhile nursery scenes now to be vital landmarks.

Another seal bobbed nearby. Engrossed, she took little notice until it snorted with pleasure, her sightseeing disturbed, when she turned with a swirl. She knew the sleek golden head and, in familiar eyes, sensed the warm recognition. The second-coater swam to her. Delightedly, the pair bussed, clapping flippers together, Niamh's greeting impassioned. Wingfoot gurgled her joy, charmed to find a companion. Their celebration complete, they trod the swell side by side, happily rubber-necking.

A little seal-crowd had gathered, other juveniles in it, now expectantly bobbing. There was a strange air of interest and Wingfoot watched them, intrigued. Faces turned out to sea, they flecked the crest of the bay as if awaiting events, as if some pageant impended. Distantly, gulls were squealing, but the calves could not see them. At last, above the far point, a white cloud of birds billowed and as their bickering grew *Goosander*'s prow cleared the headland.

Wingfoot pondered the vessel, flippering to see better, much impressed by the sight as if the rusty black boat was the grandest thing afloat. She watched a spluttering bilge, caught a glint from the wheelhouse. Gulls were thick at the wake, tumbling, raking the sea, climbing up as they clamoured. Across the hummocky flow the young seal could hear voices.

'I'd shoot the brutes' – from the helm.

'A few more days, they'll be gone.' Calum's tone was placating.

'Until next summer, the robbers.'

There was a pause then the boy said, 'He isn't kidding us, is he?'

'Gorme hates seals,' confirmed Calum.

'He'd really shoot them?' asked Donnie.

They were on deck gutting fish, slitting them at the neck before opening the bellies and removing the entrails. 'I wouldn't doubt it,' said Calum, who pitied the youngster. Donnie's hands were all thumbs, the sharp knife deployed crudely. It was not boys, Calum thought, it was men the boat needed, but then Gorme was too stingy. It was not Donnie's fault. 'For sure,' the big man harked back, 'he's killed a few seals, the skipper.'

'But isn't that . . .'

'Hold it this way. Each fish should take you ten seconds, by God, not two minutes.'

'You know the seals are protected?'

'Maybe,' muttered Calum.

'By law,' the youth aired his knowledge, affecting

Calum's calm manner. 'Autumn through to December.'

The man made no further comment, his knife at work on a codling, his hands surprisingly deft though of rugged appearance. There was a lingering silence and Donnie, secretly watching, wondered not for the first time what Calum was thinking. Did he dwell on the sea, the hazy shapes of the isles or the tall, dreamy wife whose good looks the boy reverenced? Calum's silences puzzled. They seemed to Donnie profound, as awesome as the grey swell; perhaps all seamen were brooding.

Yet when the man spoke again his words were hardly of moment.

'Soon be back with your girl, son.' It caught the other off guard and Calum gave him a grin. 'She promised you she'd be waiting.'

'Aggie?' Donnie said, reddening, and then, confused, 'She's a kid. She's not my girl,' he insisted. 'I've got no girl on the island.'

Calum shrugged. They worked quietly.

The boat plunged on past the seals, whose faces watched from astern. Niamh had turned on her back and scratched her chest as she floated; Wingfoot viewed the Atlantic.

A large grey cow was returning, breasting home after hunting, heading for the cove's shelter. It was Bragela in haste, the old seal's approach urgent. Surfacing to take bearings, she curved down under the swell then checked her course closer in, once more rising and diving. A seal could cruise in this fashion at five or six miles an hour but Bragela was racing, unsparing of effort.

As she came up to the others she was near to exhaustion. Without a glance she powered on, labouring to the shallows, while several older seals followed. The less experienced watched, a sense of danger pervading. Wing-foot looked at Niamh, then at the sea's rolling roof. It was suddenly bare, every head having vanished, and with a splash the pair plunged, shooting downwards in panic.

Finn was there, agitated, keeping close to the rocks. Other seals passed at speed, arrowing to safe waters. The grizzled Cellach barged by, Pebble sweeping beside him; the testy Treshnish torpedoed. As Wingfoot chased them in fear, she glimpsed a dark calf retreating, ploughing through a sea garden. It might have been the black Oisin, but then again it might not. Of Niamh she was quite certain for they were side by side fleeing – from what, she had no idea, but she did not pause to rest till she was back at the breakers.

From the wheel of *Goosander*, skipper Gorme pointed seawards. High dorsal fins cut the waves, triangular and forbidding. 'Killers,' Calum said, watching, 'a school of killer whales, Donald; half a dozen, I'd say, the old man and his harem. Seals are meat to a killer, he'll cut a seal clean in half.' It was said matter-of-factly. 'With a single bite, laddie.'

'Will they enter the cove?'

'Ach, not far, there's the rocks, they'll be wary of grounding. They'll wait around till the winter when the seals are at sea . . .'

'Then they'll have them,' bawled Gorme. He eyed the boy and laughed fiercely, the sandy beard breaking open. It was, thought Donnie, tight-lipped, the first time Gorme had brightened.

Calum's words proved correct: the killer whales shunned the cove and soon the seals had calmed down, the older ones back at rest while the young went exploring. At a couple of fathoms, Niamh and Wingfoot were dabbling when a fresh surprise met them.

Niamh, searching the rocks, had discovered a hole. Now, inserting her nose, she backed away with such speed that Wingfoot's interest was caught and she advanced with bravado. The niche was gloomy inside, the great eel lying doggo, its curving sinew at rest in the watery chamber. It was a forty-pound monster, thickly coated with slime, and it studied her coldly, its head broad and dark, the contemplative eye glassy. Gradually, very slowly, the conger's mouth opened.

The silver seal did not linger. No less shocked than Niamh, Wingfoot scurried astern, falling in with her companion. Abashed, they mustered their nerve and, brisk with outrage, rushed forward. It was no more than mock-courage, for though they darted and charged they stopped short of the opening. One day, many tides on, they might feel up to the eel but now the juveniles shammed, their discretion prevailing.

Tired at length of their antics, they turned away from the rock to find that they had been watched, a young seal close behind them. It was a black-coated male, sleekly handsome and fit – without a doubt the calf Oisin, his self-confidence brimming.

But he did little to charm them. As they paddled towards him he turned away with a swirl, mimicking their charade, feigning toothy aggression. Niamh simpered, still loyal, but he evaded her rudely, flippering in her face, clearly pleased when she flinched for he repeated the insult. Then, to show off his pace, he made a dive and zoomed at her, forcing her to twist sideways.

Confused, she scurried to Wingfoot, taking refuge beside her. It was too much for the storm-calf. With a quiver of rage she flew head-on at the male, who drew off looking startled. For some seconds, put out, he hung in marble-veined space, considering retribution. But when he tried to return, both the females went for him, united now in their wrath, and he quickly lost interest. Throwing a final taunt at them, a lazy roll and a flip, he withdrew to the sea-dunes.

Wingfoot surfaced and floated. Only two seals upset her, the bumptious Oisin and Treshnish, and she did not dwell on them, or the baleful cave monster, for the sun was a balm and the sea's lilt was soothing. A hazy warmth wreathed the cliffs. Beneath them, cormorants preened and oyster-catchers were sleeping while old Macrae scraped his boat, the faint noise cricket-squeaky.

Niamh had wandered away, lost on a lavender bay, and the silver seal dreamed, now and then blowing quietly. If this was life, it was good; she could support its vexations, the odd and transient scare, a windy night, a rude neighbour. Autumn's languor beguiled and she beamed up at the cloud-hills. Presently, feeling sportive, she cast about for diversion.

There was a buoy off the point, a favourite perch of the sea birds, and Wingfoot swam to it. Playfully the thing rolled but she clambered aboard, to be ditched as it tilted. Flippers splayed, she remounted, was thrown again and heaved back, a wave lifting her neatly. For the next ten or so minutes she frolicked, the game to her liking. Then, by way of a change, she ducked under the buoy, found its chain and swam down it.

As the rocks came in sight she clutched the metal-linked cable and hung above them, eyes popping. The sea was full of choice fish, meaty meals, their fins fanning. The islanders called them saith, these of two and three pounds with mouth-watering flanks, long green backs and pale bellies. They made the silver calf drool. Along the sides of each fish a thin line of dark colour trimmed the elegant livery.

The school faced into the current which, curling through rocky gullies, bore a feast of small molluscs and other rare titbits. Intent on snapping them up, the fish had not noticed Wingfoot. Now one would sally and gulp, another veer off and gobble. They were a glutton's delight and she wriggled with glee, poised to race in among them.

Had she been older and wiser she would have scorned the wild plunge. It had no chance of success and, in the blink of an eye, at speeds no seal could have matched, the fish had vanished. Floating dismally down, Wingfoot flopped on the sea-bed. Her failure left her depressed, for, clearly, serious fishing was not the sport she had imagined, like playing tag with the calves, but something yet to be learned. It called for skills she must master and all the cunning born in her; it called for wilier ways and next time she must test them.

She was still brooding below when opportunity beckoned. As she surveyed the sand glumly, a little flurry erupted and, from the gravelly debris a new quarry ghosted.

This was no streamlined saith but a delta-winged phantom, the brown-topped sails flapping slowly, sharp spines on their surface. The fish, a thornback, flew low, a foot or two off the floor, and at a leisurely pace, unaware of the seal-calf. Its eyes, both dorsally-sited, afforded no downwards vision, so that by hugging the sand the seal could follow unseen.

And this time she was cautious. She moved with

smoothly snaking thrusts, her flippers flat at her sides, now with the studied restraint recent failure had taught her. She had to wait and keep patient, put her bungling behind her. This was the chance she must seize if she would rise above dabbling, prove herself in the chase, for the quarry was worthy – more than worthy, imposing.

A big thornback could give an adult seal trouble and though this fish was not vast it looked to Wingfoot no weakling. Its lazy strokes suggested powerful reserves, the competence to fight back that she had not yet encountered. More, as she closed peering upwards, it seemed to grow with each second. Its tail was thronged with keen spikes and its thorny disc bristled.

For an instant she paused, hesitating, then set her jaw and swam on. Now her whiskers were tingling. They felt the wash from the fish as its wings laboured down, almost touching her nose, the flat hull slap above her. The time, she judged, had arrived; a savage thrill surged inside her.

With a hoist of her neck, Wingfoot drove her teeth home. They sank in soft underbelly and she braced for the struggle. The flatfish jerked and was still, then lashed out with its pinions. As they belaboured her cheeks, she smothered them with her flippers, wrestling her prey on its back so she straddled its body. The spiny tail whipped her skin. She was protected by fat and now too frenzied to care, her muzzle terrier-fierce in the wound she had opened.

There was no sentiment in her; the rip of tissue inflamed and flowing blood fuelled her fury. To every kick of the fish she responded with violence, subduing the thornback. Then, in a daze of success, she dragged her mangled catch upwards, gained the surface and gorged, tearing strips from the disc until the creature stopped flapping.

She ate the steaks to the last, retrieving those she had dropped by scooping them from the sea, her greed surpassing her hunger. And now, too bloated to swim, she turned and lazed on her back, licking the taste from her breast where the thornback had struggled. She had expunged her frustration. She watched the marker-buoy bobbing, pitching this way and that, an age away in her mind, the age of Wingfoot the bungler. In all of five brutal minutes she had left her calfhood behind, become Wingfoot the huntress.

A lot remained to be learned but she was past the beginning.

Aggie watched the sea-swallows. The little birds skimmed the dunes and turned over the bay, leaving now for the winter. She leaned a while on her bike, her thoughts back in the shop, her mother's quiet voice remembered above the cry of a curlew.

'You'll stay away from that pier, child.'

'Oh Mam, no, you don't mean it?'

'Uh-huh,' the woman had said, making the syllables briskly. There was an obdurate strength in Mrs Fraser's mild accents.

Alone now, watching the sea, the girl recalled the scene, pouting.

'I don't see why I can't meet him; Calum's wife always meets them.'

Her mother's calm face had straightened. Both of them had strong minds but, as the child would concede, when Mrs Fraser held 'views' she did not brook opposition.

'You'll not go out on the pier. It isn't proper at your age, hanging round for the boatmen. Be good and stack up those jams, it'll save me an effort.'

'Oh please, Mam, won't you let me?'

'Be sure the labels face outwards.'

'I promised Donnie I'd meet him.'

Her mam had counted stamps quickly, working in the Post Office, a small recess near the sweets. She seemed to Aggie severe and depressingly ancient: forty soon, thought the girl, worse than being thirteen which was bad in all conscience. Her mam's lips had tightened. She had turned stamps with neat hands, making notes of the totals.

'Not the pier,' she had said, 'the pier's no place for you, child.'

'Then why does Calum's wife wait there?'

'Mary isn't a girl.'

Lucky her, had thought Aggie; that was the age to be, Mary's, and do as you fancied.

'In any case, that's her business. If she wastes time on the quay, mooning there while they fish, it's no decent example. A childless woman like that should be working and useful. Besides, now Donnie's left school it's time you left him alone; he'll want to be with the boatmen. You'll not have too much in common, a child whose head's in the clouds and a wee fishing laddie.'

'I like him.'

'Ach, he's nice enough, bairn, but don't go chasing him round. I know the life on the boats, for did your father not choose it? The sea's a cruel workplace, Aggie. Donnie's gone his own way; you've years of studying yet and you'll be doing some growing. I'd say you'd plenty to learn before you think about fellows.'

'As if I think about fellows . . .'

She did, of course; mainly Donnie.

And now, alone with her bike, she watched the terns and felt sad, less for herself than for her mam, whose man had drowned at his work and left his wife with an infant. Her mam had toiled like a slave to bring her up wanting nothing, and sometimes Aggie would weep for what the woman had missed, startled by her own tears, the fierce and eye-scorching love that welled up out of ambush.

'Damn,' she said to the bike and pointed it down the cliff-path. Leaving it at the bottom, she searched for the 'captain'.

When she had shouted his name she took a peep in the dwelling. She had to squint in the gloom, its smoky atmosphere thick. There was a glow in a hearth mountainous with grey ash and, on a soot-blackened hob, a big old-fashioned kettle, its lid-knob long missing. In the single small window, grimy panes shed a light which coddled secretive shadows, vague shapes against walls, under beams and in corners.

The place was cluttered with junk. Chests were piled up with boxes, the boxes with rubbish. There was a plain wooden chair and a crudely painted table. Dusty books lay with charts, oilskins hung from a hook, empty bottles filled niches. On the floor side by side, two dark cats raised their heads, staring up with green eyes. A third sat on a ledge, its tail curled round its haunches.

'Willie?' Aggie called quietly. 'Have you seen Donnie MacDonald?'

Willie must have slipped out.

She took a couple of steps, peering round with distaste. What would her mother make of it? 'Lord, Macrae, but she'd die; it's a sty,' she reflected.

She blew the dust from a chart. It showed a strait between islands, the Isles of Jura and Scarba, and was smothered in tea stains. Between the isles, in large type, was printed 'Gulf of Corrievreckan', where her father had perished, and someone had written, 'great overfall on the flood', and the pithy phrase, 'flood race'.

She did not wish to look at it, even think of the subject, preferring her dream isles. She liked to think it was calm, calm as the Sea of Green Glass, where her dad was now sailing.

Oppressed by Willie's dark croft she went back to the open. A few young seals were ashore, resting up on the *mul*, and as she started towards them her gaze fell on Wingfoot. The pearly coat caught the sun, unmistakably brilliant, urging her to rush on leaving the hovel behind. Owlishly, the seals watched her.

A grey-lagged calf gave a grunt and as she drew near the group she could see a golden head, Niamh waving a flipper. Wingfoot's hiss was less trusting. At first the silver seal snarled, then, recognizing the girl, gave a yawn of indifference and waddled nearer the water. Aggie strolled the sand with her. 'Soon,' she promised the beast, 'I'm bringing Donnie to see you. I thought he might be here now. Don't you snarl at my Donnie.'

A rising wind swept the cove, making several calves restive. It caught her freshly washed hair, wrapping strands round her forehead. Wingfoot paused by the creamers.

'Don't go yet, not so quickly.' Don't leave me stranded,

thought Aggie, when I've no Donnie to talk to, not even Willie Macrae.

But the seal lifted forward, floated up by a wave, and swam strongly. She was, the girl mused, at home, no longer awed by the breakers, as confident as an adult. It had not taken the creature long to find out where she belonged. And now, as if to agree, she pushed up proud from the swell and stared back, blowing out of her nostrils. The other youngsters were moving, coming down from the shingle.

One by one they went in, following her example, until the beach was deserted. Soon the girl was alone, the animals drifting from her.

As she watched, the breeze stiffened, blowing full in her face while, far off, the sky clouded. Seals were leaving the rocks, slithering from the skerries. She saw Bragela slide down to bob up some yards seawards. Finn was farther out still, his capacious snout lofted. There was a restlessness in them as if the ocean was calling, as if the Westerlies beckoned. She sensed a certain hesitation, regret in glances cast landwards, but slowly they were receding. Even Cellach the Abbot, the last to give up his throne, finally took to the water.

The child could see Pebble near him and Treshnish beyond them. She could no longer see Wingfoot. Then, the heads growing distant, she lost all track of individuals, the grey armada a blur straggling out of her vision.

'Hey,' a husky voice slurred and Willie came round the croft. 'Aye, you there,' he hailed hoarsely.

She let him stumble towards her, wishing it had been Donnie.

'I couldn't find you,' she said. 'Are they leaving us, Willie?'

'Eh?' he growled. 'Are who leaving?'

'The seals,' she snapped as he swayed. 'I might've known you'd be drinking.'

'That's no' verra respectful.'

'Oh, you're disgusting,' she muttered.

She viewed the western horizon, a sea remote from her dreams, a sea three thousand miles wide, seven deep in some places. That way lay the ocean, the daunting heart of the tempests. All winter now the seals would hunt, diving under the storms, fattening up after breeding before the impregnated cows returned again to give birth, the big bulls to attend them. Meanwhile they faced frightening dangers.

She did not want them to leave. What would the cove be without them, bereft of their bobbing heads, empty of its seal music?

'At least,' she willed the right answer, 'the young won't go, will they?'

'You think not, Aggie Fraser? Well let a sober man tell ye – if they stay here in the gales they'll soon wish that they hadn't.'

For three days nothing happened, then the wind started droning, a low mysterious sound that Wingfoot found disconcerting. Sudden gusts swept the bay, making boisterous incursions. True, the sun could be seen but it was rayless and pallid, veiled by spare wolf-grey clouds hounding eastward. Beneath them gulls fled the sea, streaming back to the coast, while, where the buoy tugged its chain, the cormorants were departing.

Macrae had winched up his boat. It now lay close to the cottage, tarpaulins lashed on it. He knew the power of the waves when gale and tide coincided, charged by the swell of the Atlantic. The water's weight would be huge, hammering at the cliffs, hurling shingle like bird-shot. He had seen it break over sixty-foot crags and, battening down, the man waited.

Wingfoot swam to Niamh, who was sniffing the weather. Her head yo-yoed on the bay, floating up with each crest and plummeting in the troughs, but she did not seem concerned, as unruffled as usual. The silver seal was uneasy. The swell was running in fast and all the time getting higher, already burying rocks under spuming white fountains. Even the *mul* was awash, the ground she thought of as sanctuary. Worse, the two were alone and they should not be, sensed Wingfoot.

35

She trod the water and blew, salty air whipping past her. It had an unpleasant sting as unfamiliar to the seal as the sea's lumpy malice. Each rise and fall grew in scale and they were being swept shoreward, the whole bay seeming to tilt as the mounting waves canted. The movement heightened her fears and when the spray stabbed her eyes Wingfoot dived for asylum. What she found brought slight comfort, for in the cove's shallow pan there was no ducking the turmoil, its force all-embracing.

Soupy sandstorms were spreading, whirled up from the bed; murkily, the depths wrapped her. She glimpsed Niamh being tossed, a plaything of the water. And then the sea swung her round, a mighty tongue pressing down, and she was floundering herself, bowled along in the onrush.

Suddenly rocks were looming. She tried to flipper and veer but the torrent's grip held her, too powerful to fight as the boulders rushed forward. There seemed to be no escape no matter which way she thrust, however wildly she strove, until, as impact looked certain, she saw a gap in the stone and somehow steered herself at it. The breach, though barely seal-wide, obviated collision. She felt its walls scrape her flanks, then she had squirmed through unharmed, the flood racing ahead as its next impulse gathered.

The shock left Wingfoot bemused, aware that she had been lucky. Another wave could be crippling, for crueller rocks lay in wait, rocks with flesh-ripping teeth and no friendly rifts in them. Desiring Niamh's calm presence she probed the sandstorm in vain; the swirling silt was too thick, the sea's floor in confusion. Nor, when she surfaced again, could she spot her companion.

The heaving greyness was empty. All round the seal

the air roared, maddened water was crashing and she could make out no life save a dark sea bird skimming, wings immobile, a comet. It was a startling image. The gust propelling it shrieked, already greater in force than any wind she had known and still relentlessly freshening. Lifted onto a peak, the silver seal felt its violence.

Danger rampaged the cove. The inlet's treachery stunned her, her world no longer secure but raging fiercely against her, its cradling arms now a trap, the shore barren of refuge. The older seals had foreseen it, moving out to deep water, and she must follow or suffer, battle into the weather. She looked once more for Niamh then gave up and turned seaward.

Wingfoot's progress was slow. She had no knowledge to call on and faced the gale's wrath unseasoned. Hills of water marched at her, the wind and tide in alliance, intent on forcing her back. It was her first trek to sea and it could not have been harder. When she dived it was dark, the bay churning with silt; when she rose the waves towered and she wallowed in canyons. Everything was against her. She could not tell as she strained, muscling into the flood, if she was gaining or not. Only gradual fatigue served to measure her toiling.

The fifth or sixth time she surfaced she rested after recharging. The swell had grown, running higher, and the wind's war-chant deafened. As the sea pitched her up she had a view of its ranks, the long-plumed giants coming on, rolling out of the murk, a few crazily tumbling, others grey walls of anger. There was no solace ahead, and when she threw a glance back, only greater commotion, the land now lost to her view amidst wave-caps and spindrift. Bobbing down, she plunged onwards.

Working under the swell, she kept the flow in her face,

the only aid she possessed to maintain her direction. She had no bearings to guide her; the sun was blocked by the cloud, coast and sea-bed obscured. Once, perhaps in delusion, she thought she saw a dim shape, another seal on course with her, then again there was nothing. Slowly Wingfoot swam on, periodically rising, scarcely daring to stop though now heavy with tiredness.

At last the brine became clear, the sand in it subsiding. She had moved far from the cove and the sea's depth had deepened, now a vast waste below while above the gale strengthened. Alone and empty of air, she sought once more the wild surface.

Almost up, she felt thumps, a boat's propeller vibrating, and then the wind bellowed at her. A cable's length from her nose pitched the familiar *Goosander*.

She saw the craft top the waves, teetering in the flood with half a rusty hull clear before it plunged in a trough, black and squat as a shag, the mast swaying. Up the vessel was thrown; down she slid, her wake frothing. Oil-skinned figures clawed round, lurching as the deck angled. They were less welcome than seals but they were better than nothing.

She followed, riding the crests as the fishing-boat battled. As if to blow off her head, the wailing winds tore in low and now and then the seal ducked, quickly back looking on, the craft's presence a comfort. Its throbbing pulse gave her heart, its snatched voices tugged at her.

'It's awful rough,' anguished Donnie. 'My, the sea's awful heavy.'

'Eh, a mite,' answered Calum. 'You'll not be scared of it, will you?'

'Me?' The lad shook his head.

'Well, that's good, for it's healthy; it blows the dust from your tonsils.' Calum swayed but kept balance, the vessel suddenly rolling.

Donnie's stomach rolled with it. The boy tried whistling a tune until another wave struck, splashing in down the deck with a sound like feet running. The engine's pitch seemed to change and he said rather too shrilly, 'You're right, it's bracing is this; it's a healthy blow, Calum.'

'It clears the lungs,' said the man. 'You'll get used to the lumps, you'll see them higher than that. It's no' but par for the season.'

Wingfoot hovered to leeward in what shelter was offered. The *Goosander* was plodding, making less than four knots, and the seal kept abreast, mesmerized by the vessel. Now the bulwarks would dip so the sea brimmed above them and then the wheelhouse would vanish, only the tip of the mast still above the flood's shoulder. Then back again she would come like a great porpoise leaping, to flip her stern in the air, green cascading from scuppers.

Gorme peered out from the helm through a curtain of water. A black pipe burned in his beard and periodically he grunted. On one occasion he bellowed, 'How's that sheet on the hold? Take a look at the devil.'

At which the other man moved, weaving over the deck, hanging on where he could while the boat again plunged, the shock jolting her timbers. He scrambled back leaning steeply, swaying to the sea's motion with a ponderous grace as if in some abstruse ballet. Donnie, watching him, marvelled; the fellow seemed fearless.

'Man, she's fine, she'll not slacken.'

'It's freshening,' Gorme observed, spitting. 'I hope the stores are secured. If the stuff's spilled around, the boy can pay to replace it; I'll not replace tea and sugar, nor drink washy coffee.' He contemplated the youngster. 'Is he ailing? He's ashen.'

Calum's wet features glistened. 'He's finding it a touch heavy.'

'Heavy?' Gorme said at length, as if the word was new to him. Then, with a sniff of contempt, he eased the wheel, glaring forward.

The seal drifted astern. Vertical in the flow, her nose just breaking the water, she gave herself a brief rest and watched the boat roll ahead. When the black hull had gone, Wingfoot sprinted to catch it, making up half a cable. Resuming station nearby, she bobbed again on the swell, escalating and falling, smothered by its escarpments, flung high on its mountains.

Donnie's countenance froze, incredulity on it.

'Calum . . .'

Nothing else came and Calum turned his head, waiting.

'Well?' he asked.

'Over there. There's someone there, in the water.'

Calum muttered and peered, the weather hammering at him while Donnie swayed, pointing dumbly. The boat had tilted abruptly and they were thrown on the wheelhouse, the port bulwark descending, allowing sea to flood over. As it creamed and dispersed, Calum said, 'Someone there?' and with his slow, thoughtful smile, 'Rather them, son, than me; it's no day to be bathing.'

'A face, I swear to it, Calum.'

'The waves play tricks.'

'It was there.'

'A drifting float or a seal. Aye, a seal very likely.'

Donnie stared, unconvinced. 'It wasn't dark, it was pale – like a human face, Calum.'

The wind droned eerily past, Wingfoot lost in the tumult. A massive summit advanced and she was shoved and borne down, swamped beneath a grey wall under which she mined briskly, boring back to the daylight. She saw *Goosander*'s screw rise, screaming clear of the flood, then once more scatter froth as it carved through the surface. Determinedly, she kept pace.

'You get to think that you see things.' Calum's tone was reflective.

Donnie said, 'I don't know,' and then, confused by the sea, 'Will it last for long, Calum? Can't he steady her up, put her head on, or something?'

'Waste fuel? Gorme?'

'Till it calms.'

Calum grinned again at him. 'Not a chance in hell, sonnie.'

It was, thought Donnie, absurd: they were far too complacent, Calum grinning and lurching while Gorme sucked his pipe. The sea had got to their brains; it had affected their judgement, dulled their sense of the dangers. Had they no proper fear, no idea of the perils? He watched the walls of sea tower, sickening in their height, and told himself, 'It's no joke, the rotten boat's near to helpless.' It seemed that only he cared, that the others were witless.

He had been wary of Gorme but he had trusted big Calum. And now the man simply grinned. The boy crouched under the gale, convinced *Goosander* was doomed; the boat would flounder and sink and each would surface a while like the face he had seen, the pipe still in Gorme's beard, Calum's smile idiotic, before they went down for ever. He tried to blank out the vision.

'Calum,' Donnie said, gulping.

'Aye, my lad?'

'Is she safe?'

'Safe as most,' laughed the man. Then, with compassion, 'She's safe, son.'

Donnie whistled for courage.

'She'll not be safe if you whistle, it's worse than cutting your nails or not helping a seagull. Never whistle at sea. Mind, I'm no' superstitious . . .'

Another wave hit *Goosander*. Wingfoot rolled and submerged, diving under the bluster. Though loath to let the boat go she was by now drained of effort, in need of more than a pause to replace her spent vigour. Reluctantly the seal sank. As she slipped down into twilight the vessel's thrumming grew faint and heavy drowsiness claimed her. She seemed to drop a long way, at first through dimly lit depths then to virtual darkness, before she felt the sea's floor and, on its calm cushion, slumbered.

She slept for ten to fifteen minutes, gently rocked by the current. At last, oxygen-depleted, she stirred and rose to the waves, the wind a boorish reminder that little had altered. She was lost in a waste, the seals gone, the gale hostile. It screeched and wailed on the swell, and *Goosander* was nowhere.

Coming out of the gale the girl pushed hard on the door, shutting it with a struggle. Before it closed, the wind entered and several paper bags fluttered, an inner door banging. Across the shop from the child, Mrs Fraser was startled. 'For goodness' sake,' she complained, 'must you make that commotion?'

'It's not my fault there's a wind,' Aggie said, looking ruffled. 'You should feel it outside.'

'Could you not stay indoors?'

'I went to check on the cove.'

Mrs Fraser said, 'Uh-huh. And were you dragged through a bush?' She made the paper bags tidy. 'You're a sketch to behold, worse than Willie Macrae, child. You'll not have got the cash from him?'

'I couldn't get down the cliff.' Aggie shrugged. 'It was murder.'

'You might've guessed that beforehand.'

'I went to spy from the top, to see the calves had left safely.' Not that she had seen much with the wind in her eyes and the waves breaking madly. But she had crawled to the edge and spent a while peering down without, thank God, spotting bodies.

Her mother said, 'They'll be gone; the creatures know what they're doing. Now go and salt the potatoes, we're going to eat when they're ready.'

Aggie tugged at her hair, clawing knots from its ends, vaguely eyeing the saucepan. She always hated the winter, always missed the sea people. She hoped the depths would be calm and they could rest from the gale amid the sea's plankton meadows, or on the plains of the bottom where butterflies winged and small shell creatures scrambled.

In her dreams she wove pictures, saw wee shrimps and giant squids, submerged castles and glens, science mingling with myth in her vision of mystery.

It was her world of enchantment. It was the world of the diatoms, drifting beasties so small a hundred thousand a day could be consumed by one copepod, a barely visible plankton; a realm of strange tasselled marvels, the flagellates of her school studies, some minute balloons on strings, some like Christmas tree baubles. Others glowed in the dark, the 'night-light' and the 'fire-whirler'.

Her mother's voice broke in firmly.

'Get the eggs ready, Aggie, I'm shutting up in a minute. And you can grate us some cheese; if there's no cheese you'll be gloomy. We'll have the cold apple-pie. Put the cream on the table.'

She heard the rasp of a bolt and then the woman was with her, briskly washing her hands, saying, 'Not a good day, we've taken next to no money. They've stayed at home, who can blame them, they're not as daft as you, Aggie.'

Her daughter's thoughts wandered off, unheedful of the egg-beating as Mrs Fraser got on, never one to waste time, and an omelette was soon sizzling.

'D'you think the calves will be safe?'

'Uh-huh. Go and sit down.'

They ate their meal in the kitchen where they did much of their living. There was a radio there and a few potted plants unobtrusively thriving among the crocks and utensils, and a spike on a block which held the household invoices Mrs Fraser paid monthly with keen attention to discounts. A rather ugly black dresser displayed the best dinner service, plain but spotlessly shiny, one or two china nick-nacks – souvenirs of a mainland outing – and some long-serving books: a well-thumbed dictionary, a tome on home medicine.

They scarcely spoke throughout the meal, Aggie eating robustly and her mother more slowly, an ear to noises outside, the creaks and rattles the wind made. Loose fitments were knocking, an unnerving rat-tat as if the gale wished to enter. Once, the woman said sharply, 'You didn't salt these potatoes; Lord alive, what a dreamer.'

Aggie passed the salt-cellar. 'I was thinking of Wing-foot.'

Mrs Fraser frowned at her. Over tea, when they had eaten, she said, 'You need a new interest, a handicraft for the winter.'

'Oh Mam, I've got interests.'

'Forget the seals now they've gone; they won't return till next year.'

Outside the shop the wind whistled. Rat-tat-tat went the knocking, making Aggie uneasy.

'You can't forget them like that; I can't forget that they're out there.'

'Creatures,' huffed Mrs Fraser. 'Beasts are beasts, they're not people.' The child would learn, she supposed. 'It's the seamen I think of, that poor lad,' she let slip – just when the subject was buried. 'But that's enough about that, they'd not thank us for brooding.'

'Won't they shelter?' asked Aggie.

'Of course they will, to be sure. He's in good hands with Calum.'

'Willie said it would blow; he said the seals saw it coming. The boat should never have gone. That man Gorme doesn't care; don't you think he's an ogre?'

'Indeed, my girl, I do not, nor would I use such a name. What would your father have thought? Mr Gorme knows his business, he's always been a good seaman.'

'Mam . . .'

'No more of your blather.'

'Mam, its howling, just listen.'

'It's only freshening, my child, it's no longer the summer.'

'But poor Donnie, you said.'

'Because he'll maybe feel queasy, being new to the fishing.'

'Oh,' said Aggie less glumly. She paused then murmured, 'Not Donnie,' thinking of him on deck, every inch the bold sailor. He would have laughed had he heard them, her sturdy Donnie MacDonald whose very name echoed heroes, rugged Lords of the Islands. He would have scorned her forebodings. She said, 'He'll not mind the sea. I've never known Donnie frightened.'

'Then let's be getting on, shall we? Will you be washing up, Aggie?'

She slopped about at the sink and thought of where they might be, the grey seals and *Goosander*, the former under the swell, the latter anchored off Mull or some such friendly island – Tiree, Coll, who could tell? – in the lee of a coast where the ancients had sheltered. She felt a tingle of pride mixed with lingering qualms. Suppose the young seals were lost? Suppose *Goosander* was stricken?

Aggie hung up the dishcloth and climbed to her bedroom. The window was rattling. It faced the quay and the waves, a sea still running wild, flicking spray in the dusk as night closed on its spleen, filled her view with its greyness. Spires of spume flanked the pier where dark stone shone with water. A single figure stood on it. The head was lost in a hood and full skirts flapped and streamed, tightly strained by the wind against long, gale-braced legs.

Like a spectre, thought Aggie, was Calum's tall woman, a strange, spectral beauty.

All that night the wind blew. In gusts its strength reached force 9 and it took maybe three inches off the sea at such moments. From Malin Head to Cape Wrath the dark waves pounded the cliffs, battering at the islands from a fractious Atlantic. Then a shade before dawn, as the first farm lights glimmered, a sudden calm seized the air and the swell became greasy. It would not subside quickly but its slickness was soothing.

Surfacing at that hour, Wingfoot noted the change and stayed up for the daybreak. Soon a steely gleam spread and, as the sea rolled towards it, the east became brilliant. Far-off islands rose dimly, hummocky and unreal, sea birds sallying from them, though the seal could not see them. All she saw was the swell beneath air barely moving.

So intense was the peace, the flow's monotonous rhythm, that she swam in a trance, her gale worries forgotten. Dreamily the waves see-sawed, their new smoothness blissful. Alone and lost she might be, but she had weathered the squalls and they had proven her strong, boosted her self-assurance. Now, a pale sun appearing, she lay back and relaxed, stabilized by her flippers.

For half an hour the seal basked, at intervals sleeping lightly. After that she submerged, plumbing eerie green depths as she dived to find breakfast.

At first the larder looked bare, then from a weedy sea-garden a dark pedestrian ventured. Clad in tight-fitting armour, it marched with delicate tread, powerful pincer-claws brandished as Wingfoot descended. It was a new creature to her and she struck with discretion.

To the surprise of the seal, who made her pounce from above, the lobster promptly reversed and sped backwards, tail whirling. By the time she had turned, it was lost in the weed, and though she searched with persistence, rummaging the plantation, the meal had escaped her.

Frustration quickened her hunger. Glumly threading the fronds, she peered out for fresh quarry.

Luck was with her that morning. A foot or two from the weed a large and full-bellied wrasse was at rest in deep water, its fins idly twitching. It had been feeding inshore, catching limpets and crabs, when the gale had disturbed it and now the pudgy fish dozed, unaware of its peril. It was no piscine beauty. Thickset with large scales, it had a long spiny crest and the face of a gargoyle, the lips coarse and ugly.

But it was all of three pounds and to the seal doubly tempting for its cumbersome aspect. No elusive saith this, nor an armoured back-pedaller, but a gift for the taking. In spite of which, Wingfoot waited, her avidity bridled. A tiny change in the current was slowly turning the wrasse, swinging it in suspension to bring its tail towards her hideout.

Patiently she held on, the weeds trembling round her. Only when her plump prey was stern-on did she break from the plants, lashing them as she sortied, the fish at once running. Accelerating, she snatched the wrasse with such force that a macabre cloud billowed, the swirling blood of the fish a green plume in the tide-light. Then in heady ascent she bore her kill to the sun, her sea-slicked skull gleaming.

For a time she felt good, full of food, the gale over. She was happy to lounge with a blue sky above her. But presently the waves irked and she tired of inaction.

By noon contentment was fraying, loneliness nibbling at it, and Wingfoot wished she was home, paddling around with the others. She missed Niamh and their companions, the sport they shared when together; she missed the herd and the elders, the comfort numbers engendered – Cellach high on his rock, Finn patrolling the beach, Cuchulainn on the skerries. She missed Pebble's flecked face and Bragela's sea-anthem.

Even Treshnish or Oisin would have broken the spell, the barren sighing of waves, the bleak converse of gulls. If only she could look up and see bobbing heads near her.

As if conjured by longing, a grunt broke the silence. Startled, Wingfoot stared forward and, as the swell gave a lift, saw the faces regard her, their whiskered snouts twitching. There were a dozen or more, the nodding seals in a group, and, flippering with excitement, she rushed on to meet them. 'Augh,' the sound came again and with pleasure she answered.

An instant later she halted. The joy had sloughed from her.

The seals were glaring and snorting, peering angrily at her. Some were showing their fangs while a juvenile hissed, loudly beating the water. Wingfoot studied them dumbly. They had oddly snub noses, were smaller beasts than her kindred, of more uniform colour. These were common or sand seals, no lovers of greys, and their greeting was hostile.

In its teeth, the calf dithered. She was preparing to bolt when they appeared to lose interest, glancing round at the ocean. Suddenly they were jumpy, straining up to see better, some half out of the water in their agitation. Seconds later they scattered, a number porpoising madly, others diving so swiftly they left sparkling fountains. Bemused, the silver seal watched, soon alone on the surface.

49

The sand seals' flurry disturbed her, raised a shadowy memory of Finn in full flight, Bragela leading a rout, the grey seals in blind panic, charging into the shallows. It all came vividly back: her puzzlement and the fear, the terror she had known then and felt now in her marrow. Tension crawled on the swell, chilled her nape, made her tingle. Then suddenly she was plunging, speeding deeper and deeper, grimly seeking a funk-hole.

She remembered the lobster, its escape in the seaweed. Emulating the creature, she lay low in the fronds overwhelmed by her dread – of just what she knew not, but it had daunted the seals and when one of them passed, fleeing dimly through space, Wingfoot almost stopped breathing. For a while she cowered stiffly, the lanky weed trembling.

Then something huge filled the flood and the half-light grew darker. A grotesque hull was looming, spreading shock waves below so the quaking fronds stooped, grovelling to the sea monster. The giant was thirty feet long, black and yellowy-white, its fins larger than Wingfoot, a deadly king of the deep, sovereign in its assurance. Petrified, the seal flinched. The brute slewed, gliding slowly, trailing unctuous currents, churning silt as it passaged.

Perhaps a cable ahead, the killer whale turned and quartered, to Wingfoot's horror returning. Now she saw it face-on, its scoop-mouth leering smugly. It had consumed its first seal and the killer sought others. She saw it swerve, its eyes cold, then wheel again overhead, blasting grit from the bottom. Appalled, she lay doggo, as had the lobster before her.

Thrice the giant passed the fronds as if scenting her presence. Finally it made off, intent still on the sand seals, its dusky shape dwindling. Once, it seemed to turn back before, faint in the gloom, it forsook Wingfoot's vision. She did not budge for five minutes and then her movement was brief, a swift clamber for air, the return to her hideout.

Another hour had elapsed when, sufficiently steeled, she abandoned the weed and swam close to the bottom, making use of its cover. By now the sea-bed was shelving and she followed the rise, desperate in her fright for the safety of the shallows. It was to be a long haul. At periods she glanced round, afraid she might be pursued; now and then she rose quickly, seeking land, seeing nothing.

And yet she travelled in hope, for the sea's depth diminished.

At last her toil was rewarded. There it was, grey and ragged, a chimera of wild cliffs sharpening as she swam, growing hearteningly solid. But there was no friendly strand and she was forced to plunge on, following the cliffs tiredly. When next she blew they were gone, a small island before her, a place of squat little hills where a stony bay beckoned.

Here, to Wingfoot's relief, clear green shallows appeared, a mosaic of bright pebbles.

Snorkelling to the beach, the seal flopped on its shingle.

The priest had perched on a boulder, a fishing-rod at his side as he studied the scene, slowly munching a sandwich. He watched the young seal in silence. Another pilgrim, he thought, to the shrine of St Columba who, nineteen centuries ago, had landed just where the seal had, trudging over the stones to raise his church where the burn ran.

The wee beast would have pleased him: a tough old

fellow, Columba, but a friend of dumb creatures as well as of poor people. The calf's arrival was fitting, a happy touch to the bay, the ancient rock of the faithful, historic Iona.

In spring the wild flowers bloomed on it, primrose and wild orchis, and then the larks sang their praises. Now, the seashore was quiet and a silver seal rested.

The breeze was quiet as a mouse but deceptively cold, and groups of gulls sat puffed up on the quay's huddled buildings. Aggie's pink nose felt icy. A small bird hopped among the rocks, plucking off periwinkles. Far away on the sand, dark against a chill sky, a lone figure was digging. The girl had watched from the shop and now, reaching the beach, made her way through the stones. On the wet strand she sprinted.

The lad was forking for bait, leaving thick greyish mounds like bleak forts on the shore where a creeping tide glittered. Above the short-handled fork, Donnie's face was intent, his hat low on his brow, spikes of fair hair escaping. As the girl scurried near, he glanced up, sighing deeply – the sigh a busy man gives when his privacy's threatened.

'They'll hear your feet,' he complained. 'Must you come clomping round? They're senstive to vibrations. I'll catch no more lugworms.'

In a box on the sand they were wriggling, reddish things with large heads and, as Aggie had seen, nasty watery innards. 'You're doing well,' she approved. 'Would you like me to help you?'

'Jigging round doesn't help. I can't dig where you're prancing.'

'I'll come along if you like, if you're going off angling.'

'No thanks.'

'Oh, go on,' the girl wheedled. 'I scarcely see you now, Donnie.'

'You can see that I'm busy.'

'That you're hard,' she protested, scuffing sand with a foot and throwing in, 'I think of you. I thought of you in the gale.' Her voice was plaintive. 'I worried.'

Donnie failed to respond.

'For you,' she spelled it out clearly. 'I couldn't help it. I worried.'

He drove the fork. 'It was nothing. Hold your tongue now, I'm digging.'

He pressed the prongs down and heaved. The worms were not far below, in the top eighteen inches. The trick was choosing a cast and forking half a foot from it, vertically through the sand, then quickly turning the pile. As he gave it a flick, the lugworm squirmed in the heap. Donnie stooped, an arm stretched, and the worm joined the others.

'The waves were high,' murmured Aggie.

'Waves?' he said, looking up. He thought of Calum's indifference. 'You don't suppose we were bothered? We're not kids on the boats; a few waves don't concern us.'

'I told my mam you'd not scare.'

'We don't think of the danger.'

'I'm sure that I would,' said Aggie. 'You're a cool one,' she marvelled.

'Ach,' he said, not displeased, almost glad she had come, 'I don't know, maybe, Aggie.' He played it Calum's way, calmly. 'You can't be fretting on boats, it's no job for the nervous.'

'That it's not,' exclaimed Aggie. She had a strong urge to please him.

In the heap by his boots she saw another worm move and she pounced, fingers scrabbling. 'There you are,' she said proudly.

Donnie leaned on the fork. He was at last smiling at her. 'You wee daft girl.'

'It's more bait.'

'It's a ragworm. You've the wet sand all down you.' He clasped her hand and yanked roughly, pulling her to her feet. 'You can't mix them like that. You put that in the box and it'll kill all the others.'

Aggie squealed as she rose, startled by his quick jerk. For a moment she giggled. 'I didn't know,' she gulped, quietening.

'Now you do.'

'Yes,' she answered. Her fingers were tingling. 'I'll remember that, Donnie.'

'Aye,' he said, 'lugs and rags,' and he carried on digging. She watched him, stroking her hand, and thought the sea agreed with him. His face was tanned, with less spots, his plump cheeks seeming firmer. She thought her voyager bonnie, not that that was what mattered or she would moon over others. There was more to it than that; she did not know what it was. Her mother called it a 'crush'; he had, for sure, crushed her fingers.

She said, 'You know a lot, Donnie.'

'Bait?' He sniffed. 'Bait is child's play. You learn a lot more at sea. At sea you see things,' he told her.

'What?' she urged.

He let her wait while he dug. Presently he said, 'Things,' with a mysterious squint, adding, 'Things in the waves, like faces peering up at you.' He saw her gawp. 'People's faces.'

'People?' echoed the girl.

'There was this drowning face staring, all white and drained,' Donnie whispered.

Aggie broke the spell briefly. 'Another worm,' she intoned; 'you've gone and put the fork through it.'

'That's no good, it won't keep. They're no good once they're damaged.' He took her back to the story. 'It's true,' he said. 'In the gale, you ask Calum, he'll tell you. I saw it plain as your nose. You get to see things like faces.'

'Sea people,' she murmured.

Donnie worried a worm-track, forking round it with vigour. He missed the lugworm and scowled.

'It's like the tale of King Lochlann; do you remember that, Donnie?'

He shook his head, so she told him – how Lochlann's first wife had died and he had married another who loathed her several step-children, consumed by jealousy of them. Resolved to spirit them off, she had got hold of a potion that would turn them all into fishes when next they went bathing.

'But,' said the girl, prattling on, 'she had broken the flask and, scooping up what she could, had only half the stuff left to put into the goblets.'

Donnie straightened and grunted.

'So?' he said to indulge her.

'So it only half-worked. Next time they swam in the sea each one was partly transformed, half a fish and half human.' She paused, eyes on him. 'Sea people.'

'A fairy story.'

'Seals, Donnie.'

'The worse for them,' he observed. 'What I saw was no seal. It was white-faced, I told you.'

'So's Wingfoot, or very like it, she's silver. You must have seen her at sea. I think that's wonderful, Donnie, it means that Wingfoot's alive. It's a lucky encounter.'

He frowned, his own yarn upstaged. 'Think what you like,' he returned, sternly sloping the fork, 'I'm off to fish from the pier.'

'I'll come too.'

'No, I'll likely meet Calum.'

'He'll have his wife with him, Donnie.'

Donnie picked up the box. 'Just me and Calum,' he grunted.

'She's always there on the pier; she was there in the gale. Mary's always there waiting. Why can't I come if she's there?'

'It's different,' said Donnie.

Aggie saw his cheeks redden. She faced him fiercely, chin rising. 'Yes, you fool, she's a woman and you're sixteen, Donnie. You know what you've got – a crush. If you don't want me, then go. See if I care, MacDonald.'

Wingfoot took little heed of the priest. Hauled out on the shingle she spent much time asleep and he never disturbed her, getting on with his fishing. Once or twice a monk joined them. The monk did not bring a line but would sit quietly nearby, his head cowled when it blew, reading a paperback novel. Soon the priest left Iona, his sabbath there over.

Alone, the seal roamed the coast from her pebble-shelved haven. At either end of the isle were little hills and rough glens, a flat strip in between broadening into *machair* in the north-eastern quarter. Across a wintery sound the Ross of Mull clenched its fist, a brawny arm punching west from the roofs of Lochbuie.

There was plenty of fishing. The sole and flounders were good; there were wrasse in fair numbers. Though Wingfoot yearned to be home, she ate well and was safe in the priest's reef-strewn inlet. Loath to risk a long trip, she hung on at Iona.

The seal spent countless hours hunting. At other times she hauled out or would sleep underwater, sheltering from the weather. Great clouds reared and winds screamed, icy calms gripped the islands, gave them wintery mantles. Every once in a while, dawn would bring a false spring and they glowed on the sea, but more often they loured, sleet or rain blurring outlines. Then the ferry-boats slouched and the trawlers passed dimly.

She met the sand seals again. The creatures loomed from a storm, company in their way, but she did not dare to join them. They stayed for almost a fortnight, ignoring her presence, then moved off up the sound for the lochs to the north and the banks which they favoured. Another time, farther west, she fell in with porpoises, undulating beside them. Though friendly enough they soon left, speeding south after mackerel.

By January, still lonely, Wingfoot thought winter endless. And then, one fine early evening, a flight of dark birds appeared, skirling back up the sound to their spring breeding places. They had thick horny beaks and came fast into sight, powering low overhead before, extending their feet, they rocked down to the water. There the razorbills sailed, line-abreast on the swell, ducking under in mass for the fry they had sighted.

Before long others joined them, puffins, petrels and gannets, homing after their travels. The little shearwaters came, knifing over the waves, flicking this way and that to show glinting black backs and then contrasting bellies. It was the moment to leave, to seek the cove of her birth, and yet the seal hesitated. The call was strong, the skies kind, but could she find her way back? She had made off in disorder, swept up without bearings and was lost for direction. Would instinct preserve her? Should she risk the sea's dangers?

A starry night mocked her doubts. Decked with bright astral knowledge, it lit the swell with its sheen, but its wisdom escaped her. Stretching out on the beach she dozed in short restless spells, as fidgety as the tide with its constant lap-lapping. 'Come,' it said, and then, 'Stay,' drawing out and returning. She lay ashore until dawn and then went to the water. It rolled in out of a mist, vapour filling the inlet.

Wingfoot swam on the surface, flippering through the greyness. A patchy blur marked the reef and as she slowly approached something stirred on its brow, large and ghostly. With a snort she ducked down and went on, peeping up in a moment. The hazy form was still there and she was turning away when its scent reached her muzzle. In disbelief she swung back, nosing cautiously closer. At that point the mist swirled and a gap opened in it.

The ancient seal gave a yawn, his huge neck stretching up, awesome in its blotched girth, blubber-ringed, scored and pitted. Down his scarred Roman snout Cellach threw her a glance as his narrow eyes watered. Then, statuesque in the dawn, like some creature of legend, he lapsed back into slumber.

Astonished, Wingfoot swam round him. The mist was coming and going and now the Abbot was lost, now thrust back into sight, now a dream snatched away then ineffably solid. The old bull at Iona. It took a while to sink in; the implications took longer. He would not be on his own, that seemed very unlikely. There would be others around, grey seals back from the depths, grey seals bound for the cove, for Seal Island, the skerries. She was no longer alone; she would travel with guidance.

'Hooo,' she called from the mist. Her ears strained for an answer.

For a while there was none, then 'Hooo-oo' came an echo and, as the sun burned the haze, there they were on the waves, at least a score of grey seals, their distinctive heads shining. Many of them were youngsters, their first dispersal survived, meeting up as they homed with their friends of the autumn.

A golden head broke the ripples. Wildly Wingfoot advanced, her flippers meeting wet shoulders, her darting kisses profuse as Niamh's daubed her muzzle. Exuberantly they bussed then examined each other. Both were into their moult, their third coats well advanced, and neither beast had changed colour. More than pleased, they rubbed snouts and went back to embracing.

The rising sun made them gleam, dazzling as they cavorted. Leaping high they hurled spray then tore down through clear depths, jinking over the stones, paired like twins as they sped, every caper and tilt celebrating reunion. Backs arching, they raced, swerving, waltzing, zigzagging, their eyes as round and as bright as the pebbles beneath them. Suddenly they turned upwards as one, shattering the jewelled surface.

Joyously Wingfoot twirled, her long loneliness over, her completeness regained as a gregarious creature. Elatedly the seals flew in their dance of the water. Side by side they let rip, hurdling waves and switchbacking, then in line they played tag, the old game of calf days when all life was amusement. Every now and again they would pause, clap or buss, then once more they would frisk where the swell flared and sparkled. They were young, wild and free; it was spring and home beckoned.

On the reef, Cellach scratched. His days of madness were gone and he ignored their behaviour. He was drained of excitement. Today he bowed to few urges, not even to those of late summer, the time of mating in earnest. If he was bound for the cove it was not to disport at the great spring assembly but to safeguard his seat, Cellach's throne on the skerries. There he paid his devotions not to seasons or passions but the gods of old age, idleness and reflection and, mightiest, slumber.

Now the younger seals waited, watching for him to move, for they trusted his knowledge. None of them was so travelled. He knew the waves of Tiree, Little Minch and the North Channel. He had indeed reached the outposts, Sula Sgeir and The Hunters, and probed the south past Kintyre to the mouth of Loch Ryan. And he had braved the dire roar, the dread wrath of Corrievreckan. He knew the soundings and tides and was a skilled navigator.

So when the old one bestirred, many youngsters took notice. He left his couch with a grunt; an explosive splash followed. It made Niamh pause and stare, halting Wingfoot's exertions. The Abbot's grizzled head bobbed. In a moment it turned and the V-wake stood seawards. The breathless pair eyed each other. Already some seals were moving, making off to the south, and when Niamh gave chase her companion soon followed.

They set out in high spirits. There was an air of excitement, a race to be with the leaders as the shore fell behind them. Wingfoot swam with Niamh. Others thrust alongside, some as young as themselves, some at eighteen months old grown as large as small adults. A few mature cows went too, due to calve in late summer. There was the odd untried bull and, at the head of all, Cellach, his pace surprisingly brisk, achieved in long shallow dives with short spells on the surface.

When the first rush eased up, the seals cruised resolutely.

Niamh's mood was serene. Gliding under the swell she seemed to lack any qualms, any fear of the voyage, as unworried as ever. This was not true of Wingfoot, who remembered the killer. Her glances were anxious, becoming quicker and keener the farther shelter receded, the deeper the water. There was comfort in numbers but as the journey went on so the convoy thinned out, until, patchy and straggling, it was less reassuring.

The more she looked for support, the fewer creatures she noticed. Only Niamh stayed close, calmly ploughing the flood, and Niamh was no safeguard. They were small and exposed and when a flurry ahead indicated seals turning, leaving course at high speed, Wingfoot's fears seemed well founded. For a moment she stopped, then relief forestalled panic. They had run into a shoal, a large movement of codling, and the mammals were pouncing.

Wingfoot's greed overcame her. Below, a second school browsed, quietly nosing the bottom. The meaty cod were enticing, up to two feet in length, three or four years of age, green on top with dark spots. Barbelled chins near the floor, they were harvesting sandworms and when she plunged they split up, the surprised swimmers bolting.

So eager was she in chase that she did not spot the net, the peril draped in the depths, until too late to avoid it.

She struck the thing at full tilt, nose and flippers entangled. Suddenly she was struggling, wriggling like the fish as the clinging bonds bit, every twist and turn binding. Frantically she contorted, complicating the muddle. At last, in shock, she held still, her plight bearing in grimly: her oxygen running low, no escape from entrapment.

The other seals had moved on; of Niamh, she saw nothing. In heightened terror she threshed, wasting crucial resources. Then, like a fly in a web, she gave in and just waited.

She was near suffocation when the net started rising.

'There's something there,' muttered Gorme.

'That's for certain,' said Calum. 'And more than fish, by my reckoning.'

Donnie watched the net dripping.

'Come on, boy, don't doze off.'

'More than fish?' the lad queried.

Calum pulled his leg quietly. 'Could be an old German mine. Not the first we'd have netted.' The man pondered gravely.

'Mine? You don't mean a live one?'

'Aren't they all? Ask the skipper.'

'You're joking,' Donnie said tensely.

Calum's face did not yield.

63

'Ha, you're kidding me, Calum.'

'You'll find out. Work her steady.'

The net sucked up from the sea. It seemed to come with reluctance and Donnie was nervous. Water socked at the bulwarks. With a squelch it fell back, the swell torpid and fleshy, the boat's shadow writhing. Donnie viewed the sea bleakly. Even when it was calm its immensity menaced like some leering great thug, always flexing its muscles. He could believe any story, anything of those depths: monsters, mermaids or mines, spouts and maelstroms, drowned treasure. Drowned men, come to that; Aggie Fraser's drowned father.

Calum chested the gunwale. 'Ach, you're safe, that's no' mine.' He peered down at the tangle. 'Do you ken, lad, look there.'

Donnie glimpsed the trapped creature. Its frightened eyes met his own, its face pale, the mouth gaping. 'A silver sealie,' he breathed. She had said it was silver.

'I'm damned,' said Calum, impressed. 'Keep your hands back, she'll have them; she'll have those bairn's fingers off you.'

Gorme was thundering. 'Kill it.'

Helplessly, the seal struggled.

'Kill the thieving brute, Calum.'

Still the pale face was staring and Donnie felt frightened. It was the face from the gale and he could hear Aggie saying, 'I think that's wonderful, Donnie, it means that Wingfoot's alive.' It was grotesque, like a nightmare. The seal was hissing, eyes weeping.

'Kill it, man, let's get on.'

Donnie gulped.

'Pass that knife, lad,' growled Calum.

The sea was splashing and slurping. In the net, cod were flapping. Donnie passed the knife dumbly and saw its razor-edge flashing. He was too scared to protest, the blade's shimmer mesmeric. As he watched, Calum moved, blocking Gorme's line of sight, then the knife slashed the net, deftly freeing the captive. With a plop the seal vanished. 'Damn,' said Calum, 'she's gone. Broke clean loose as I stuck her.'

Poker-faced, he eyed Donnie.

'How's the net?' Gorme asked, scowling.

'Nae too bad, it'll mend.'

'She'll no' live,' Gorme reflected.

Calum shook his great head.

Gorme said, 'Verminous thieves, they need culling ashore. I'll get round to it one day.'

Later, gutting the fish, Donnie studied the big man. Calum worked without talking, his expression remote and, like the sea, uninviting. The hush seemed unnatural. 'I thought,' the boy broke the spell, 'that you were going to do it. I thought you would for a moment.'

The other barely glanced up.

'Calum,' Donnie confided, 'you know I've seen her before — saw her face in the waves. They're like sea people, eh, Calum?'

'Mind where you're throwing those livers.'

'I mean,' Donnie persisted, 'don't you think it's uncanny?' But Calum did not reply and the spell remained potent. It had all happened quickly and yet each detail was vivid: the creature's eyes, the bright blade, every sharp image haunting. At length the lad said, intrigued, 'I didn't think you would save her. You had your reasons, I reckon.'

'I had my reasons,' growled Calum.

'Will Gorme really cull them? He'll need a gang on it, won't he?'

'Ask him, son, don't ask me.'

'You'd not join them, eh, Calum?'

The man clammed up, his frown daunting. He said no more until they landed and he had joined the tall woman, then he called from the quay, 'No girl waiting, MacDonald? A handsome lad should do better.' The woman smiled at the youth as if, he thought, they were friends, and he damned his hot blushes.

When they had gone and he had washed he made his way to the shop, needing someone to listen, to share the trip's strange excitement. He could not talk to the men, not about such a matter – a wee silver seal – for they would think him soft-headed. They would laugh at his tale and make fun of his notions. The girl would understand best; such odd happenings enthralled her. The silver seal was her pet. She would be hugely impressed and he could not wait to tell her.

'The child's gone out,' said her mother, watchful as he peered round. Was there something he wanted? Mrs Fraser perturbed him. It was her businesslike manner: it always made him feel awkward.

'I just had something to tell her.'

'Will you not leave a message? You know she's lots to do, Donnie; and so must you have, I'm thinking.'

'Would you know where she is?'

'I wouldn't, Donnie MacDonald.'

He put a hand to his brow and crushed the spiky hair backwards. 'I'll try to find her,' he said. 'I've some news, Mrs Fraser.'

'Well, just remember she's busy, so if you meet her

don't keep her. I've got more errands need running. You send her home now, you hear me?'

He cycled over the dunes and took the path to the cove, pausing high on the cliffs where a large stone protruded. Half-hidden by growth, it had a boat on its face, carved in shallow relief, and showed men killing seals with long, primitive cudgels. It was no novelty to him; he had grown up on Seal Island with its reminders of slaughter, not all of them ancient.

Pushing on he free-wheeled, bumping down to the seal strand. The girl was standing with Willie and listened, thrilled, to the story, past anger forgotten. 'Now,' she said, 'you'll believe me, now you've seen her so close. Donnie, isn't she special; have you known a beast like her? She wasn't harmed, you're quite sure?'

'He never touched her, I watched.'

'Good for Calum,' said Aggie.

'I was surprised that he freed her.'

'The fellow's soft,' said Macrae. 'The man's been daft since a laddie.'

'You're daft yourself,' Aggie bridled.

'Not as simple as Calum. I'll tell you this much, wee lass, I wouldn't work for a Gorme nor be as soft in the head as to wed yon weird Mary. As for cutting a net — I'd no' have damaged a net, not for king nor for country.'

Aggie said, 'You've no heart,' and drew closer to Donnie.

'Take no notice,' he told her, 'you shouldn't listen to Willie.'

Macrae's expression was evil. 'You've no respect, either of you. And nor have they, the wild devils.'

The bay was filling with seals, their spring carnival starting. As the travellers returned they made sport in the cove, pairs and groups water-dancing, racing round, switching partners. Maiden females disported, virgin bulls showed their paces. Older females, though pregnant, caught the spirit and flirted while seasoned warriors mingled, tolerant of each other. It was no time to draw bounds nor for stuffy decorum at the great spring reunion and all was prancing and kissing.

'Look,' cried Aggie, 'there's Cellach; Cellach's back on his seat. And there's Cuchulainn, too.' She clutched Donnie's arm, jigging. 'There's Niamh, see, with Oisin. And Pebble and Treshnish. Oh, but can you find Wing-foot?'

'They're a plague,' Macrae grumbled. 'There'll be no peace here tonight, just the de'ils caterwauling.'

'Singing,' Aggie corrected.

The dancing continued. As they tired, the seals beached, lying back in the sun and scratching where they had moulted, some watchful, some dozing. Many napped on the skerries, stretching out near the Abbot. Soon refreshed, they bounced up, off to twirl with new part-ners. The youngest frolicked in sets, giddily cutting circles, Oisin chasing Niamh, trying hard to impress her.

'I've seen Bragela,' said Aggie. 'Oh, but Donnie, where's Wingfoot?'

He raised a hand to his eyes, shading them from the brilliance. Far away by the buoy a seal had rounded the point, taking bearings and diving, then surfacing closer. A silver head caught the sun. 'Coming in,' he exclaimed. 'Look, out there, past the rocks. That's the sealie for sure; you could never mistake her.'

'Yes, that's her, she's arrived.' Aggie's arms rose in triumph. 'Safely home,' the girl crowed, 'with the winter behind her.'

'Winter?' scoffed the old man. 'A few winds? She's seen nothing; the brute's like you, scarcely lived. She'll no' be safely home yet, no more'n you while you're living. When you're my age you'll know. While there's life there's worse brewing.'

PART TWO

The Cauldron

There was, this day, a great bull-fight. It had been threatening since dawn, the rival animals surly. The crippled gull saw it coming and raised itself from the beach where it had stood, its stump dangling. The nursing cows sensed it, too, and drew away with their babes across the festering kelp to leave a space in the crowd, a little sandy arena washed by jittery wavelets.

Swarms of small flies hung low, flitting as the sea creamed, aggravating the calves and infesting the seaweed. From the croft round the bay came the sound of a hammer used in unhurried blows, like a metronome swinging. In a while the blows stopped: perhaps the old man was drinking.

Now the warriors came, the lustful lords of the nurseries. They were proclaimed by their scent, the tarry smell of the rut, their bloodshot eyes disputatious – Cuchulainn of the crags and big Finn the beachmaster. Since Cellach's powers had declined, there had been none to out-fight them.

The first emerged from the surf, the second humped from the shingle. At the sea's edge they stopped, its line at low tide their march, and Cuchulainn's avid glance swept the females assembled. Incited, Finn took the ring, his shuffle heavy with purpose. There he issued his warning, the territorial challenge, stretching out a vast neck with his toothy mouth open.

Many a concupiscent poacher would have run at that moment, but not the laird of the rocks, not Cuchulainn of the skerries. Cuchulainn feared no rival, a beast whose many war victories were only equalled in number by his sexual conquests. When still young, long ago, he had usurped the ageing Abbot in a fight still remembered, a battle lasting two days and terrible in its damage.

Today the gull screamed above and on the strand the cows waited. The cove was hot, the sun high, a breathless bight so subdued its puny rollers collapsed, trundling in enervated. In their froth the bulls paused, Finn the dark-skinned contestant, the other bleached by the years like a grizzled old tusker. They were the giants of the herd: nine hundred pounds took the ring, each bull seal an eight-footer.

For several minutes they glared, their chests broad on the sand, then with a heave of their arms the big males attacked headlong. The thud of flesh as they met struck the cliffs and resounded. It was as if two great trees had been felled so their trunks struck each other. The shock, fragmenting the waves, sent a pall of mist skywards.

At first both beasts held their ground. They fought with teeth and clawed flippers, their rolling eyes showing white, their fury rained on thick necks uglified by bygone contests. It was a ponderous tussle. They gnashed at blubbery rolls, the rings of fat that each carried, already scarred like worn tyres and soon doubly disfigured. Raking short curly manes, they wrenched the tufts in their rage and chewed at skin like starved monsters.

Neither growls nor cries left them, their violence eerily

quiet, the only sounds from the sea and the calves when they bleated.

When one white calf strayed too close it was snatched swiftly by Finn, shaken hard for its pains and hurled back at the spectators. A few regarded the mite but left its mother to claim it, her anxious wail skirling. Most remained unconcerned until the fight veered towards them, then the nearby seals fled to crowd those ranged behind them.

Now the beachmaster reeled, the sand luridly reddening. Another round had begun and Finn, forced from the sea, had his back to the shingle. Thrown off balance, he turned, bent on switching his ground, but Cuchulainn seized his tail, fiercely biting the flippers. At this the other stopped dead, quivering in his torment. Galvanized, he tore free, wheeling on his opponent, the run of battle reversed as a maddened Finn sallied.

Once more the waves rinsed their wounds, churning over their shoulders. A fiery sun made them gleam and beat down on the shallows. Here and there, farther out, bobbing heads strained to watch while splayed flippers trod water. It creamed the backs of the giants, fell in sheets as they reared, sluiced from huge barrel forms as the brute frenzy mounted. Both were curtained with blood, their flesh injuries grisly. Viciously they attacked, spurred by the damage inflicted.

For maybe ten or more minutes they slanted up from the tide, powerful jaws working grimly. Locked together they lurched, twisted round and lashed out, raising scaffolds of spray, steely as the sun met them. At times they leaned on each other, at times one would draw off to crash back with fresh fury. Neither creature gave way, though, slowly, stamina weakened and the breaks between rounds were longer and more frequent. Cuchulainn would crouch down, Finn submerge in the water.

Once, in this fashion hidden, Finn made a sudden assault, catching Cuchulainn's chest, the curved fangs piercing deeply. Surprised, the laird towered and swayed, his eyes widening in anguish. And then, in pain, he dived steeply, crashing down through a wave to turn, seeking revenge, speeding back on the bottom. The surging charge left a wake, two diverging swells rising, spreading out overhead as he speared at his rival.

As he shot from the foam he seized Finn by the throat, almost bowling him sideways. Again they wrestled and threshed, brine and blood intermingling, the cauldron seeming to boil with repulsive pink bubbles. The necks of both were macabre. The craters in them were raw, chunks of blubber removed, the fat striped with claw-furrows, and from Cuchulainn's breast hung a great strip of skin like a wind-bereft pennant.

They struggled on for an hour, their strength gradually draining. Each was weary and blown, reserves already decreased by several weeks of patrolling, the endless duties performed in a long mating season. Nostrils flared, the bulls puffed, breathing ever more deeply. Then, as a stalemate looked certain, the decisive blow landed.

Somehow Finn found the strength for one more wild offensive. Lumbering at the foe, he feinted, ducked and drove home, catching Cuchulainn's nose with a hammering flipper. It was enough for its victim. Dazed and shaking his snout, Cuchulainn turned away, heading back for the skerries. Unrepentant, he slouched, his reluctant strokes sulky. A final gesture remained, the ritual act of the victor.

Slowly dropping his head, Finn let out a low hiss, at last breaking the silence. Then, where the smallest waves lapped, he eased himself on his side and rolled triumphantly over so that he faced up the beach, the territory defended. Battered, torn but unbowed, he regarded the females.

Wingfoot still found him awesome. Two years after her birth, that bleak night of the storm-calf, she was not charmed by such hulks or their inelegant battles. Though now as large as some cows, a seal of striking appearance, she was of immature status with three more years as a maiden before the urge to breed roused her. True, she came to the nursery for its memories haunted, but like most of her age she kept apart from its passions, whiling time round the point or the farthermost skerries.

When the fracas was done she dived for peace to the depths, gliding through the sea-gardens, searching rocks for crustaceans. Coming soon to the cave she peered inside for the eel, recalling how, with Niamh, she had first found its dungeon. And how the conger had scared them. She was prepared for it now; indeed, the prospect excited, the thought of thick meat enticing. But the eel had withdrawn, out of reach in its labyrinth, and she was frustrated.

Surfacing near the point, she saw a seal on the buoy and swam over. The platform rose and fell gently and Wingfoot, meaning to rest, had begun to climb up when its occupant snapped, causing her to slip backwards. Flippering in the trough, she took a look at her assailant. She might have guessed it would be Treshnish, that least friendly of neighbours, a beast who seldom drew near without expressing resentment. So far Wingfoot had borne it, though her patience was shrinking. One day, she thought . . .

But not now.

Now the warmth made her yawn and she fell back on the current, drifting lazily off until she heard a soft splash and, looking up, caught sight of Niamh and Oisin. They were cavorting in circles, sporting brazenly together. They made a handsome young pair, long and lithe as they turtled, the bronzed flank of Niamh brushing Oisin's black torso. The male was setting the pace, his companion delighted. Their rapport nettled Wingfoot.

Suddenly Oisin saw her. He sped across in a flash, tossing spume, showing off, jostling her as he gambolled. He poked his snout in her face, slapped her neck, flipped beneath her. She did not care for his attentions and let him know with a hiss, obliging him to move off. Then she turned to Niamh, looking for her approval.

But Niamh's eyes were for Oisin. As he turned she rushed to him, falling in at his side, and they were gone, leaving Wingfoot forsaken.

The lad had filled out a lot lately, more a man than a boy, but then he must be eighteen, three years older than Aggie. Of course, the years hardly counted, for Aggie made him seem childish. What exercised Mrs Fraser was not the poor lad's intentions but where her daughter might lead him.

'She won't be long; sit down, Donnie.'

The youth sat down, his arms folded, dumbly viewing the dresser.

'She'll be upstairs titivating; goodness knows what

she'll look like.' There was no way of predicting, the woman reflected. 'She's at that age,' she confided.

Donnie's glance was perplexed and Mrs Fraser felt for him. He was a good honest boy but soon the girl would outgrow him; he was too dull for her now, though Aggie still led him on – like a dog, thought her mother, regarding his patience.

'Will I make you a coffee?'

He shook his head and she asked, 'Have you plans to go somewhere?' for the girl had said nothing.

'To the cove, Mrs Fraser. She wants to see the new calves.'

'Oh well,' the woman replied, 'then she'll be occupied, won't she? She'd spend all day watching seals.' She gave a smile of relief. If all they did was watch seals, the child would be out of mischief; the beasts were still her first interest. 'See she behaves herself, Donnie.'

He gave a grave, courtly nod and Aggie entered the kitchen. She looked, her mother thought, pretty. She wore a short cotton dress, her thin legs as brown as chestnuts. A coloured band held her hair in a semblance of tameness.

'Wake up, then,' she exclaimed. 'I'm not idling, Donnie.'

Donnie rose, his grin sheepish.

Mrs Fraser tut-tutted. 'It's you who've idled, my girl, sitting up there and preening.'

'He could've cycled ahead, I'd very soon have caught up. He's as slow as a cart-horse.'

'And you can slow down yourself.' The woman straightened her shoulders. 'Now look,' she said, the words measured, 'I want you home for tea, Aggie. You be sure she is, Donnie, I'll not be having excuses, for Mr

Muir will be here. He's coming in from Oban and we'll be sitting down promptly. After the voyage, he'll be peckish.'

'Yes, yes,' Aggie said briskly.

'And don't you forget, child.'

As boy and girl crossed the dunes, the first asked who Mr Muir was. 'Oh, no one,' Aggie threw back, 'the man who comes for our orders, a traveller from the wholesaler. He brings the samples and so on. It's not important, don't worry.'

'You'd better be there,' said Donnie, for whom her mother's words mattered; he had not lost his awe of her. He cycled on, ruminating. Oyster-catchers were feeding and a distant sea sparkled. 'I wouldn't care to upset her,' he owned on reflection.

'It's me you'd best not upset.' Aggie laughed but it was meant. 'We'll go home when we're ready.'

Despite the band, her hair blew as her legs pumped the pedals. There was an ominous glint in the look that she gave him. Though still attached to the youth, time had opened her eyes and, glimpsing faults once unseen, she was crusading with zeal to improve the flawed model. The woman in her was talking: 'If it's a choice, Donnie boy, you'd better not choose my mother. Unless,' she trilled as she flew, 'you tire of me by the evening.'

'You're bloody daft,' Donnie muttered.

'Well, hurry up, you're so slow.' She raced ahead, calling back, 'I haven't seen them all week and there'll be new calves for certain. I can't wait; pedal faster.'

But the loose sand sapped her strength and he rode by her one-handed, an arm stretched out to her back, shoving her through the drifts. She liked the feel of his assistance. At last they freewheeled downhill, a long wild cruise to the cove with Aggie's squeals trailing back, then dismounted elated. Gulls were sailing far out and, from the beach, Macrae hailed them. 'Come on,' the girl said, 'ignore him. Look, the nursery's crowded.'

'Let's take a peek at his boat.' Donnie strode across the shingle.

'We came to see the seals, Donnie.'

'The beasts won't budge.' He walked on. He shared her interest in seals but boats were boats and came first. 'A quick glance at her, Aggie.'

She trotted by him, annoyed. He had a stubborn streak in him, something needing correction. She noted it with a pout. 'It's just a wreck,' she protested.

'He's done years of work on her.'

'More fool him, the thing's rotten.'

But Donnie shrugged off her views. She might be brighter than him but he was safe on this topic. After two years at sea he knew a bit about boats and did not need her opinions. He told her now, without malice, 'It takes an expert eye, Aggie, you'd not be trained to judge points.'

He viewed the craft, his gaze knowing. 'She's looking better then, Willie?'

'You'll see a change,' Macrae boasted.

'Aye,' said Donnie professionally.

'I thought you would, young MacDonald, you're no' the fool you were once.' The 'captain' puffed at his pipe. 'You've learned a few things at sea.'

'One or two,' agreed Donnie. He hoped that Aggie was listening. She seemed less struck with him these days, a harder girl to impress. He said, 'You're making good, Willie. She'll be a smart wee boat shortly.'

'When I've painted her, eh?'

The pair of clowns, Aggie thought. She showed her mounting impatience. 'Come on, Donnie, I'm waiting.'

'Yes, in a minute,' he said, obstinately unhurried. He gave the craft a fresh survey. 'Is she ready for painting?'

The 'captain' stroked his chin-stubble.

'Of course she's not,' the girl snapped. 'You can't put paint on bad wood, and if you could there's no paint. Where would Willie get paint? He spends his pension on whisky. Where would Willie get money?'

'Aye,' the lad said, 'where, Willie?'

The old man spat, looking sly. He said, 'Don't fash yourself, laddie, I'll find the paint, that's my business. I'll handle that when I'm ready. It's not the paint that's the problem; the only problem's the engine. I've no head for these diesels.'

Aggie turned, her voice grating. 'Are you coming, MacDonald?'

'Yes,' he said, 'half a minute. We might as well take a look.' He scrambled into the well, his head bent to the motor.

She could go off him, the girl thought.

Donnie said, 'It's a pig. You've a problem here, Willie.'

It was a pig of a muddle. Most of the casing had gone – two wooden sides and the roof – revealing something inside that should have been on a scrapheap. At all events, the boy mused, it was no prize to be salvaged. Thick black oil hid the metal, oozing down to its moorings, smearing leads and the shaft, running out in the bilge from where a thick reek of derv rose with a mixture of salt and a stench vaguely fishy. Rags were serving as gaskets and spanners lay rusting. To the throttle was fixed what appeared to be fence-wire, this extended with twine to a nail near the tiller.

'What it needs,' growled Macrae, 'is a diesel-man on it.'

'Or a bomb,' observed Aggie.

'Are ye demented?' he answered. 'That's a powerful good engine. She's the throb, when she's right, of a strong woman's bosom. Ye'd no' remember her running.'

Donnie clambered back out. He was visibly gloomy. 'She's not the best,' he admitted. 'She needs a bit of attention. She'd maybe want the odd part.'

'Could you manage it, laddie?'

'Me?' said Donnie, astonished.

'Man, it's no big proceeding, a case of tinkering with her.' The 'captain' knocked out his pipe. Stowing it in a pocket, he drew a flask from his hip and uncapped the container. 'Take a dram,' he invited and, when the lad shook his head, 'Maybe later,' he wheezed, 'when you've done sizing her up. You'll have the need to think clearly.' He took a tipple himself and replaced the cap slowly. His expression was solemn. 'If you've done planning the work, we'll have the terms to consider.'

Aggie wished she could kill him. Instead, she said with calm force, sounding much like her mother, 'I'm waiting, Donnie MacDonald; will you leave him this instant?'

'Ach,' Macrae interrupted, 'let him hear the proposal. You're no' your mam's girl, wee lass, if you'd not hear an offer.'

'She'd have the ears off you, Willie. She'd want no part of your scheming.'

Donnie gawped, torn between them.

'Just hear me out,' the man wheedled, 'there's a partnership for him. You couldn't quibble at that: a partnership for his trouble, a trifling job for an expert. That's awful generous, Aggie. A partnership with Macrae once the engine's in order. No more working for Gorme; a fair share of the business. Aye, you're thinking I'm soft, an old soft-hearted fool. Well, I've a place for the boy and I mind he'll be useful. He'll do all right in my business.'

'Your business, Willie? What business?'

'Why, the boat here, the *Peg*. You understand we'll be fishing.'

Donnie's mind caught them up. He said, 'Our own fishing business? Just you and me, Willie? I'd give that serious thought. Man, it's terrible tempting.'

'It's crazy,' Aggie retorted.

'Why?' said Donnie, beguiled. 'I reckon I'm just the man. I'd not be beat by an engine. She'd take a while but I'd manage.'

'She's not so bad,' Macrae added. 'A little job for the evenings.'

The girl could hardly believe it. 'It's daft,' she said. 'Drop it, Donnie. You'd give him all your spare time and end up smothered in grease. You needn't think I'd be waiting.'

The youth looked anxiously at her. For a moment he dithered.

'But if you were,' urged Macrae, 'you'd be the first to sail in her. We'd take you out round the seal rocks.' He eyed the girl, his grin foxy.

'There, you see.' Donnie brightened. 'You could watch the seals, Aggie. We'd follow them in the bay, go where Wingfoot was swimming. We could visit the skerries. Willie's right, you'd come with us.'

'Willie's mad, the *Peg*'s finished. Even with a good engine, she'd sink in two minutes.'

Disgruntled, Donnie flared up. 'Be damned,' he said, 'I'm not dim. How would you know?' he asked her.

'Are you coming?' she snarled. 'If not, I'll go on my own. You and him can talk nonsense.'

She turned away, walking slowly. She hoped that Donnie would follow and, when he failed to, cursed quietly, damning him with foul oaths, striding out in defiance. Among the seals she stood fuming, taking little heed of them. Small white calves slept or stared and one scratched a damp nose. Others lay in the pools, drowsily blowing bubbles. A big grey cow snorted at her. She was too angry to care.

Glancing back at the boat she could see Willie still babbling and that fool Donnie listening. Then they strolled to the croft and she watched the oafs enter.

Aggie scowled and mooched back. Poised on the seat of her bike, she heard their voices inside, the drunken idiot croaking, 'You'll take that dram with me now? Ye'll toast the partnership, laddie?'

'Since you're insisting then, Willie' – the other idiot blabbing.

She stamped the pedals and left, labouring up the incline, growing damp with exertion, her flimsy frock sticking to her. The front wheel scraped on a rock and she swore like a trooper. The noise stampeded a blackbird. There was a breeze at the top and, removing her headband, she flicked her hair in the draught as if to shake the fools from it. Her afternoon had been wrecked. She would make Donnie pay dearly; she doubted she would excuse him.

More than spoiling her outing, he had ruined the future, pledged to futile endeavours to please an old boozer. Ditched, she thought, for an engine, the *Peg*'s stinking diesel. Inexcusable, that was.

Unless . . .

She pictured the skerries with Cellach high on his slab, Wingfoot snoozing nearby, others resting like statues – and on a tranquil blue bay the painted *Peg* chugging round them, a chastened Donnie aboard, Aggie Fraser commanding. She might forgive him in that case.

And pigs might fly, she thought grimly.

She flounced indoors through the shop and a man rose to greet her. He was stout and quite bald, plainly straight from the steamer. He wore a light suit and tie and had a glittery wristwatch. No one went round like that unless they came from the mainland. Mr Muir's face was pale; it had a moonlike beam on it.

'My, you're growing up, Aggie.' He was clasping a sherry.

Mrs Fraser beamed too. She had put on her best dress, the one with heathery patterns. She said, 'Good girl, nice and early.'

Mr Muir said, 'Well, well, and what has Aggie been up to?'

'Looking over a boat.' She tried to hide her vexation.

She saw her mother's eyes narrow.

'Willie's *Peg*,' the girl grated.

'Oh, I see. Well, that's pleasant.'

Mr Muir drained his sherry. He was determinedly jolly. '*Peg*?' he cried, his face glowing. 'Well, well, well – Willie's *Peg*. Is that a blush we see, Peggy?'

At last the eel was exposed, caught away from its labyrinth, and Wingfoot dived swiftly. As she speared through the flow she could see the beast travelling, a thick and muscular brute, broad of head and large-eyed, its armed jaw at the ready.

Closing in, she bit fiercely, her fury primed by Niamh,

her mood as evilly-disposed as the bull seals in battle. The conger, prowling for food – sea-worms, fishes, crustaceans – had left its rocky retreat at an inopportune moment.

The huntress felt it recoil. Its snaking body was smooth, clad in thick greasy slime which the seal now encountered. It smeared her lips as she snapped and drove home her incisors. At which the serpent lashed out, its tail beating her body.

Wingfoot clung to the neck, rendering the mouth harmless. Nonetheless she was dragged, the eel's power and weight testing. It yanked her forward at speed, then, as she fought to hang on, abruptly shunted astern, its great torso contracting. Before the move could be stopped, her prey had latched to a crag, a tusk of limpet-scabbed rock which a greasy coil circled. In this way, firmly anchored, the eel refused to be budged no matter how Wingfoot tugged at it.

Infuriated, she heaved, hauling it from all angles until, frustrated, she paused and, releasing the neck, stormed the conger's coiled body. At once the creature enwrapped her, daubing her with its slime, a ferocious head darting. Savagely, she snapped back, re-addressing the neck, shaking it to and fro in such a frenzied attack that the brute uncoiled from her.

Twice it tried to break free, jerking round and convulsing; twice Wingfoot denied it, her teeth closing tighter. Though they sank to the bone, they did not bring submission.

Driven mad by the mauling, the serpent twirled and contorted, twisting her as it turned until the tide seemed to spin and a darkening roof slanted. Giddily, Wingfoot leeched, the eel bucking and rearing, scissoring to escape to the rocks, reach their sheltering crannies. But the huntress gave nothing. The struggle veered towards shore, flailing over the bottom through the tide's dusky flow, amid the swaying plantations, the haunts of odd little fish, of the blenny and goby. The conger failed to break free but its efforts continued.

Thwarted, Wingfoot bit deeper. It did not stop the eel thrashing and still they whirled on the bed, scattering sand and pebbles. Only near to the shallows did the tussle diminish. Now the sea serpent tired and the seal rode it upwards, but as they broached the flood's roof the eel's struggles redoubled. It fought this time in short bursts, dragging downwards then resting, always striving to dive with the rocks its objective.

Again the seal surfaced with it.

The sun had set, the bay calm, an afterglow on the skerries. Distantly, seals were hooting.

And again the eel wrestled. But its spasms were flagging; each whipping burst was short-lived, more resigned than the last, and the seal edged ashore bent on beaching her victim. Only then, on the sand, dare she loosen her neck-hold.

Purple-grey in the waves, the conger's greasy length pounded. Wingfoot wrenched the beast fiercely. Dragging it to the strand, she hammered it to subdue it. But when she put the eel down it still came up with reserves, starting back to the sea, and she had to act quickly. At the base of the skull she found her prey's spinal column and, with a final convulsion, its death-throes concluded.

Wingfoot took a long breath. With head raised she gazed round, the prize safely before her. Once the conger had scared her, now she savoured it smugly. It was more than a feast but she would scoff until full and then slumber contented. The breeze was light, the sky clear and an evening star twinkled.

The fog had closed quickly, sliding in round the buildings, filling alleys and yards and, like a sorcerer's spell,
causing moored boats to vanish. From the shop or the
chapel the quay might not have existed, or the sea for
that matter, its plops and sighs disembodied, its sweep a
grey nothing. There was no longer a headland, no shore,
no horizon. The sheds and nets were erased, the black
lobster-pots swallowed.

At last the sheer breadth of space, the island's roomy
location, became a fact in mind only, visibly undemon-
strable. Space itself crawled and clung, bewildering as a
blindfold. A woman's voice from a door sounded strange
to her neighbour; a cat came home like a phantom.
On a half-recalled corner the shades of two ageing men
discussed the fogs of the past, their reminiscences
muffled.

In the shroud of the morning a trip along the stone
pier, flanked by dimly seen bollards, was a weird explo-
ration, the ghosts of masts looming quietly, a hidden
swell gurgling. Shapes appeared, were expunged; crates
and trolleys dissolved giving way to bare slabs as the
mole's end approached, its steep plunge wreathed in
vapour. Here the light of a torch, a pale glow, blinked
and wavered.

The woman had a shawl round her, its corners draping her hips, her long skirt tightly woven, hugging her in the chill the fog's dampness brought with it. For a while she was still, vigilant in the gloom, then she prowled back and forth, her torch shining to sea, showing little but greyness. By and by she paused, listening. Faintly, seals were conversing, as if on some other planet.

Wingfoot swam to the pier, the strange light fascinating. She watched its pale blob move on, stop, then flicker a little. It was a will-o'-the-wisp, a most unnatural lantern. Once or twice through the fog she glimpsed the spectre behind it. But straight away the stuff swirled and it effaced Calum's woman.

Uncannily, overhead, the sound of wings pierced the cloud and the seal heard geese yapping. They passed above the grey shroud, barnacles in great skeins bound from Greenland to Islay, southeast of Seal Island, where many fowl wintered. Their creaking passage was timely, reminding her of the season. Again, the seals were departing, slipping off through the fog. Many followed the geese and now Wingfoot went with them, drawing out from the pier, lured away by the barking.

As she ploughed through the murk, the *Goosander* homed slowly. The boy and Calum were forward, peering into the fog, the wheelhouse dim behind them. The spooky blankness scared Donnie. Calum laughed at his jitters. 'Gorme's your man in a fog; he can smell the way, mister.'

'He'll hardly see us from there. How's he going to steer safely?'

'By his old woman's cooking. He's got a nose for his breakfast.'

'I wouldn't say that's so funny.'

91

'Man, it's knowledge,' said Calum. 'It's all experience, this is.'

'A man can't navigate blinded.'

'Ach, it won't be the first time. I mind the old Irish packet from Rosslare to Stranraer crossing once in a fog; she barely slowed for Loch Ryan, just cruised in steaming normal. Her old man had his watch out, changing course by the time. First we saw of the land was the pier, slap ahead where it should be. That's experience, Donnie.'

'A stroke of luck, more'n likely.'

'Not with some, don't believe it. There was this old ocean skipper – I met him once at Mallaig – who ran in fog every foot from Liverpool to the St Lawrence. He fetched up true on Father Point as if he'd sailed in broad sunlight. You don't do that by good luck, you learn it, Donnie, the hard way.'

'There's bad luck as well, Calum. We've rocks to clear and tides vary.'

'That's where buoys come in useful; you can judge the tides by them.' Calum grinned, keeping watch. 'Another tip for you, lad: a fog will sometimes hang low; climb a mast, you'll see over. I once looked down on a fog from the Rock of Gibraltar – this was back in the war. I could see masts sticking up but nothing else of the vessels.'

'Should we no' take some soundings?'

'You're the devil for fretting.'

'You've no respect for fog, Calum.'

'Bah,' the big man disputed. 'I've more respect than you'd know.' His gaze was forward, eyes narrow. He said, 'With reason, young fellow; with powerful reason, I'll tell you . . .' He did not slacken his watch; his voice rolled out on the vapour.

'I'm talking pre-war now, Donnie, when I was green,

about your age. I'd gone a bit off the coast in a wee boat for mackerel; just two oars and a line. You'll understand it was pleasure. At first the fog wasn't thick. I still had sight of the cliffs and the beauties were biting. Then it closed of a sudden: the shore was gone, and the sea. I couldnae count my own fingers. All I could see was bright bellies, the fish I'd caught shining at me.

'Well, I thought I'd row in, soon find gravel and beach her; it should've taken but minutes. In half an hour I was scared. I must've pulled her in circles for I'd not met the shallows, and, man, the silence was dreadful. Respect, you say? I was learning. I'd lost all sense of direction, my arms were out of my shoulders and now a tide had me hold, like the devil's hand tugging.'

Calum paused, his neck craning. 'Do you see a buoy, laddie?'

Donnie stared, spotting nothing.

'No,' said Calum, head shaking.

In a while, he continued, 'And now the devil had charge and where in hell was I heading? I could be drifting miles out, on my way to the States, or worse, bound for the rocks. I couldnae see my own knees and, man, the quietness was deathly. Respect, you say? I was praying. And then I hollered for help, sat there shouting and bawling, but the fog snuffed the racket. There was no echo from land, just a drip from the oar-blades.

'You'll understand it was calm. The sea was doom-laden smooth, as mostly happens in fog, and no bell-buoys were ringing. There'd be no warning of that sort; no assistance seemed likely. I had to sit there and stew, for rowing blindly was pointless.

'And then, by God, lad, I heard them, at first a faraway din, a distant hooting and wailing, and then a little bit

93

closer. At last I knew where I was: drifting into Seal Cove where the beasts were pronouncing. They would be out on the rocks, lying up on the skerries, sounding off like fog klaxons. The seals were guiding me in, telling me where the reefs were. I pinned my ears back and listened, and when the cries became loud, hauled like blazes to skirt them.

'Believe me, Donnie, they saved me. I'd've foundered without them. Lord, when sand touched that boat I dragged her up and collapsed, stretched out flat on the beach like a pop-eyed young sealie. I've not forgotten that lesson, nor would you have, my friend. I treat the fog with respect, though I can handle it nowadays. And I remember who saved me.'

Donnie glanced at him sideways. 'Now I see.'

'I'm not clowning?'

'No, not that – about Wingfoot. Why you spared her life, Calum.'

'Ach.' The older man shrugged. 'One good turn, boy,' he grunted.

The fog expired some miles out and the sun dazzled Wingfoot. She could still hear the geese, their gruff voices excited like those of dogs hunting rabbits. They seemed to urge the seal on, their black necks straining forward, snowy cheeks scintillating, south-bound in great spear-heads. It was a fine cavalcade, the fowl filling the sky, barnacles for the most with some white-fronts attending, the big seals below them.

Several times on the trip Wingfoot spotted companions, Pebble not far away, others bobbing and surging. She did not dwell now on dangers, the killer whale a dim memory, the fishing nets far behind. The sea ahead winked and danced, the teeming geese reassured her.

Quite soon a rocky point loomed, the northwest finger of Islay, a new land to Wingfoot. Above her, white streaks on cliffs showed where sea birds had nested: guillemots, like small penguins, and little kittiwake gulls as clamorous as they were dainty. Now the choughs held the heights, corvine-black with pink bills, quieter in their affairs, the odd raucous 'Tcha' startling.

Still the geese thundered on, calling Wingfoot to follow. They led the seal up a loch, reached the flats and descended. Rocking air from their wings, they came in skeins from the blue across pale cloud-reflections to join a congress of backs which, like a huge dove-grey mat, marked their winter assembly. In tens of thousands they spread, landing, taking off, wheeling, some resettling to browse where the winter growth sprouted.

For many days at Loch Gruinart, Wingfoot lazed and went fishing, often diving with Pebble, a mild, friendly creature. Once, as the weather grew cold, a pair of eagles flew over, a dying sun on bronze plumes, their broad wings scarcely stirring. Languidly they slid east towards a neighbouring island. Far away, beyond sight, highland peaks had turned icy.

Next day, seeking fresh shoals, the seals swam on round the coast, down the west side of Islay. It was the time to catch whiting, which came inshore at that season. The fish, whose flesh tasted sweet, fed near the beds of the bays and the seals captured many, sometimes squabbling for prizes. When Oisin stole a steak from her, Wingfoot turned on him, snapping. The dusky male gave a snarl but withdrew, gulping quickly. He was already a poacher, the cause of Niamh's desertion, and Wingfoot abhorred him.

But there was much else that pleased her; the hunting that month was sporty. The sea was cutting up white, a stiff Atlantic breeze blowing, stimulating the fishers. Along the coast stretched small hamlets and little crofts on their own, reminding her of Seal Cove and the old 'captain's' dwelling. Farther in lay broad fields by woods whose leaves had now gone; and east again, wild deer forests on hillsides of quartzite.

Unlike Wingfoot's own home, it was a big sprawling isle with lochs and great sweeping bays, and she explored them with relish. Then, the Westerlies strengthening, the rollers starting to pound, she gained the heel of the reach and slipped round it to shelter. As if rewarding her zeal, another loch offered welcome.

Broader than the goose-haven, it was no less a bird kingdom. In places far up its banks the swims were speckled with duck: merganser, goldeneye, teal, bands of eider and wigeon. Scaup were gathered in rafts, hundreds feeding together. Mute and whooper swans cruised; herds took flight, pinions throbbing. And on the strands waders foraged, turnstones levering pebbles, redshanks mingling with curlews, godwits ready for snow in their seasonal whiteness.

But the seals did not stop. Somewhere thunder was growling and as the western storms rose the older beasts in the group headed on round the south, past the stern crags of Oa, towards the east of the island, the side best screened from the weather. Only one or two dawdled and when they finally left, the Mull of Oa looked ugly. Its hanging jaw glowered through rain; the noise of thunder was louder.

Along a stretch of five miles, four grim points of rock challenged and Wingfoot grew anxious. So far winter had flirted, now its onslaught was earnest. The rolling clouds crashed and smoked; through a deluge, bolts sizzled.

Wingfoot swam close to land, avoiding fierce tides to seaward. The flow was kinder near in and all went well for a while, until she reached the third point. Here, with ominous force, a current clawed from the rocks, completely cutting her path before, transcribing an arc, it precluded evasion. She watched its rip through the downpour. A flash of fire lit the cliffs and they seemed to leap forward.

No small boat in safe hands would pass close to the Mull with any kind of sea running. Though less at risk, the seal faltered. She did not want to turn back, already trailing the others, and to dive could be dangerous; the flood was dark, rock-infested. At last she brazened the rips, thrusting shallowly at them, all her strength called to bear as the tide's flood embroiled her.

The current's belt was not wide but, while it lasted, exhausting. It pushed her far from the shore and fighting back drained her strength, the weather steadily worsening. The lightning flashes were blinding. They raked the waves with their glare, left the murk even darker. The rain came sheeting in squalls and she had no one to guide her, no Cellach or Finn, no experienced elder.

Beyond the last of the points she sought somewhere to rest. There was a cave in the cliff, a black and secretive gape, and she struggled towards it. By the flare of a bolt she could make out a smooth flow, a deep and shadowy throat, strangely calm and remote. The darkness slithered and slopped, the least flurry resounding. With caution, she entered.

At first the dungeon oppressed, its chill limits

constricting, but soon, despite the deep gloom, a sense of space could be felt as the chamber expanded. The rocky floor must have sloped for soon the water was sparse and, when her belly touched ground, Wingfoot climbed the slabs round it. She did not mean to stay long; long enough to draw breath. With luck the others would rest and she would soon overtake them. Meanwhile, sprawled in the dark, she could hear vexing noises.

She thought that something was moving. There was a sound in the pool as if some creature was stirring, a rhythmic squelch at the rim. It made the silver seal nervous, its gurgle persistent. She snorted, straining her eyes, but could see only shadows; smell only the cave's breath, its own dank exhalations.

Suck-slap, the sound taunted.

Then, growing used to the gloom, the traveller picked out a shape, long and grey in the water. It reclined half-submerged, its head dry on the stone, rolling as the brine lapped it. It was the corpse of a seal, not long dead. With each roll it squelched quietly. Wingfoot watched fascinated, curious yet repelled. In the end she humped nearer, stretched her neck and sniffed quickly. The scent received was familiar, indelible in her system.

Beyond the hole, lightning torched, fleetingly penetrating. Then once more it was dark and, in a warp of her mind, she was alone, three weeks old, left to fend for herself as the charging waves threatened. Never since, until now, had Wingfoot met her mother.

The silver seal sat and wailed.

From a rock draped with weed she cried out to the sea, then again when unanswered. There was no sign of her companions. The storm had passed, the rain gone, but the wind was still stiff, hindering vocal contact. She had moved north from the cave, continuing up the coast until the green water narrowed, another island now close, rearing up beside Islay. Down the sound between shores, the offending draught funnelled.

Against this, running north, a tidal stream battled strongly, the sea accordingly steep and confused in appearance. The sight did not entice Wingfoot who made instead for the new island, a weather shore beckoning. Here she stopped to find food where the water was quieter. Surfacing with a crab, she lingered partly consoled, munching it on her back while nearby, long and wooded, the Isle of Jura kept guard, glaring south to Kintyre and the high fell of Arran.

Some way off, in the storm, a ship had split on the rocks. Now, as Wingfoot searched on, she smelled oil in the distance, a sickly scent she disliked, reminding her of the *Peg* when a breeze would waft from her. Marking time, she took stock, the reek slowly increasing. A small black fowl sailed towards her. The stricken bird floated by, flapping when she reached out, and she allowed it to pass, its soiled feathers repulsive.

Farther on, she saw more: a cormorant and some gulls, then a shag flapping weakly. A few were dead, more resigned, one or two stretching wings in forlorn oily gestures. Surprised, the silver seal stared, charier of proceeding, for something shimmered ahead the like of which mystified her.

She was about to turn back when from the gleam on the swell a frightful image approached, an awful black-besmeared head, its eyes pale and bewildered. It was a gargoyle of Pebble, a travesty of the beast, and when it coughed, the mouth opening, a stream of dark fluid filled it. Casting round in her fear, Wingfoot saw the stuff spreading, slithering on the sea, flanking them with its arms like a lubricous monster.

Uncertainly, she submerged, hanging under the oil slick. She did not know what to do. The tentacles had moved on and now the ooze was unbroken, a roof of total pollution within the seal's vision – for all she knew, for miles round, since she had seen nothing like it. The water's surface was dark with iridescent streaks in it, a sight as strange to behold as a rainbow at midnight.

But night's black wing was not noxious; it did not stifle the birds or stick their feathers together, and had no power to choke Pebble. This was the darkness of death, more dangerous that *Physalia*, the Portuguese Man-of-War, or the giant squid of the Atlantic, many-armed *Architeuthis*. This black plague was not quick but a slow, clinging killer. The dappled Pebble had gone: carried where, to what torment?

Two or three fathoms deep, Wingfoot grappled with crisis. She had an urge to swim blindly, search for gaps in the slick; another mind to save air, her precious oxygen levels, by resisting such action. After all, fog dispersed; perhaps the slick would just vanish. And were there gaps to be found, and if so would she find them? Confusion settled the matter, its outcome inertia.

Overhead the oil hovered, as black as octopus ink, its smooth gloss nauseating. For many minutes she watched, hoping the ceiling would clear, but if it changed it got darker. And still the silver seal waited.

Had she been told she was drifting, just as the oil was above, she would have known that delay could bring her nothing but peril. Without a wind to bring change, the evil film would stay put while every moment that passed reduced the oxygen in her. Soon so little was left that she could feel her ribs tightening, feel a panic inside that made the oil secondary. In the end, air came first; air at any cost to her.

Her eyes were starting to pop and her heart was protesting. Inching nearer the ooze, she braced herself to accept it. She was a few feet away when, scarcely trusting her sight, she saw seals far below, calmly mining the current. They had a dreamlike appearance, a kind of lazy indifference. Heading into the tide, they were led by Bragela, the oldest cow of the herd, whose seamanship rivalled Cellach's. She was no stranger to slicks. Bragela knew that her course must take her well past the oil and to the rear of its passage. Without a glance to the side, she stroked the depths with assurance.

Frantically, Wingfoot followed. She was a breath now from stifling but took their lead, chasing wildly, demons pounding her skull, hammering at her eyeballs. Hanging on in a daze, she seemed to pierce a grey blur, barely conscious of swimming. Stars were flashing ahead; her whole body was bursting. And then a dozen suns blazed and with her guides she was climbing, clambering through the tide, an unblemished roof dazzling.

As the freezing air swirled, Wingfoot gulped it and wallowed.

The men stood round on the front exchanging grumbles and insults. They thumped their arms to get warmer. The snow had come in a flurry before it tumbled in earnest, the flakes no longer propelled but falling plumb in big blobs on the harbour and buildings. Soon the pier turned to ice and crews dispersed to their homes, some delayed by their thirst and a much-pitted dartboard.

Gorme said, 'I'm for a drink,' his breath defrosting his beard. 'We'll have a drink on the boy. I pay him money for nothing.'

The man made Donnie upset and Calum's grin did not help, infuriatingly neutral. Were they boatmates or not? Both worked hard for too little but Calum never took sides, merely grinning inanely.

'Another time, Mr Gorme. I'm off now,' Donnie mumbled.

'Off?' growled Gorme, nudging Calum. 'Off to where mighty sudden?'

The lad glanced down at his boots; there was snow sticking to them. He did not wish to reply but said, 'Seal Cove,' adding quickly, 'It's Will Macrae – Willie's poorly.'

'You mean his boat's poorly, son. I've heard you're quite the nurse these days.'

Donnie glared at them both; Calum's grin was moronic.

Gorme enjoyed his discomfort. 'I've heard you're strong on compassion if not on skill, laddie. I wouldn't bother too much; you know it's terminal, don't you? Macrae's boat's terminal poorly.' The skipper relished his wit. 'Bah, get off to your cove. And while you're there, kill some seals. I'll be along one fine day, me and some of the others, to sort out those robbers. They'll all be terminal cases.'

Donnie left, his mood surly. As he slouched down the front he heard the rasp of Gorme's laugh and strode on in a temper. At length the scenery soothed him. The crystal flakes whispered down, then in a while the sky cleared and their crisp blanket twinkled. He had to walk to the cliffs, the snow too deep for a bike, giving time for reflection.

The day of reckoning would come, the day when Gorme found him missing. He kicked the snow with a grunt. He would be out in the *Peg*, a partner in his own business, and Mr Gorme would be damned before he found cheaper labour. A little tractor came by, trundling on the *machair*, and Donnie waved to the driver. He dreamed again of his share in 'Macrae and MacDonald'.

When he got to the croft he found the girl in with Willie. The man sat over the fire, his furrowed features morose, and Aggie Fraser looked flustered. She turned as Donnie came in, plainly thankful to see him.

'Lord,' she said, 'he's a pig. Will you make him see reason?'

'Reason?' muttered Macrae. 'Where's the reason in women?'

'I brought his goods for him, Donnie, and that's the thanks that he gives me. He ought to be in his bed with someone cooking him something. I've said I'll cook on the fire. He isn't fit to be up; there's a temperature on him.'

'I'm warm; it's warm by the hearth.' The 'captain' spat in the embers. 'I can do without fussing. Send her packing, eh, Donald?'

'There,' hissed Aggie, 'hear that? Knock some sense in the pighead.'

'Aye,' said Donnie, 'come on, you've a chill in you, Willie. You're lucky Aggie came down; she's more use here than I am.' He caught the girl's fleeting smile. 'You should thank her for caring.'

'For provisions, maybe.'

'She wants to cook you a meal. Man, you ought to be grateful.'

'Bank the fire up,' said Aggie. 'I'll warm some soup and fish for him, just something light he can swallow. If he'll not go to his bed, you can draw a rug round him.' She held the boy's eye again. 'Will you take hot tea, Donnie?'

'Thanks, a mug for outside. I must look at the engine.'

He rummaged round for a rug. Amid the smoke and the gloom – the chests, the charts and the rest – it was a difficult search and dark cats watched from crannies. 'On the bunk,' croaked Macrae. 'You'll need to slide the door, damn it.' The bed was littered with junk: empty bottles, a box, and parts of some old device, perhaps a ship's echo-sounder. Donnie backed from the depths as Aggie poured the tea for him. He clutched a torn army blanket.

'There's sweet tinned milk,' the girl offered.

'I've paid for that,' moaned Macrae.

She turned her back. 'Aren't you partners?'

'By God we're not, not as yet. We're partners when the job's finished, and that's a lifetime ahead. I'll likely die before that the way the boy's going at it.'

'He'll be doing his best; it's you to blame if you perish.'

The girl passed Donnie the mug, getting on with her cooking. He had not seen her like this, no longer Aggie the tomboy, almost motherly now, and he found it alluring. It made him feel safer with her and happier in himself, not so overwhelmed by her.

For a moment he watched, then went out to the shingle. There was a seal in the bay. One or two had hauled out: the few who lingered through winter, on the more distant skerries. The covered boat was white-mantled.

Wrestling with the tarpaulins, he threw them off with the snow and exposed the stripped engine. It had kept dry through the downfall. Astern, some flakes had blown in to leave a powdery drift, and he started to clear it. In a while Aggie joined him, a woollen scarf round her neck, her short duffel-coat buttoned.

'It's cold,' she said, 'there's more coming.'

'Yes,' he said, stopping work. 'You should've stayed in the warm. Have you had enough of him?'

She pulled a face. 'The great fool, he's eating now that I've cooked it. I could murder him sometimes. If mam could see him, she would. We'll have to watch him, you know; he could go down in this weather. He'll take no care of himself.'

'You've been good to him, Aggie.'

The smile she gave him was wry. 'You wouldn't think so,' she said. 'I'm glad you came when you did; I might've walked out and left him. He's got no right to act that way.'

'Ach, the fellow's all right.'

'He'll catch pneumonia next and that'll be the end of him.'

She was not joking, thought Donnie. He said, 'I'll keep an eye open; I've got an interest in Willie.'

'That remains to be seen.' She viewed the boat, unconvinced. 'He's got an interest in you but it seems to be fading. He thinks you're taking too long. Can you really repair it?'

The other leaned on the gunwale. He could excuse Aggie's doubt; why should she understand? Willie ought to know better. 'Yes,' he said, 'given time. It won't be done by tomorrow: parts to find, the right tools. There isn't that much spare time. There's more to fix than he thinks. I'll get her right in the end but he'll have to be patient.'

'Oh well.' His confidence touched her. 'I guess you know what you're doing. I still don't think the boat's worth it.'

'She's no great shakes but she'll serve; she'll last a while, earn some money. If I can put a bit by I can look for another, get a better one some day. I'll never save on Gorme's money.'

'Gorme,' said Aggie, disgusted. 'I don't know how you can stick him.' She gazed to sea for a moment. 'Were you serious, Donnie? I mean, about you and me – about a trip round the seals and sailing out to be near them.'

'I wouldn't lie to you, would I? I'll take you out to their haunts; I've seen them from the *Goosander*. There's lots of places they go: to Iona and Islay, lots of rocks round the coasts. We'll visit them in the boat; we'll see what Wingfoot gets up to.'

'Get away from this place.' Aggie warmed to the notion. 'It would be marvellous, Donnie.'

'Eventually,' he advised.

'Oh yes, I know, not next week. I've got more patience than Willie.'

The girl went in and washed up. A lot more snow was about and Donnie fixed the tarpaulins, then carried peat to the cottage so the fire would keep burning. He said, 'We'd best leave him, Aggie, it's time we got on our way.'

'He'll be all right won't he, Donnie?'

'Yes, he's snug for tonight. I'll look by in the morning.' Climbing back up the cliff the couple paused at the top. The island switchbacked ahead, a white land in grey water. Here and there chimneys smoked; flakes were swirling already. The youth glanced back at the cove, then kicked snow from his boots on the stone which stood near them. Ice had stuck to its face, the carved relief of the sealers. Aggie turned her eyes from it.

'I hate that thing,' she exclaimed, 'those men killing the creatures. I couldn't stand it,' she said. 'It doesn't go on now, does it?'

'I shouldn't think so,' said Donnie, afraid to mention Gorme's threats.

In the blizzard, she asked, 'You'd not slaughter them, would you?'

'You know me better than that.'

'Yes,' she said, 'that was daft. It's the cold — I can't think.'

'Then we'll get you on home.'

'I wouldn't scream,' Aggie vowed, 'if you cuddled me, Donnie.'

In the blizzard far north six black fins cut the waves, faced at length by Cape Wrath, a monstrous bulwark of rock little short of the Arctic. Since first the oceans had formed, its cliffs had fought the Atlantic, slowly maimed and defaced, a monument where the land stopped to the sea's brutal nature.

The killer whales tracked towards them. The male was thirty feet long, his dorsal fin five feet high, triangular in its shape, those of his females recurved as they followed the mammoth. Though not as large as the bull, the cows were equal in greed and at least as voracious.

For a while they stood east as if to plunder the Orkneys, then veering back round the Cape they streamed south for the Minch, the Western Islands their aim, the herds of seals there enticing. Periodically blowing, the *Grampii* dived near to Skye and, terrorizing the deep, rose again off the Cuillins.

The steely crags caught their mood, the heights dark on the swell with snow adhering to clefts, tongues of cloud on the corries. From the slopes slithered winds which with whistles and shrieks urged the pack to fresh action. At Loch Scavaig sand seals fled; Ergol's crofters stood watching. Then the fins turned away, spearing now for Ardnamurchan and the grey seals of Treshnish.

There they harried like Vikings in sight of long-crumbled forts and the ruins of Lunga, their kills quickly swallowed. From the bleak volcanic rocks they could be seen moving on, immense appetites whetted. But at the next place of call, the cove where Wingfoot was born, they found the rookeries bare and, prowling now to the south, sought their prey about Islay.

At last, rounding the Mull, they came close to the herd, the seals now working back north up the long Sound of Jura. Abreast, the plunderers followed, sweeping up through the straits, the straggling island to port, a chilly mainland to starboard. Ahead the water was clear, greenish-blue and breeze-ruffled.

Wingfoot had hauled out. Grown fat on good food, she was sprawled on a beach, a draughty corner of Scotland, the coldness lost on her. Other seals lay nearby, the small strand littered with them. Across the sound to their front the snow shimmered on Jura, a spine of white running north to Corrievreckan's fierce waters. Behind the herd, trees were bare, sheep with black faces foraged.

To this place long ago had come the first of the Scots, a tribe out of Antrim, colonizing the coast, sailing lochs, hunting forests. Undeterred by the Picts, then engaged with the Romans, the Scots had carved out their realm, naming it Dalriada. By the time of Columba it had stretched far through Argyll and its chieftains had flourished.

Aggie's sea people slept, scratched their flanks, aired their flippers. Some were veteran cows, others immature females. A few big bulls drowsed among them, passionless and content, lions of lust in the rut become docile in winter. Cuchulainn gave a yawn, caring not where Finn rested. A languid Finn twitched his nose, full of cod and indifference.

Wingfoot lolled on her side, recent crises forgotten. She was regarding the sea when a familiar head rose, drawing close through the waves, and the silver seal straightened. Momentarily pleased, she concealed the emotion, leaving Niamh cold-shouldered. For Niamh's fickleness rankled. Doubtless Oisin had gone, again changing companions, and she was back to make up as if nothing had happened.

But to Wingfoot it had. She had been shunned by her friend, ousted by the brash male, and she showed her displeasure. As Niamh tried to approach, the silver seal curled her lip and, when the hint was ignored, made it plainer by snorting. Abashed, the other held still, sidling back in a minute. Again the overture failed and its enactor looked sad. With moist eyes she withdrew, flopping not far away, her jowls pressed to the sand and her longing gaze owlish.

Wingfoot took little notice. The seals grouped near them were sleeping and only Treshnish aroused, vexed as Niamh moaned quietly. The prickly Treshnish reared up. Ever quick to chastise, she promptly seized the newcomer, falling on her irately and rudely waking their neighbours. Astonished, Niamh was squashed, her assailant across her.

It ended Wingfoot's aloofness. She might be vexed by Niamh but Treshnish angered her more, fanning smouldering fires, the glow of early resentments, to brisk conflagration. Revengefully she pitched in, punishing the aggressor and causing her to back off so Niamh could recover. Allies now in the scrum, the friends of calf days attacked, smiting Treshnish together, settling scores with the scold who was forced to retreat and soon afterwards routed. As she fled through the throng other seals, lashing out, made her pay for old wrongs, grievances they had harboured.

Wingfoot looked at Niamh; coyly Niamh eyed Wingfoot. Then touching noses they sparred, feigning battle like weaners, frolicking on the sand in their double elation, the joy of Treshnish's dismay and their lively reunion. Presently the pair snoozed. Side by side on the beach they might have been at Seal Cove, pudgy infants again, their small world without cares, all annoyances trifling.

Even when one appeared, waking them an hour later, it was only a dog, little more than a pup. Romping down from the fields, it scurried round the herd barking, too afraid to come near but enjoying its outcry. The seals put up with it briefly. Disdainfully a few sighed, none concerned to move far. But as the yapping went on, increasingly aggravating, it got too much for their nerves and they began to hump seawards, sloshing into the surf, shouldering the green breakers. At last the dog reached the brink, hopping up and down braying.

By now the seals were afloat. Their streaming heads formed a fleet, slowly drifting away, sailing out on the sound as the killers slid nearer.

On the quay the snow was melting and Calum's wife trod in slush, some of which had made puddles. She had noticed the killers. As they passed the pier's end she had watched, her eyes brooding. Most people were busy. Behind her many were shovelling, clearing steps and the paths, others off to the shop now conditions were better.

She heard the door when it chimed, and the babble of voices.

'I've not been out since last week' – this an elderly woman.

'It was the ice,' said another, one of Donnie's relations.

Mrs Gorme said, 'That's gone but don't be thinking it's over, there could be more my man reckons. I wouldn't argue with Gorme.' She had a grey ewe-like face and a querulous nature. 'You've over-priced the greens, Peggy.'

'Fresh produce is scarce.' Mrs Fraser smiled grimly. She was doing brisk trade, glad the new stock was in, thanks to Mr Muir's promptness. 'Try the cans on the shelves, we've a good canned selection.'

Aggie came from the back and crossed the store like the wind. She aggravated her mother. To Mrs Fraser's regret her daughter still lacked deportment, so important in business. 'Now, young lady, less haste; let's be calm while we're busy.'

'I've seen them, Mam – the black fins.'

'Take a breath and speak slowly.'

'Half a dozen together.'

Mrs Fraser said, 'Uh-huh.'

'Killer whales,' blurted Aggie.

Her mother frowned, weighing cheese, wrapping it on the counter. She smoothed her apron with care, a sign of her irritation. 'The child's concerned for the seals. Now stop worrying, Aggie.'

'They'll be killed,' the girl anguished.

'I mind,' recalled one old woman, 'when I was just a wee bairn they cut a killer whale open.' Her words were gritty with relish. 'They found fourteen seals in it – what remained of the creatures – and plenty else with them.'

Mrs Gorme's thin lips snapped. 'They flay them once

they're inside. The skins,' she cried, 'are disgorged.'

'God,' the girl said, dismayed, causing mumbles of censure.

Mrs Fraser lost patience. 'The seals have gone,' she exclaimed. 'Do get on with you, Aggie.'

There was a pause in proceedings, as after prayers in the chapel, then Mrs Gorme pronounced harshly, 'Seals are nothing but vermin,' a text she took from her husband. 'You'll have to learn, Aggie Fraser.'

In the silence that followed, Mrs Fraser spoke quickly, before her daughter exploded. 'Aggie, make yourself useful, you can put up the orders. Take the things for Macrae, he'll be anxious to have them.' She touched the girl on her arm. 'The seals will be here next spring. Some get killed, others flourish. It's nature's way, child. Stop fretting.'

'I can't bear to think of it.'

'Then stop thinking, you ninny.' Peggy Fraser clucked softly. The girl was melodramatic, highly strung, thought the woman. She did not know who it came from.

'Yes,' said Aggie, subdued. She glared at Gorme's mean-faced wife; Gorme deserved her, she brooded. But none of that would help Wingfoot or save her old favourites, nor would being at sea where there was nowhere to shelter. She thought of Finn and Bragela, of Niamh and Oisin. She had grown up with the seals, known many of them as calves, watched their births in some cases. And now the killers had gathered.

'She's young,' said Mrs Gorme coldly. 'You'll have your problems there, Peggy.'

'She's a good, helpful girl.' The rebuff was as chilly. If Peggy Fraser had problems, she did not share them with neighbours. She had started with nothing and built her business unaided with the same quiet resolve she now brought to the counter, hard-working and deft, a boon to them and they knew it.

'I hear,' persisted the other, 'she sees a lot of young Donnie. My husband's mentioned it lately. I hope the boy's work won't suffer.'

'And should it, now, Mrs Gorme?'

'A wee impressionable lad. They're very young, very young.'

Aggie's scowl had grown darker. She reached for eggs from the back, for she could make Willie eat them, and packed some tins of milk for him. She could have punched Mrs Gorme.

Peggy Fraser worked swiftly, checking produce and change, filling bags with loose items. She said, 'The girl's got a head; Aggie's bright and trustworthy.' Her tone was mild, her glance daunting.

Mrs Gorme smiled malignly. 'Then she'll grow out of the nonsense.' She added scornfully, 'Seals . . .'

An aged female MacDonald pushed in for attention. 'I'll take some rashers, my dear. The poor lass, she's upset. She's missed a father, poor bairn, for he'd have talked about seals, he'd have told her about them. A canny fisherman, Peg, a good man I mind well.'

'He was,' the widow acceded. 'A good and principled husband.'

Without a smile, Aggie thought, in a frame on the sideboard, an irrelevant issue. What could he do to help? She doubted he had liked seals any more than the others.

The tough old woman was mumbling, 'Sixteen years ago, was it? Ach, the time passes quickly and still we don't know what happened. He wasn't careless at sea, no one called him that, Peggy.'

'He was not that, not my husband.'

'The Lord will know,' Mrs Gorme said, kindlier in her manner, the subject bonding the women. 'The Lord could tell, and Corrievreckan, but that gulf keeps its secrets. If Corrievreckan could speak instead of roaring and raging. They say the noise can be heard four miles off in some weather.'

Mrs Fraser sliced bacon. 'It's not our business to question; if we were meant to, we'd know. I'm thinking God takes the good ones, leaves the bad to the devil.'

'He leaves the Willie Macraes,' Mrs Gorme said succinctly.

One or two of them nodded. Only Aggie demurred, breaking silence to shame them. 'He's sick,' she said with emotion, 'so maybe you should pray for him.' She pressed it home, her voice fraught. 'If you don't care about seals you might care about Willie.'

'Now,' her mother said firmly, 'that's no way to be talking.'

'Mam, he is, the man's poorly.'

'We all know Willie Macrae; he'll not be perishing yet, child.'

Aggie snatched up her basket. Her eyes were misty with anger, and panic swam in them, a fearful vision of seals, Cellach, Cuchulainn, Treshnish, the killers behind them, and worst of all in her mind the silver seal wild with terror: the only silver seal living. She clutched the goods for the croft and turned to run, her cheeks burning. As she passed the last shelves she grabbed Willie's tobacco, then her feet were in slush and the bike was before her.

She crossed the yard in a rush and dropped the pannier home, slamming it in the frame. Damn them all, Aggie thought, they did not care, those old women. The place was full of old people. They were stuck in the past; all they cared for was ghosts, ghosts with unsmiling faces, God-fearing and callous. It was the young ones who cared but they were few on the island.

'Aggie . . .'

Aggie swung round. Surprised, she said, 'Oh, it's you. I didn't know you were there.'

Mary's haunted eyes stared. She seemed to Aggie misplaced, somehow lost off the quay, her habitual location. She was a curious woman, the childless wife of big Calum, her loveliness almost startling yet tempered with sadness, for which the girl saw no reason. She was, she thought, not quite real, like seal music in mist or a moon before sunset.

The others gossiped about her: she tied her man to her strings, dogged his steps when he landed, stood in wait on the pier lest another might snatch him. They said she spoke of sea sirens, of mermaids and suchlike; that she was barren, did nothing, was work-shy and so on. Of course, the old ones were worst. Aggie damned the old women.

'The silver seal, Aggie . . .'

'Well?' she said in a hurry. She wished to get away quickly.

'Calum mentioned the seal.' The rapt eyes were inquiring.

Aggie mounted the bike. She felt the woman's gaze on her. 'I've got to go. Sorry, Mary.'

'Wait and tell me.'

'I'm sorry . . .'

*　*　*

The hour of feasting had come for the black-finned cetaceans. They sensed the seals now and surged, beaming calls to each other. The seals were many, they droned, a fine herd for the cull; a hunters' banquet, they crooned, the reward for long searching – the grisly feast of the depths only *Grampus* could handle.

As they closed on their prey they were tracking up-channel, the tidal streams running strong. It was the time of the springs and from the sound's western shore, far out into the middle, the flood stream was swift, racing north with the killers. They were in seventy fathoms. At times the depth touched a hundred.

Shoals of fish passed their flanks; they showed no interest in fish. The food the grampuses stalked came in hundredweight portions.

The seals had followed the shoals.

Drawn far out on the sound, Wingfoot swam near the top, unaware of the danger. The first she knew of the whales was a commotion below – several cows at full stretch – then the giant was beneath her. Its great black fuselage swirled and as its tail rose and fell she was bounced by the wash, jostled up willy-nilly.

Bobbing high on the crest she saw dorsal fins speeding and watched the killers veer round, dashing after their quarry. She glimpsed no more for a moment and then the sea opened up, another mighty back rising, the brine streaming from it. It formed a ponderous hump before thundering downwards.

Barely had it submerged when a seal, in its fright, leaped clean out of the current and curved like a salmon.

Soon more fins streaked and dived, pandemonium spreading. It was a scene of confusion and it had happened in seconds: a moment earlier, peace; suddenly, fear and panic. In all directions seals fled while everywhere the giants harried. Wingfoot, stricken with dread, saw Niamh breach the swell, rubber-necking in terror. Though their glances converged they held only distraction.

Next thing, Niamh had dived, kicking up her hind flippers, the spot marked by bubbles.

Other heads rose and blew, drawing air in deep gulps. Like stranded fish the seals gasped then were gone in a flurry. The rout took two main directions. One group of seals followed Cellach, its flight a bid for the mainland. Many bulls took this course, young and old toiling fiercely. The other group, with Bragela, fled north up the sound, the fast flood stream assisting. This, at up to eight knots, was the flow which drew Wingfoot.

She had to fight to keep up. There was blood on the tide and stampede was contagious, her frantic comrades flat out, the marauders behind them. In their fear the seals flew, making long shallow dives, frenzied in their exertions. Several hurdled the waves, rocketing in their anguish. Those behind were possessed, those ahead were urged faster.

Wingfoot plunged beside Treshnish, passing her in the trough, of the two seals the swifter. Maidens overhauled cows, were themselves overtaken; juveniles scrambled with them. There was no thought to save strength or to pace their endeavours, just a rush to survive, to escape from the mayhem.

As Wingfoot charged at the flood its green wall seemed to thicken, a screen of mounting resistance as heart and lungs laboured. She was approaching Bragela, catching up with the leaders, when through the flow loomed a giant, its horrendous flank flashing. A bucket-mouth opened slowly. Suddenly it had snapped and a dark blood-cloud billowed.

The silver seal saw it spread, coiling into the current. Solid pieces flowed with it. A severed flipper made off, quirkily turning turtle. She did not wait to see more, for, as the killer mopped up, another brute was approaching, now shifting towards her.

It came on like a ship. Seals were panicking near her, desperate to escape. In their antics some clashed, Treshnish crossing her path so her impetus slackened. Another toothy mouth opened. She tried to make up lost speed but her force had been spent and she seemed to slide back, slip towards her attacker. Despondently she cast round, catching sight of Bragela. The veteran cow was crash-diving and with a lurch Wingfoot followed.

There was no time to look back. Instead, she chased the old seal, striking down through the flow, trying hard to keep contact. Bragela knew all the tricks; the young animal dogged her. As they sank it grew dark, gloomier with each fathom. Determinedly they descended, plunging farther and farther.

When they had reached eighty fathoms, the silver seal hesitated. She was unused to the pressure and instinct urged caution. At nearly five hundred feet she stopped diving and waited.

Cellach's group had run east, turning back for the dog beach. The Abbot swam bravely. Not far off, Finn was toiling, hammering at the waves, while his dusky son Oisin, rudely stripped of assurance, charged in frantic disorder. Younger males straggled round them.

A rainy front had blown up bringing cold drizzle with it. In dirty sheets it trailed in, darkening the sea's surface.

Suddenly from this brew a great snout rose and snapped and another seal vanished. Two more fins tracked the group, pirate sails on its flanks. Gradually they eased in, terrifying the convoy.

Oisin yawed as he laboured, heaving forward in torment. Seeking safety in numbers, he hurled himself behind Cellach where the seal pack was dense and the big bulls might shield him. Some were streaking ahead, burning up their resources, but Cellach's progress was steady, a stern and rhythmic retreat that seemed almost phlegmatic. Perhaps he lacked greater speed, now too ancient to sprint; perhaps, so long wooed by death, he scorned to dance to her bidding.

As the killers closed in he blew loudly and dived, leaving Oisin above. Straight away the giants plunged, their trajectories converging, and Oisin saw the sea heave, a red stain spreading on it. Wearily he pressed on, something floating back past him: the gory tail of a bull seal. He quickened pace in dismay, loath to look at the object.

Finn had surged at his side and the two swam together. They bored just under the chops, surfacing in the rain, glancing fearfully round as the misty cloud lowered. There were now fewer beasts with them. Some the killers had taken, some had drifted away, made obscure by the drizzle. And still the terror was prowling. Oisin missed Cellach's presence, steadfast and symbolic.

Then through the pall to his front he saw the Abbot loom up, ploughing doughtily forward. It was a sign and he rallied.

Wingfoot rocked in suspension. She had tried once to resurface but had been forced to stay low, the marauders still swirling. She had hung on, reserves draining, and now could hang on no longer, her need of air urgent.

Again she rose from the depths, drifting up through the twilight. She startled olive-green fry but saw nothing more frightening. At last the rain touched her face, its grey web blurring vision, screening out the far coasts so the seal had no bearings. She must have been taken north for the current was hustling and she could hear a faint roar, Corrievreckan now closer.

She did not care where she was as long as there were no killers. The muffling drizzle fell softly, barely tickling the sea, disconcertingly creepy. It clung like dew to her whiskers. Minutes passed, nothing happened. Then, disturbed by a snort, she stared hard at the vapour.

Another seal had come up, its head dimly familiar. Anxiously, she steered nearer.

Wingfoot peered. She felt frightened.

It was a quaking Niamh whose eyes rolled and who twitched, who was demented by fear – a Niamh who fled wildly. And instantly more seals splashed, leaping high, panic-driven, and she was back in the nightmare, the dread unabated. Distraught, she joined them in flight, once again racing madly.

Somewhere back near the tail a sickly beast laboured feebly. The oil-drenched Pebble had ailed, lying up among rocks, eating nothing for days, keeping touch with the herd but infirm on its fringes. Now, polluted lungs failing, she wallowed exhausted. The bull whale ended her pangs, one abrupt crunch sufficing.

When he had gorged he powered on, coming up behind Treshnish. She too had grown tired but her terror recharged her. At fifteen knots Treshnish zoomed, shooting clear of the water. Thirty feet of whale passed, streaming by underneath her.

Cuchulainn rolled and dived. Unlike most of the males

he had stayed with the cows, heading up the sound with them. Spiralling, he plunged steeply, hit sixty fathoms and flattened, mining on in the dimness. He swam without wasting effort, barely stirring the depths, as a submarine saunters. Just ahead and below, a shadow glided as smoothly, one as wily as he: the old sea-fox Bragela.

Wingfoot swam near the surface. Behind her, others made haste but the panic was lessening. Several killers were full or clearing up in the rear and, though she did not relax, there was hope in her now, a growing faith in her swiftness. Curving shallowly down, she ripped up through the flow, skimmed its brow then dipped back, her symmetric lines gleaming.

Ahead the channel divided, Corrievreckan to port, a broad inlet to starboard, the aperture of Loch Craignish. Where Craignish Point split the ways, rugged islets stood guard, craggy sanctuaries beckoned.

The silver seal headed for them.

Suddenly the sea darkened. The darkness deepened and grew and fleetingly she was puzzled. Then the phantom took shape and Wingfoot's hopes turned to horror. The dusky shape was alive, a killer charging towards her, their courses set for collision, a monstrous mouth gaping.

At her back seals were scrambling, scattering left and right. Once more Treshnish zoomed up; Niamh wheeled, bolting sideways. In the swirl of the tide, young and old raced anew, fled as sprats before mackerel. Those behind turned about, in their haste threshing water.

For Wingfoot, space had run out, there was no room for evasion. The killer was on her. At the last instant she dipped and struck a huge lower jaw, swept on down the white bib to a barnacled belly, scraped and bumped as she rolled, before, almost unconscious, she felt the brute's tailfin strike her. She seemed to sink like a stone.

After that she knew nothing.

When the girl reached the cove it was empty. The wind had recently freshened and the sea had grown restless. There were white manes on the waves but no seals, she lamented. If only they had been there; if only she had seen Wingfoot, and Cellach up on his stone, and bobbing heads in the shallows, safely inside the skerries. If only . . .

Donnie's voice reached her. She saw him wave from the *Peg* and come hurrying over.

'You're here,' he said. 'I'm glad, Aggie.'

'I couldn't stay in that shop.'

'It's Willie,' Donnie went on, 'I don't know how to mind him.'

She read his worried expression: it meant that Willie was worse. 'Oh,' she said, unprepared, the seals still her misgiving. 'What's happened; how is he?'

'Not so good – in bed, Aggie. He took himself to his bunk and the man won't stop moaning. He's rough now, I reckon.'

'There, they didn't believe me.' She thought of the women. 'They didn't care,' she said harshly. 'I told them Willie was poor. If he's in bed . . .'

'All day long. I haven't known what to do.'

'You should've got me here sooner.'

Donnie smiled at her lamely. 'Aye, you'll know how to cope. You'll be able to manage.'

'Perhaps,' she said, less convinced. She did not relish the prospect, the pigsty scene that awaited. 'Oh Lord,' she sighed with bad faith, 'come on then, bring the basket.'

She drew a breath at the door; what a dump the man lived in.

The smoky gloom pricked her eyes and the peat fumes were stifling. In spite of which, she supposed, she should be thankful for dimness; at least it hid some things. The cats were mewing like waifs, as if mourning their owner, and softly from the low bunk a deep groan rose and wavered. She peered ahead, her heart sinking.

. The bed seemed piled with old clothes. The bundle under them turned, half-exposing a face, and the drapes fell back from it. The 'captain' sprawled in his shirt, collarless, the neck open, one arm flung from the heap so a hand trailed the floor, bony talons extended. In his cheeks burned small fires and he stared like a demon.

'Willie?' Aggie said, frightened.

'It's Aggie,' Donnie said, louder.

She took command of her nerves. 'Willie, how are you feeling?'

'Go away,' the man answered.

'We're here to see you get better.'

'I'm dying, leave me alone.' The hand jerked up from the floor and fixed itself to a blanket. 'Can't I die in peace, damn you?'

Aggie took a step nearer. She felt his brow and stood back, rather pleased by her calmness. 'You're in a sweat,' she asserted.

'Sweat?' the man croaked. 'I'm sinking.'

'You'll not be dying yet, Willie.'

125

'No,' said Donnie, relieved.

Less assured, Macrae cursed, swearing quietly but fiercely. 'Let me go on my own; clear off out, I don't need you.'

The girl glared back, her fists clenching. 'We'll go whenever we're ready. And don't you swear at me, Willie, I haven't come to hear swearing. I've come to mind you with Donnie, who's worried about you. He's concerned, you old pig.'

'He's concerned?' the man echoed. 'He's hardly started that engine. A lot of good is MacDonald. I told you, girl, this would happen: I'd die before it was finished. The man's hardly started.'

'That isn't true,' complained Donnie.

'Never mind about that.' Aggie turned to the fire. The cats were wailing up at her, their grey faces pleading. 'Take no notice,' she snapped, 'he's a foolish old pig. Give these cats something, Donnie, there's milk in the basket.' She glanced across at the bunk. 'At least he's in the right place; he should've gone to bed quicker.'

'Right,' growled Donnie, 'you said so.'

'I'm going to get him a drink. All that sweating, he'll need one.'

The 'captain' lifted his head. 'Get the whisky,' he grunted.

'You're not to touch that stuff, Willie. I'm going to make a warm drink and I've brought you some aspirin. Then you'll sleep, sweat it out.'

'Get the whisky and leave me.'

Aggie did not reply. She put a pan on the hob then withdrew to the door, the air outside it refreshing. The tide was flowing and boisterous, its spray high on the rocks. Donnie came and stood near her. 'Phew,' he said, looking strained.

'Have you quietened those cats?'

'Yes.' The lad's smile was anxious. 'Is he bad? He looks scuppered.'

'I'm not a doctor,' she answered.

'You know the best way to manage.'

The girl was vexed by his trust. 'Grow up, Donnie, how can I?' She gave a shrug, sorry for him. 'Well, feed a cold, starve a fever – I do know that,' she relented. 'Make him drinks, keep him warm; hope he sleeps, I suppose. See the fire's well banked up.' She observed the sea glumly. 'The waves are big,' she reflected.

'Westerly, blowing rough. We shan't be sailing, that's one thing.'

'He'd not be got off the island. I mean, if he needed moving.'

'To hospital?' Donnie asked.

'I don't know. Yes, maybe.'

'Then you do think he's bad. D'you think he really might die?'

Aggie turned on him, anguished. 'Don't you start, not you too. Don't you start talking that way.'

'No,' he said. 'He talks daft.'

'Yes,' she said on the move. 'I must stop that pan boiling.' She paused, her gaze on his face. 'What's pneumonia like, Donnie; have you seen someone with it?'

He shook his head.

'We need help. You'd better go for my mam. She's nursed people, she'll know. She's got a book about medicine. You'd better go for her, Donnie.'

'Aye,' he said, 'if you think so. Will you be all right, Aggie?'

'Yes, go on, don't waste time. Go before it gets dark.'

She went back in to the fire. 'Now,' she said, 'your drink, Willie.'

'Where's wee Donnie MacDonald? Is he fixing that engine?'

'No,' she said, 'not just now. He's gone to bring out some help.'

'Can't he fix it himself?' Willie moaned and writhed damply. 'The man's no use, no damned use; not the brains of a rabbit. Who's he going to bring out? I'll no' have Gorme near my boat. If it's Gorme . . .'

'It's not Gorme.'

'Ah,' he breathed, staring vaguely. He was feverish and rambling.

Aggie crouched by the bed. 'Here,' she whispered, 'drink this, it's sweet, Willie, and warm. Just a sip, then you'll sleep.'

He glared past her. 'Who are you?'

Dear Lord, she prayed, give me strength. She could see the cats peering. It had grown dimmer inside and outside the wind hooted. She wished that Donnie was with her. 'Come on, Captain,' she begged, 'you know me, Aggie Fraser.'

He took a couple of swigs, spluttering on the liquid. 'It's poison, woman, be off.'

'Then just you settle and sleep.' She pulled the blankets up round him.

He flailed an arm and sank back. She did not catch his next words, then he croaked, 'Who's he bringing? If it's Gorme, you can't trust him.'

'Hush now, Willie, I know. Gorme kills seals,' she said quietly.

'Seals?' He managed to cackle.

'Get some sleep. I'll be with you.' She took a spill to the fire and fumbled over the lamps. They made the shadows jump round, shining dimly on cobwebs. The final gleams of the day filled the single small window.

From the bunk the voice mumbled, 'You'll have an interest in sealies?'

Aggie sighed and sat down. 'You know I have. Try to sleep.'

Willie groaned. 'Reeking devils. Can ye read? On the table . . .' He gave a heave and was quiet, restless still but now dozing. From time to time his lips moved, then his breathing grew deeper and Aggie thanked her God softly.

She did not shift for a while, determined not to disturb him. At last, for something to do, she took the book from the table and flicked through its pages. It was a yellowing diary he had shown her before, kept by Angus, his father, a man of parts in his lifetime. Trimly ruled, sloping neatly, the script was signed on page one: *Angus William Macrae*. There were twelve entries, by months, the year 1897.

Aggie read from October.

Most of the birds have now gone and our cliffs are deserted. Some gulls and cormorants stay and while the Westerlies blow the fulmar lands to take shelter. Our crops are housed, with much straw but the grain yield is meagre. Potatoes few and diseased. All the field work is late and no fuel has been gathered. The weather treats us unkindly, yet many seals come to breed and we have readied our boat, sure of one timely harvest. The men are eager with clubs and there is rivalry in it . . .

The seals have grown increasingly numerous. After many poor crops and the dismal weather, everybody looks forward to autumn's bounty: oil and seal grease, skins for shoes and pouches and other items. Some will welcome the meat, which is dark in colour.

We crofters – along with the Gormes, who own the best boat for sealing – have been planning the slaughter for several days. Now the tide suits the seamen and business beckons.

Accordingly, in the wee hours after sabbath, we make our way to the clifftop and wait for daybreak. Skeins of mist twist and swirl; they hide the skerries. A single seal voice arises, a sleepy reveille, but there is no sign of movement and darkness still lingers, the headland gloomy.

At last a crow winnows over, its black wings silent. Planing to the beach, it is joined by another in search of the refuse the seals have scattered. Soon the first gulls are arriving, a faint glow spreading.

Below the cliff, beyond the sands of low tide, the sea is drowsy, the mist upon it. Crags and bluffs emerge now in the greyness, the beasts beneath them. Long humped shapes can be seen on the strand and in the quietness men count them, the numbers pleasing.

The herd is large; many creatures are nursing, inclined on their sides as the infants guzzle.

Contentedly the small white beasts push and suck

with wrinkled noses, sometimes blessed with a grunt or maternal pat. A few of the cows feed adopted orphans beside their own calves.

Other youngsters, past the age of being suckled, are asleep or, if awake in the dimness, remain impassive. Many lie in nests of soft fur as their first coats moult. Like cherubs they blink and yawn as dawn wakes them, the seagulls mewing.

There is, I must confess, a tenderness in the groupings, a touching intimacy I cannot gainsay. It is as if some fellow tribe of the sea has sought respite on the island. But life is hard in the winter, our hearts are unyielding. We watch in silence.

Pools are gradually brightening and, where the sand becomes lighter, worm-casts are appearing like dusky pimples.

A man coughs and quickly covers his mouth: a choking splutter. The crows have heard and take off, cawing as they fly over. The noise must startle the seals – but, no, they take little heed, the cows still nursing their young, others peacefully sleeping.

Through the now rising mist we look out for the boat.

The splash of oar-blades comes first, then the sound of coarse voices. This time the herd fidgets. A large bull splashes off, scurrying through the shallows. Most of the beasts hold their ground, looking no more than puzzled. We curse the Gormes for their din and feel that we have been lucky.

Soon we see the craft dimly, drawing out of the vapour. As it grinds on the beach its crew leaps in the waves, wading, sloshing and swearing. The Gormes are rude and uncouth, much disliked by the rest, especially by my son Willie, who fancies the sea life. They tend to pick on the lad and their youths have fought with him.

Now, though clumsy about it, they do their job well enough, forming a straggling cordon to stop the beasts bolting, while we finger our clubs and look down with impatience.

Some of the seals are afoot. Three or four of the creatures, more alarmed than their friends, have moved down from the shingle. Intent on gaining the sea, they press on and one is hastily bludgeoned, its cries disconcerting.

The wails set other beasts moving and we again cuss the Gormes who, by bungling the killing, have got the whole herd in turmoil. As they belabour the runners, the rest draw back on the stones, staring round in their panic. A few continue to flee but most retreat up the beach, the bemused infants bleating.

There is much blowing and 'hoooing', the seals in distress. Many make for the cliff in their labouring fashion. Undulating and straining, they glance in fear at the boatmen then heave on in spasms to eddy below us. They seek escape in the rocks but their struggling is futile. Some just turn on the spot, others make wider circles.

Mothers call to their calves; the white infants are weeping. When the young fail to move, their parents nudge or wait by them, their fussing pathetic.

There is no time to dwell on it. In the dawn we are moving. Suddenly, from the cliff, we start like troops down the gullies and crumbling tracks, form again at the bottom and lift our cudgels.

At this the seals lie quite still, scores of them in a

huddle. Confused now and distraught, the beasts are helpless against us, cut off from the sea by the Gormes, forced to watch us approaching.

Pudgy moulters, rolling onto their flanks, raise small flippers in anguish. Tiny infants, full of milk and bemusement, gawp innocently. At their sides the cows gaze in despair, showing the whites of their eyes. They can do nothing but wait; lie and wait in their terror.

I have to say I feel for them. Life has not left me callous, blind to God's gift of nature, but we have to survive and our lives can be brutal. Around me faces glaze over, men's features are rigid. Gulls are screaming above, their intense clamour piercing. We trudge on slowly, sticks lofted, to where our victims are clustered.

They seem resigned to the end, bound by a fatal inertia as we weigh in together, crofters joined by the boatmen in a pitiless onslaught. As if a frenzy has seized us we strike again and again until the sweat runs on brows and our veins bulge with effort.

Grimly the massacre mounts, ponderous and grotesque. Stones grow slick with the blood; the dead and dying are piled among those yet to suffer. There are swift executions and there are grisly bunglings. Beasts are finished with knives, others struck many times before death overcomes them.

Mouths agape, cows are clubbed beside the calves they have suckled, little creatures who peer in trusting ignorance at us.

And now, thank God it is done, I write honestly of it. I think our haul not excessive. Others kill larger numbers. At North Rona, above the Butt of Lewis, and on neighbouring Sula Sgeir, hundreds of seals have been taken. On Haskeir, off North Uist, there has been 'infinite slaughter' writes the High Dean of the Islands.

Enough, I say, is enough, for the faces haunt me.

A gull was wheeling above, screeching to its companions. It saw the wallowing seal and thinking that she was dead made a low, scudding pass, weighing up the food prospects. Just then Wingfoot revived and her flippers moved slightly. She saw the gull as a streak, a white flash on awakening, then was conscious of waves and her own rolling motion. Disabused, the gull quit, to leave the groggy seal rocking.

She lay a while on one side, shoved and tossed in the troughs, barely sensible now and imperfectly balanced. She neither knew where she was nor, in truth, what had happened. The rain had gone, the sky glared. It formed a roof in her eye, an all-encompassing dome, indigo then steel-grey, then an ominous umber. The wind's incessant chant strengthened.

The gulls knew just where they were.

Four cables' length to the north a little hilly-spined island, Ris-an-tru, was their home. Farther east, off Craignish Point, the tide raced like a river, but if one looked for wild water one took the flood stream north-west to where it entered the throat between Jura and Scarba, the awesome Gulf of Corrievreckan. That was well named the Cauldron.

It rumbled now like a beast, heard at twenty-five cables, a raging tumult of brine caused by the difference in heights of the tides in the region. This was five feet in places, the overfall aggravated by disparities of depth, with shoals of just fifteen fathoms and sudden drops to a hundred. In the resulting confusion a vessel, even a ship, could be turned in all directions, forced ashore if unlucky.

Gorme respected Corrievreckan, while according to Calum, a traveller in wartime, Pentland Firth plus Portland race at their worst were nothing after the Cauldron when west winds were blowing. Then, caught up in the flood stream, a boat whose engine had failed could be drawn to the gulf, struck by seas from all angles.

Such facts meant nothing to Wingfoot, her senses still fuzzy. She had lost blood from a wound and was the worse for concussion, impressions coming and going. She swam a little way feebly then once again wallowed. She had slight notion of place and time was not in her reckoning. Jellyfish floated by; drifts of smoke smudged the skyline. Once, a tramp ship lurched past with a mien of drunken triumph. A pile of rivets and rust, she had outlived the U-boats.

Straggling seals laboured landwards. At last the killers had gone, turning back whence they came, and the survivors re-grouped, sheltering at Ris-an-tru and the other small islands. Unknown to her friend, Niamh had found a wild inlet and flopped on the rocks. Close to her was Bragela with Cuchulainn not far off. When they had rested a while they would move north through Scarba Sound, reach the open Atlantic and steer for home waters.

Now they called from the crags, summoning other travellers. Wingfoot heard them and stirred, trying hard to make headway. But she could raise little strength. There was a mist in her mind and a deadening pall on her. The slightest effort fatigued and, slipping into a faint, she would drift from her bearings. Each time her senses returned she had to puzzle anew, grasp a fresh situation. Sometimes the calls would assist, giving her a direction; more often there were no calls and the Cauldron's growl haunted.

Helplessly, Wingfoot listened. Increasingly the waves swamped her; she fought to keep her head rising, to hold the buoyancy in her. Porpoises passed in line, streaming north effortlessly, and several seals paused to look then cruised on to the islands. 'Hooo,' a distant voice summoned.

Wingfoot strained to respond but her sinews were flaccid. Very slowly she swam, making weak thrusts and resting, often stunned by the waves, painfully inching forward. With every stroke she felt spent, yet for a time she kept going. She was urged on by her will – her will to reach Ris-an-tru – and the desultory seal calls. 'Hooo,' they wailed as she struggled, their winding music her guide, but she was soon forced to stop, and the calls seemed no closer.

Once again the seal strove, jerking on a while longer. Once again her mind dimmed, its dark curtain encroaching, her fragile movements mere gestures, little more than reflexes. And then the chops swept her up, spindrift veiling her limpness.

On the rocks, Niamh slept; Cuchulainn stretched and yawned. Others fitfully drowsed, twitchy still from their traumas. Treshnish hooted a while as if it brought her relief, then dropped her muzzle and sighed, like the rest of them sleeping. Only Bragela kept calling, her plaintive notes low and strong – perhaps a cry for the Abbot, or in her primitive way a requiem for the missing. Even she napped eventually.

Wingfoot came round abruptly. The spume was stinging her face and no one called from the island. It might
have ceased to exist, for she could see only waves and
the ubiquitous sea-spray. She had in fact drifted west
towards the wild north of Jura and, since endeavour was
futile, resigned herself to more floating.

This she did on her back, periodically blowing. She
could not know at this stage the speed at which the tide
travelled, since she had no point of reference, but as it
happened it raced, the flood galloping with her. For here
the stream set northwest directly into the gulf, a surging
one-way career to the thundering Cauldron. And like a
straw in the flow, like a leaf in a culvert, the seal was
borne by the sea, all her efforts exhausted.

She barely knew she was drifting. Much of the time
she knew little, slipping off into sleep – more than sleep
– then returning, the hours and seconds confused, the
blank spaces unnoticed. A great black sea bird swept
over and little fishes came up, slyly mouthing her body.
She was oblivious often; light-headed when conscious.
Then, above the sea's sounds, one sensation persisted,
the rising roar in her ears, vociferous Corrievreckan.

By and by, her mind clearing, the clamour alarmed
her. The stream had veered to the west and high coasts
flanked its channel, their headlands forbidding. On either
side rose stern bluffs through which the sound ahead
funnelled, becoming steadily louder. She had no chance
of back-tracking, no protest left in her; the Cauldron was
calling.

From cliff to cliff the blare echoed, and as she entered
the rips they closed round in their riot. She tried to steer
to one side, ride the aberrant flow down its less troubled
paths, but the surge swept her on and the din had grown

deafening. The waters leapt in their rage, cascading on her in torrents, a scrum of hooligan waves piling in from all quarters.

The narrow channel was crazed, falling in on itself, whirling round in wild eddies. Like the sea of her calf days, when she had cringed from the breakers, the sudden violence appalled, her own weakness alarming. Spume was rising like smoke, blotting out the gulf's walls and obscuring the heavens. Beneath its plumes the flow boiled, a foaming frenzy of brine in which bubbles erupted, blew up in vast blisters.

Ahead it bellowed and seethed, its delirium mounting. Here the chaos was caused by subterranean shoals which, deflecting the race, shot the flow from the depths to collide with top currents – a gross Neptunian freak, fearsome in its dementia. Dizzily, Wingfoot twirled, hurtled into the ferment. Had her true strength returned, miraculously bestowed, it would have happened too late: nothing now could avail her.

She was bound by the race, the demon hand of the gulf, its *opus magnum* approaching.

A mighty barrier met her, a glassy wall of sea, streaming suddenly upwards. Defying gravity's rule, a cataract in reverse, the soaring prodigy heaved, lifting her like a gull, bearing her to its summit. She seemed to hang for a trice then was tumbling on, rolling, cartwheeling madly, all sensation receding. Again the black curtain dropped and when it rose her ears drummed; she was describing an arc, carried round in a circle.

She thought the crags and cliffs waltzed, a nightmare carousel whirling. She was by now beyond caring. At least her passage was smooth, a curving, velvety glide that grew steady and soothing. The clamour round her went on but now the ferment had gone and the seal swung sedately. Round she swirled and once more, spared the buffeting tumult. For at its perilous heart Corrievreckan was subtle, insidious and unhurried. With each rotation she made, Wingfoot's journey got shorter, the maelstrom's coil tightening.

When her numb mind caught on, she could only flap weakly. There was no flight from the tow, its sleek clutch unrelenting. Faster now the seal spun, the huge whirlpool in charge, drawing her at each twist ever nearer its vortex. The rolling eye did not blink. Wingfoot gasped, her mouth opening. At last she came to the rim, made two loops and went down, sucked below through the opening.

There were few secrets more dark than those kept by the Cauldron. Mysteries lurked at its bowels and on a rock not far off, where the cliff-face was steep, a black fowl pondered bleakly, bemused by the waters. It saw, that day, the seal sink, then the sea bird sat watching.

As it waited it preened, accustomed to the pool's rhythm, the growl of the channel. The hustling westerly moaned and dusk crept on the islands. At length the gulf, growing bored, tossed aside its limp victim, casting her on the shore over which the bird brooded. At first the seal did not move, then she stirred and blew feebly, pummelled, wretched but living – a state, the fowl might have vouched, she was lucky to cling to.

With a cry it flew off, skimming down like a sea ghost.

The old man was still sleeping, his face a mask in the lamplight. At times he mumbled and moaned as the heavy door rattled, the wind slamming at it. The cats had crept round the hearth, their grey shapes dimly striped as if sketched in soft pencil, and Aggie hunched with them. She dared not think of the seals, already fearful enough. Suppose that Willie died on her?

No, she told herself sternly, it was not going to happen. He was a fool, the old pig, but he was never a quitter, too bloody-minded by half and too fond of a tussle. He was a man of the isles and would die hard like his forebears, folk once feared for their toughness, once the scourge of the mainland. Had not Donald of Islay, the Lord of the Islands, led his men across Scotland, their battles honoured in memory?

The 'Grit Donald' of ballad:

> *Richt far and neir baith up and down,*
> *Throw mount and muir, frae toun to toun,*
> *Allangst the land of Ross he roars.*

And so was Willie a fighter, a roarer, she reckoned. He would cuss again one day, and guzzle the whisky, and she would give him a scolding – tell the rotten old fool he had had no right to scare her. Damn the man, the girl brooded; get well, Willie, she urged him.

The fellow moaned in his sleep. 'Where's MacDonald?' he mumbled.

'Hush.' She pulled up his blankets. 'Hush now, Willie,' she soothed him.

He thrust an arm out, still sleeping. 'D'ye hear me, MacDonald?'

'He won't be long,' Aggie whispered. 'Just you rest and get better.'

She looked outside when he was quiet, taking with her a storm-lamp. There was no sign of the others. The wind played loose with her hair and she flinched, the chill biting. The sky was vast, the sea dark, in the gloom spirit-haunted. The pulsing breakers frothed dimly, glimmering in long ranks, and a glow marked the skerries, their distant caps foaming. Somewhere, Aggie imagined, Columba might yet be praying, Vikings roaming the night, torches flaring from rocks where the old chieftains rallied.

Were they there in the murk? On islands now long abandoned, did unseen children laugh quietly?

Or did they weep for the sea people?

She could not block out the seals, her fear the killers might take them. Perhaps they already had; perhaps her favourites had gone, lost to the cove and the herd, some in calf, some too young, not yet five years of age (when the creatures first mated). Was the silver seal dead or was she after all safe? And had young Oisin survived to court the likes of her one day?

She fretted over their fate, shivering as she anguished.

But now the old man came first and he must not be left longer. She went back in and for warmth made herself a hot drink, mostly milk strongly sweetened. She eyed the book on the table. She did not care for the book, a grating voice from the past – 'The men are eager with clubs' – but then the man had no taste. Since when had Willie had feeling?

'Is that you there, MacDonald?'

The creature stirred and peered round.

'No,' she answered, 'it's Aggie. Are you awake? I'm still with you.'

'Ah,' he pondered, 'the girl.'

'Will you moisten your lips? Shall I fetch you some water?'

She filled a mug without waiting and heard him croak, 'Is it done: has the boy fixed the engine?'

'Sip up, Willie, don't talk.'

He dribbled liquid and choked. 'It's time he finished,' he spluttered. 'It's time he had her to rights.'

'You can talk to him later.'

'He's not got Gorme with him, has he?'

'No,' she said, 'don't be daft.'

'Daft, you think? I could tell ye . . .' The man looked up, his eyes bleary. He made a mumbling speech, incomprehensible to her, then pushed the mug from him. 'I'm daft enough if that's whisky; fetch me whisky,' he grunted.

'Hush,' said Aggie again. 'You're not having it, Willie.'

'Just a dram.'

'No.'

'I'm dying. A final wish.'

'Heavens, Willie . . .'

'A final dram, lass, I'm dying.'

A gust of wind filled the croft and a hand-lamp was flashing. Then Mrs Fraser was speaking, her breathless voice rasping. 'No one's going to die and no one's touching a bottle; quite right of you, Aggie. You can stop blathering, man, I'm more concerned for my daughter. Child, it's time you had food, stuck out here all the evening. Why, this place is . . .' Words failed her.

'It's not kept tidy,' said Donnie, coming in at her shoulder. 'It's not our fault, Mrs Fraser.'

'Of course it's not,' snapped the woman, 'it's the way the man lives. I've not seen anything like it; it isn't fit to set foot in. I wouldn't keep a hen in it. Dear Lord, the place turns me over.' She sniffed the gloom, her lips tight, and unbuttoned her sheepskin. 'Take my coat,' she told

Aggie, 'you'll need it, bairn, for the journey. You're going home with the lad – and see you get a meal in you.'

Peg Fraser pulled up her sleeves. 'Let's have a look at the patient.'

She took his pulse with a frown and placed a palm on his forehead.

'I'm bad,' he whined. 'I'm weak, Peggy.'

'No worse than Florrie Maclean.' She straightened up with a frown. 'And several others,' she told him. 'You've got the flu, Will Macrae, it's not so nice when you're old. Especially,' she tacked on, 'when you've abused your poor body, neglected what the Lord gave you.'

'He scared me, Mam, with that fever.' The girl's relief left her vexed. 'He frightened me with his moaning.'

'He's in a pitiful state and he can thank himself, Aggie. The way he lives it's no wonder; we'd all be bad living this way. But I'll take charge of him now; you get along with the boy, and mind the path in that wind. I'll be here till the morning. If I'm not back in good time you can get the shop open.'

'If she gets flu?' Donnie worried.

'I'll not get flu,' Aggie blustered.

'We'll have to see,' said Peg Fraser. She placed her hands on her hips. 'If you feel poor, stay in bed. I'll see that this one pays for it.'

The man stared up with a wail. 'Don't leave me, Aggie, she's hard; you've got a fearful hard mother. I need to talk to MacDonald.'

'You'll talk to no one, Macrae.' The woman turned to the youth. 'On your way,' she enjoined, 'and take good care of her, Donnie.'

'That I will, Mrs Fraser.'

'Hurry up, and be careful.'

When they had gone the man groaned and Mrs Fraser glowered at him. 'You'll need a wash and fresh clothes; we'll see to that in a minute.' She stoked the fire and stood by it, the wind droning fiercely. It brought the sound of the sea, like a steam-piston pounding. She viewed the cobwebs and rubbish, inspecting cupboards and corners. At length, she said, 'It's disgusting, I can't believe someone lives here. Have you no self-respect? It's a scandal, you're shameful.'

'You always were a hard woman.'

'I always had decent standards.'

'Aye,' he mused with a sigh, 'a bonnie girl but a hard one. You scorned me, Peg, for a Fraser – a stony, teetotal Fraser – and now you're back with your scolding.'

'I'm sure I wouldn't remember.'

'I'll not forget,' said the 'captain'.

The woman glanced at him primly. 'No doubt you got what you deserved.'

'You broke my heart, Peggy Fraser.'

She was unmoved by his whimper. 'And when was that?' she inquired.

'When you were just twenty, Peggy.' He raised himself on his pillow. 'I mind the sight of you, lass, like a wee boat a-sailing, all trim, pennon streaming. You'd the lines of an angel.'

'Save your breath now, Macrae. I'm not here to be wheedled.'

The man lay back with a gasp. 'Just turned twenty you were, and turned me down without blinking.'

'You were as old as my father.'

'Full of life, not like some. I'd have made you laugh, woman, made your cheeks blush like plums. I'd've seen you were merry. You'd not have moped with Macrae, you'd have known you were living.'

'In a hovel. On whisky.'

The woman stooped in the gloom and retrieved a dead bottle. She carried it to the door and as she threw it outside a cat fled through the opening. She came back in with a sniff, flicking dust from her fingers. 'I'm thinking, Willie,' she said, 'I made a canny decision. The Lord preserved me from this – from being wed to a tramp.'

'You'd have changed me, though, Peg.'

'I'd have cut your throat for you.'

He ogled her from the bunk. 'You've still a neat figure on you.'

Mrs Fraser said, 'Huh,' but slyly pulled in her stomach.

'If I had any strength in me . . .'

'Ach, you're sickening, Willie.'

PART THREE

Sea Fury

Wingfoot played on the bell-buoy. Though not far off fully grown – she was five feet in length and weighed a hundredweight and more – she still enjoyed the old games and had perfected float-riding. When as now the waves danced, bouncing up to form peaks, she would spend hours at the sport, scrambling onto the ledge, clinging there as it see-sawed. The more the bumps threw her off, the more enticing the challenge.

With a fine sense of balance she knew the tricks of the platform. By swaying this way and that she could stay on in the chops, surviving pitch after pitch like a steeplechase jockey. When at last she was thrown she would be back in a trice, sliding up on the flow to remount the iron platform. Given the right kind of sea, neither flat nor too rough, the endless pranks of the buoy made her childishly happy.

Now the sea was just right, Corrievreckan forgotten. The water jigged round the float and made loud sucking noises. It made the far beaches reel, tipped and rocked the horizon. Across the bay, in the sun, the 'captain' puffed on his pipe, pottering near the *Peg*, whose fresh paint stood out brightly. The man had finished her trim, sprucing up her name proudly. He was not back to full strength but could handle a paint brush.

Several seals were about, their heads sleek in the billows. Preoccupied with her sport, Wingfoot took little notice. The breeze tossed spray in her face and her drenched charger gurgled. By and by the bell growled, marking freshening winds, and she gave up her antics.

Drawing off through the swell, she turned turtle and floated. A head had bobbed up nearby and she saw Oisin's face peering. He had a hesitant manner. He did not rush to show off but rather hung back and watched as if unsure of himself, afraid he might not be welcome. This was not the old Oisin, the pushy male she remembered, but a much-subdued version. The Sound of Jura had changed him.

While many seals had survived – most that Wingfoot knew closely: Niamh, Cellach, Bragela – many more had been killed and Oisin's group had fared badly. He had dragged home deeply shocked, chastened by his adventures. He now displayed a reserve the silver seal rather liked and her greeting was friendly. She rubbed his nose and submerged, not displeased when he followed.

Diving under the waves, she dawdled round near the floor and Oisin shadowed her quietly, glad it seemed of a friend, docile in his behaviour. For fun she hid by a rock and he found her with pleasure. Darkly handsome, well mannered, he made a charming companion and, though she darted away, she took good care not to lose him. They played a while and then rose, surfacing close together. As she lay in the trough, Wingfoot's mien was complacent.

The sun was high in the sky and she could hear the gulls calling. Their cries impinged on her dreams, loud and wild, and she listened. The birds were hovering low, a sign that fish were about, while several larger birds gathered. Gannets plunged one by one, cormorants were submerging. She gave her neighbour a glance and suddenly they were off, sensing food as they sallied.

Their prey seemed sparse at first sight. They were slim and fast-swimming, their steely backs bluish-green with black irregular bands over silver-white bellies: sea sprinters, the mackerel. They did not usually linger. Flattening their top fins, they would accelerate swiftly, leaving danger behind, but now these swimmers were listless.

The reason lay just ahead: a mighty crowd of the fish jamming into the shallows, its flank a glittering reef stretching far out of vision. It happened every few years. The teeming shoals ran inshore, suicidal as lemmings, obsessed by some frantic urge to pile up round the beaches. The sight astounded the seals. It halted Wingfoot's advance; Oisin stared in bemusement. There seemed no end to the fish, the tide of metal-blue backs laying siege to the point, swarming far past the buoy up the coast to the harbour.

There was no sense in the mackerel. They did not turn from the shore or break ranks when approached but simply pressed towards land, squeezing closer and tighter. They filled the tide from top to bottom; they churned and flashed and broke surface, a twisting, shimmering bulwark. As Wingfoot wheeled round the buoy and stalked incredulously nearer, it seemed too good to be true, a feast day for fish-eaters.

Other seals were converging while sea birds mustered and plunged. She could see their shapes diving, carving down through the mackerel then kicking upwards, rewarded. Everywhere they were swooping, bills spearing, wings flattened. It was a predator's dream and with a sudden surge forward the seals joined the diners.

Wingfoot, charging the mass, was surrounded by mackerel. They swarmed in brilliant confusion, oblivious of her presence. Her mouth was full in a moment and, swallowing, she refilled it, roused to greed by the glut. Deepest blue and pale green, the vast mackerel-wall shimmered. She caught a brief glimpse of Oisin, jaws crammed as he turned, then the mêlée closed round him.

Overhead, gulls were dunking, banqueting on the surface. A diving gannet streaked past her trailing luminous bubbles. Seconds later it climbed, black-webbed feet paddling briskly, its powerful beak burdened. A hungry cow seal loomed, snapping, to disappear in the host, her wake filled by more mackerel. Gorging, Wingfoot barged on, overwhelmed by the numbers.

She rose not far from the pier, to find it crowded with people. Excited children were shouting, women bringing up baskets. Youths dropped lines with hooks on them; others simply sank buckets tied to ropes and hauled on them, securing fine catches. The water simmered with fish. They came up in huge swaths, forced to rise by their numbers, folding into the air, their tails thrashing.

Aggie ran up the quay, savouring the occasion. It had the thrill of a gala, with everyone out to view and mackerel shining like trophies. They lay in piles on the stones and people carried them home, filling boxes and bags, stringing them through the gills, cradling them in their aprons. Youths ran down the pier's steps, dipping basins and pans; on the beach others waded, using shrimp-nets as scoops and old tubs as containers.

The girl gazed down on the water. A man was lifting a pail, heaving hand over hand on the cord which secured it. Mackerel gleamed in the vessel. 'Will you take some?' he asked. 'There'll be plenty more coming.'

'I've got nowhere to put them.'

He eyed her clean skirt and sweater. 'No, don't worry,' he said, 'I'll drop some by for your mam. She'll need to cook them tonight while they're fresh, for your supper.'

'Thanks.' She gave him a smile. 'Do you know why they do it?'

'I reckon porpoises chased them; they've got themselves in a pickle. Last time I saw them like this was before the war started. You were still in your cradle.'

She laughed and moved down the pier, heading for the *Goosander*. The boat was ready to leave and Donnie, close to the steps, was chatting quietly with Mary, peering up at her raptly. Aggie paused, irritated. His cheeks were flushed, his lips slack, as if the woman bewitched him. He looked, the girl thought, absurd, like a big lovesick schoolboy.

Aggie Fraser watched, glowering. When Calum's wife had withdrawn, gliding on her long legs, Aggie hastened to Donnie. He was embarrassed and grinned.

'You can smirk,' she accused him.

He looked away, his shrug awkward.

'And what was that about, tell me?'

'You tell me,' he rejoined. 'I'm the wrong one for riddles.' He made a quick, moody gesture. 'About the seal – about Wingfoot. She's got some bee in her bonnet. Don't ask me, Mary's strange.'

'Is that what makes you blush? I've seen how you look at her.'

'Come on, Aggie, she's married.'

'And if she wasn't?' she snapped. She did not know why she cared, but Donnie's blushes annoyed her.

'We're due to sail in a minute.'

'You're like all of the men.' She could see Gorme

swilling tea while Calum climbed from the hatch. The streaks of grease on his face were like a circus clown's make-up. 'You might be honest at least and admit that she's lovely.'

He frowned and sulked. 'Well, so what? She's Calum's woman,' he muttered.

'You never say that I'm pretty. You look at her like a fool.'

'I'm busy, Aggie, we're sailing.' He glanced away at the headrope. 'It wasn't my fault she stopped; she only asked me some questions. They didn't make any sense. She's as daft as those fish; thinks the seal's a bad omen – thinks it's following Calum.' He squinted over his shoulder. 'She's off her head, I'm not joking.'

Aggie sniffed. 'She's still gorgeous.'

'She hasn't got your brains, Aggie. I'll have to go,' Donnie grunted.

'Huh,' she breathed, unplaced.

The voice of Gorme interrupted. 'Wake up, will you, MacDonald?' The sandy beard jutted fiercely. 'Stir yourself there, we're leaving. Let her go fore and aft.'

Aggie folded her arms. 'Go on then,' she remarked, 'get away. I'm not bothered. The harbour's teeming with fish; if you can't catch the things here then you'd better be going.'

'Ah,' called Calum, amused, 'we're after bigger than mackerel. We're after man-sized fish, Aggie.'

'He doesn't know what he wants. He doesn't know when he's lucky.'

Calum's hoot crossed the gap and she turned back past the fishers. She had, she knew, been unfair but so was beauty like Mary's. And Donnie asked for sharp words. 'Brains,' she mused with a snort: a rousing compliment that was. It was high time he improved, if he was capable of it. Or had her mother known best – would Donnie always be Donnie, stuck with admirable points but ineducable failings?

She did not dwell on the prospect.

Later, riding her bike, she made her way to the cove then crossed the beach to see Wingfoot. The silver seal had hauled out and was asleep, full of mackerel. She roused at Aggie's approach and slightly opened her mouth, its breath of protest half-hearted. The girl was known to the beast, who was in any case torpid, the victim of her own greed and not inclined to be shifted.

Quietly, Aggie walked round her, admiring the creature. The nose was 'Grecian' in profile, a smooth line back through the head to sleek shoulders and body, a line of flowing perfection like that of a bird, a great bird of the ocean. The girl crouched down, arm extended, and touched the silvery back. 'My, you're bonnie,' she whispered.

Wingfoot hissed, her teeth showing. They were strong and well-spaced, as were the claws on her flippers. Drawing back, Aggie smiled. Her silver seal was a glutton and far too bloated to move. The stupid Mary should see her – follow Calum, indeed. Did Wingfoot look like a threat, some dire warning to seamen? All she cared for was fish and a snooze when surfeited.

However, Aggie admitted, she could see how the myths started, the tales of mermaids and sirens. For, as was Mary herself, this was a beautiful creature.

'Hey there, Aggie, come here.' The 'captain' stood by the *Peg*. 'Cast your eyes on this boat. Take a look at that paint job.'

'You're not supposed to work, Willie. Didn't mam tell you not to?'

'Did she now? I've forgotten.' He watched her saunter across. 'Your mother's hard on me, lass. Mind, she still stirs my blood; she's a trim wee waist on her.'

'I'll tell her so,' Aggie laughed.

'Be damned, I've told her myself. She's a heart made of granite.'

'Let's say you're not her type, Willie.'

'Oh well,' he said, 'this *Peg*'s mine.' He viewed the boat with huge pride. 'What do you think of her now? You wouldn't call that a wreck, eh?'

'Very smart. Will she float?'

'Float?' the man said. 'She'll fly. When she's launched she'll dance, Aggie. We'll not have wasted our time, though it has dragged on lately. That boy of yours doesn't hurry.'

'He's not my boy,' Aggie snapped, still not wholly forgiving.

'Poor wee Donald MacDonald, he's disappointed you, has he?' The 'captain' eyed her and chuckled. 'Then take a look at his work, for that'll not disappoint you.' Climbing into the boat, he raised the new engine-casing. 'The laddie's slow but he's thorough, just you peep for yourself. You won't find better than that in a boat round this island.'

Aggie looked at the motor. It did not mean a lot to her but was, she thought, much transformed, neat and clean in its aspect.

She said, 'But does the thing go?' and got a petulant answer.

'Does it go? Will it float? You're like a bairn with your questions.'

'I'm not an engineer, am I?'

'D'ye think the boy's toiled for nothing?'

'No, but . . .' Aggie felt guilty. She should be kinder to Donnie. Defensively, she observed, 'You had your doubts too, remember? You cursed him, Willie Macrae, and were you not always grumbling? I stood up for him then.'

'I was sick at the time.'

'Well, if you're pleased with him, Willie.' She wished she had not seen Mary and felt especially remorseful for sending Donnie to sea without a civil farewell. Suppose some dreadful thing happened?

The 'captain' patted the engine. He said, 'I'm more than pleased with him. Why, don't you see, we're in business. A few small jobs to complete and we'll be trying her out.'

'I hope she runs well, that's all.'

'Don't you fear, girl, she'll run. It's Donnie's chance to leave Gorme. I've worked for them, those damned Gormes, and you can be sure of this: if being rid of a Gorme rests on that engine running, she's going to run like a stag. Stands to reason,' the man said.

'I wish he'd left Gorme already.' The girl had turned to the sea. 'It's getting rough; the bell's ringing.'

'They've not put out today, have they?'

'Would you not?' She swung back.

'I'd think twice. I'd maybe ponder the mackerel.'

'Why?' asked Aggie, disturbed. 'They say the porpoises drove them.'

'Do they?' Willie demurred. 'Some might say so, some wouldn't.'

When she had slept off her feast Wingfoot found Oisin waiting. He was stretched out on the stones, contemplating the rock-pool. It had seemed large to them once, now it looked a lot smaller. As Wingfoot humped to the male, a third seal surfaced in it.

They fell on Niamh with glee; they might have still been first-coaters.

The little pool took them back, hardly changed since their calf days. Here they had played submarines, caught small crabs and blown bubbles, or paddled round until bored, bursting pods on the seaweed. Much had happened since then but they were not past a romp and made sport in high spirits.

At length they tired of the game and lay watching the breakers. The sea had billowed up quickly and tall waves were crashing. As calves the three might have quaked; today they lolloped in line, struck the foam and dived under.

In the marbled green light their old play-haunts unfolded: shelving rocks, terraced views, the drowned switch-backing dunes with their rich kelp plantations. Familiar sights met the eye, the homes of rockling and goby and the den of the eel, their first frightening conger.

Ahead, beyond the sea gardens, the reef was in ferment.

The trio swam in formation using lithe body movements, the cove growing rougher. They had played tag round its crags, hide-and-seek among boulders. In this coombe or that vale they had learned to catch dabs, stalk the spiny-finned gurnard, hunt whiting and haddock.

And here, when new to the sea, they had observed their first gale, almost trapped by its fury. They had grown wiser since then.

Now, as the sand started rising, shimmying on the bottom, they respected the warning. Prudently, they took stock, surfacing close together. The wind was gathering strength and, as the swell threw them up, Wingfoot saw that the coast had a broad white frieze around it, a sign to be reckoned. The spume was high on the cliffs and each pounding wave rumbled. The time had come to move out and the silver seal flippered.

Nostrils tight, she plunged swiftly. Niamh and Oisin were with her, thrusting earnestly now, their course set for deep water. They gave the reef a wide berth. The sea was boiling above it and knife-edged crags sliced the waves, menacing in the lather. With snaking thighs the seals hastened. Then, beset by cross-currents, they had traversed the cove's frontier, the open ocean before them.

Aloft again to take bearings, they glimpsed the land far behind, a low and straggling wall that was lost as the sea rolled. They had no special objective but cruised ahead at their ease, gliding under the lumps, free of imminent danger. Other seals were about, equally weather-conscious; shoals of fish were in motion. Wingfoot saw them below but, well-fed, took no interest.

Instead she followed Niamh, Oisin running abeam. They swam a while near the top then, shafting lazily down, found a place on the bottom. There they stopped and reclined, far beneath the rough surface. Soon Niamh was asleep, the male drowsing beside her, while Wingfoot rocked on the sand watching shapes in the half-light. A massive ray winnowed past. As it dissolved in the gloom, like a white owl dusk-prowling, a tangled ball of kelp loomed, rolling over the sea-bed.

A school of cod finned above, bulky bad-weather feeders. They were fat and alluring but Wingfoot dozed, unprovoked, and in a moment they moved leaving only a waste, a wilderness of the depths in which three seals were sleeping. Several times, barely waking, they floated up to take air, sinking back semi-conscious.

When Wingfoot finally roused, the group had drifted apart and her surroundings had changed. Now the floor undulated and crests of sand-hills rose dimly. Something vast filled the murk, a grey and mountainous object, and drawing cautiously nearer she saw at first a tall funnel and then the barnacled plates, red-lead plain round their rivets. It was a ship on the bottom, a merchantman of war vintage, a gaping cave in her side where she had stopped the torpedo.

She lay listing to port, her stem deep in the sand. Apart from losing her masts, and the hole in her hull, the ship was largely undamaged. Fish browsed over her decks and passed calmly through hatches. Encouraged by their aplomb, Wingfoot nosed round the rails, curious to explore, maybe find her companions. Investigating teak planks, she followed their tracks of caulking then flippered on to the bridge through a door which hung open.

The sea inside was unmoving, funereal in its stillness. Broken glass lay about, coated green by the depths, while wooden stools, floating up, had wedged under a ceiling. She saw a mug on the boards and several heavy brass ashtrays, now as dull as the dials on corroding telegraph pedestals. A little squid darted by, taking fright at her presence, and she turned out of the door, peering next in the chart room. It had been hastily rummaged before the ship was abandoned and wooden drawers were jammed open. Their metal handles were tarnished. Scattered round in the flow were compasses and dividers.

Such things meant nothing to Wingfoot and yet the search fascinated. It raised obscure expectations. Here and there in the maze a tiny current prowled with her as if the vessel was lived in, as if not merely the fish possessed its watery dwellings. The eerie emptiness haunted and Wingfoot slid forward.

Utensils littered the galley, rusting pots, pans and beakers. There were still coals in the stove; cans and jars were unopened. Tightly clamped in its place was a cast-iron meat-mincer. In sheltered crannies and nooks little shellfish were scuttling. Cutlery strewed the mess deck where a meal had been scattered; boxes swam in aft cabins along with half-empty bottles, leather boots and hair brushes. In the forecastle quarters, the seal found tin and wood chests, razors, combs, a crew's knick-knacks. A gramophone lay upended.

She was, she sensed, not alone, and yet she saw no large creature. Perhaps Niamh was ahead, as curious as herself, or she would meet Oisin exploring. But they were not in the hold, nor where the engines had seized or round the blast-damaged boilers. She felt a pang of mistrust, an uneasy foreboding. Whatever lurked in the ship, it was not her companions.

On deck an open door beckoned, one place the seal had not looked. Swimming past it to leave, she turned back and peeped in. The captain's cabin was dim, the water's stillness uncanny. The thing was black in the shadow, an arm flung out on the wall while two bulging eyes glimmered. As the seal turned in fright the mighty octopus moved, unravelling from its lair and pumping out across deck, its great tentacles trailing. Macabrely, the brute vanished, Wingfoot fleeing obliquely.

Surfacing to take air she was tossed and wind-blinded. The sea was rowdy and stinging, hurling sheets in her face, a contrast after the depths of confusing proportions. Until she gathered her wits it seemed an empty commotion, a barren ferment of waves, and then ahead in the trough she saw a dusky stern swinging. The beamy boat rose and dipped, her short wake quickly lost. She was an old fellow-traveller, the familiar *Goosander*.

Donnie came to the side. He had a pail of swill with him and as the deck tipped he lurched; half the contents went down him. The water soaked his boot-stockings.

Calum grinned, swaying safely, his movements perfectly timed. He wore a pair of old jerseys with a torn smock above them, thigh boots and sou'wester. He said, 'You've learned how to swear; you'll find your legs one of these days.'

'Not on this trip, I shan't.'

'Now's the right time to practise.'

Donnie leaned on the wind. It moaned and whined in the rigging, plucking notes on the ratlins. With the gusts the boat rolled, ploughing deep in the swell, taking sea on her foredeck. She threw her rump in the air like a mettlesome heifer. 'It's blowing twenty knots, Calum, or twenty-five, and still strengthening. It's not my lucky trip, this one.'

'I'd say we might not do badly.'

'Yes, you would,' Donnie grumbled.

'Heavy sea, heavy fishing.'

'That won't alter things for me.' He thought of Aggie's foul mood. The sky glared at them darkly.

The other checked the nets slowly, his body rocking with ease as if faultlessly balanced. He said without looking up, 'So the wee girl's upset you?'

'It's not as if I did something. '

'She'll be touchy, that's all.'

Donnie clutched at the gunwale. Water ran round his feet, sluicing out through the scuppers. It was ultramarine with a vein of white in it. He said with force, 'I did nothing.'

'Makes no difference,' said Calum.

'Blow that.'

'Just forget it.'

'That's easy said,' the youth groused. The man did not have his problems; he had a doting wife waiting, the loveliest on the island. Donnie envied him Mary, if she was a bit dotty: she would have to be that, to dote on Calum with her looks. 'It's all right for you,' he said resentfully.

Calum was silent. A mask had dropped on his face, the blankness Donnie knew well. It was the secretive sea-face, reserved, melancholy. At length the big man said drily, 'They're not aboard with us, are they?'

Another wave hit the boat. It raced on by with fierce splendour and Calum added more kindly, 'She'll be all over you later. She'll be as bright as a kitten.'

'I suppose . . .'

'Aye, you'll see. She's a canny girl, Aggie; she's going to turn out a good one.'

A fleeting sadness returned but Donnie missed it, asserting, 'She's overbright, that's the trouble. She gets her brains from her mother.'

'You'd better stick with her, son, she'll keep you one day,' said Calum.

'I'll not need that,' Donnie bridled.

'You never know.'

'Yes, I do.'

Calum smiled. 'Got big plans?' The square face shone with spray.

'Plans?' The youth clammed up quickly, for Gorme

and Calum swapped gossip. 'I might have notions, just notions.'

'How's Macrae's old boat shaping?'

'All right.' The tone was suspicious. Had Calum heard she was ready? Or nearly so, bar the trimmings. Did they suspect he might quit? He wanted that to surprise them, especially Gorme, when the time came. 'She's coming on not too badly.'

The other hid his amusement. 'So you've notions then, have you?'

Donnie stared at the water.

'You'll need them,' Calum went on, 'if you're to keep pace with Aggie.'

'Yes,' said Donnie, then, 'Calum . . .'

'Does she approve of them?'

'What?'

'Why, these notions you mention.'

'Calum, did you see that?'

Calum pondered the ocean.

'I thought I saw the seal, Calum; I'm sure I saw the seal bobbing.' Following the *Goosander*. Or had he dreamed that he saw her? Why should she follow the boat? It was a daft proposition – as daft as Mary herself. He eyed the man, who said nothing. The wind was rising to gale force.

'There, I saw her again. I saw the silver seal, Calum.'

The boat pitched on through the wind, mast and rigging vibrating. Donnie's voice whisked away, shredded by the gale's violence. The air was throbbing with noise as if a sea battle raged and they were caught in the barrage, a ceaseless roar from the south interspersed with loud thuds as spume crashed on the wheelhouse. Calum's answer was lost and the youth mimed his deafness.

A second time, the man bellowed. 'Your sight's better than mine.' No compliment was intended, the comment sardonic.

'I tell you, Calum, I saw her.'

Calum braced with a leg forward, back bent, his head lowered. His arms flapped out from his sides as he struggled for balance. He might have been playing rugger, about to enter a scrum, but for the bulky clothes on him. Not until the gust passed, screaming on to the north, did he shout, 'If you say so.'

'I'm certain of it,' bawled Donnie.

Calum humoured him. 'Right.'

'The seal you saved from the net.'

'Did I?' Calum said vaguely.

'You know you did.' The boat rolled, causing Donnie to stagger. He ran to keep on his feet then stopped himself with a jerk. He scowled at Calum, incensed, the man's perversity galling. Was he ashamed of his kindness? 'The silver seal . . .'

'So you said.'

'I thought . . .' The vessel reared quickly and Donnie reeled to her housing, hanging on, his mouth open. He dropped the subject and brooded.

When Calum took to the sea he chose his own conversations, seldom joining in others, or simply toiled without speaking. Donnie glared at him dumbly. A wave had rushed down the deck, swamped his boots and drained out. As he awaited the next, he thought, 'All right then, don't talk. See if I care, you ape.' And yet he did, for it helped; talking broke the suspense, served to ease his forebodings.

'Damn this, Calum,' he groused. 'Damn this lot for a living.'

Calum's eyes focused on him, their striking blueness uncanny.

'This?' he yelled. 'It's not much.'

'Bad enough. And it's worsening.'

'It's not your first spot of weather.'

Donnie's lungs filled with salt, a blast that tore at his head and might have come from a power-jet. He said, 'It's time we got out; time we headed for shelter.'

'You ought to know Gorme by now.'

'I know Gorme. That's what scares me.' Not just Gorme, come to that, but the other's indifference. 'You're as bad as each other.'

Calum balanced adroitly, his complacency maddening. 'You don't catch fish, lad, from shelter.'

'The flaming boat could tip over.'

She met the trough and plunged wildly, bottoming with a jolt then, still shuddering, soared, her prow climbing the wave-wall. Pouring onto the deck a snowy riot swept aft, reached the stern and rebounded. Donnie watched it foam round him. Scudding brine struck his face and he swore like a fishwife. When he could see again clearly, the big man was smirking.

'You're punch-drunk, Calum,' he gasped.

'Don't you trust the old *Goose*?'

'Not with him in there driving.'

'Where's your faith?' Calum teased.

Donnie watched the sea towering. 'It's getting up, getting worse.'

'Ach, she's built for it, son; I've seen twice the sea round her. Let it blow for a while, it'll make her feel happy.'

'You're mad,' the youth told him fiercely. 'The two of you, you're both mad.' His voice was dwarfed by the roar and Calum's answer came faintly.

'I didn't order it, man; if you're complaining, blame heaven.'

A vast green precipice curled and *Goosander* stove through it. As the wave raced astern, Donnie, clutching a rail, saw a gleam in the swell and was sure it was Wingfoot, her silver skull streaming. He felt an eerie sensation, remembering Mary. But then the woman was touched – as if the seal would pursue them. Besides, he could not swear to it: the stormy light was deceptive, baneful through the wave-valleys, and one seal's head . . . or a float . . .

He looked again and saw nothing.

Then Gorme was gesturing at them. 'Have you done?'

he was calling. 'Is that tackle made ready?'

Calum lofted a thumb. 'Aye,' he screamed, 'it's all ready.'

'Right – inside till it eases.'

Donnie moved, arms outstretched. The sea forayed with malice. As they piled in the wheelhouse Calum shoved his rump roughly, the wind commanding a door which slammed brutally on them. Gorme did not turn his head. A pipe fumed in his beard and he was peering through glass where grey water was sheeting. Dimly framed, the bows ghosted wreathed in spray, cowled by waves, vanishing, reappearing. Donnie, gulping the fug, wedged himself in a corner. Soon his ears began burning.

'That's snug,' Calum averred. 'You feel safer, Mac-Donald?'

Donnie made no reply.

The bearded helmsman ignored them.

Every now and again, like a cartload of muck, the sea fell on the windows. It thundered down on the roof, sheeting off in cascades. Donnie felt far from safe. He thought the wheelhouse must smash, its glass shatter to splinters. They did not care, these two men, they were seafaring cretins. They would press on after fish to the brink of extinction. One day they would cross it.

Calum said, 'It's got fresh,' and glancing slyly at Donnie, 'Our expert here says it's freshening.'

Gorme stared forward unspeaking, contempt in his silence.

The housing trembled and rocked as each wave hit the craft. It was, thought Donnie, a matchbox and all about the sea pounded, a trillion-trillion tons of it. With every roll the thing canted until the sky stood on end; with each pitch he prayed quietly. It was a sickening feeling.

The floor would drop like a lift's and he could sense his guts rising, his diaphragm impelled upwards, and then the planking would heave and his whole frame grow leaden. And still the two men behaved as if nothing disturbed them.

Gorme addressed him abruptly. 'You can make yourself useful.'

Calum's daft grin was spreading.

'Behind you: open that locker.' It held a well-handled bottle. 'Give it here, and be careful.' The skipper swigged from its neck, belched and passed it to Calum. When the big man had gulped he said, 'Here, lad, taste that. That'll make you more cheerful.'

Donnie shook his head, glowering.

'Then put it back,' grunted Gorme. 'You've not learned much from Macrae.'

Calum's leer was provoking.

'Should I have?' the youth parried.

'You tell us,' Gorme invited.

Donnie watched the sea, flustered. Outside, the scene was tumultuous. A green escarpment approached and *Goosander* dug at it, tardy this time in rising. As the wave stretched above, a cringing helplessness seized him, then the cloud-wrack had gone, the whole cosmos extinguished. A roaring blackness descended in which a single light glowed, the red fire in Gorme's pipe, and for a hideous spell Donnie thought they had foundered. Slowly daylight returned, first deep green in the windows then a dirty grey wash as, with a juddering wrench, the boat hauled from the tunnel.

Her stubby prow steamed with spray and the foredeck was flooded. Gorme had not twitched a muscle. The sandy beard was still stiff, the squat pipe still protruded.

His attitude was unchanged, his gruff voice had not altered.

'Ye'd best forget him,' he snarled, 'there's not much Willie can teach you. Apart from how to drink whisky.'

Donnie's jaw had locked tight.

'Would you agree with me, Calum?'

'He's a master of boozing.'

'He'll teach you little else, sonnie.'

The boat came up with a shiver. They rolled and sea topped the gunwales, each beam in turn deluged. At least, reflected the youth, Willie understood weather: he would have forecast the winds, steered well clear of the filth, but you could not talk to Gorme and the youngster kept silent.

'Well,' rasped Gorme, 'the boy's quiet.'

Calum swayed. 'Thinks it's worsening.'

'Does he now?' The man lurched, his small bloodshot eyes squinting. 'That's not a bad sign, eh, Calum?'

'Blows up worst before clearing.'

'There you are, boy, stop moping.'

'I think his girl has upset him.'

Donnie's sullen face darkened. A sudden tilt threw him sideways and Calum's powerful arms caught him, both man and lad reeling. He pushed himself away, cursing, detesting the fellow.

'Girl?' sneered Gorme. 'He's a bairn.'

'Aye, he'll learn; he'll find out.'

The howling wind batted at them. Above the roar from outside, their shouted banter struck home.

'I'm learning,' Donnie spat back. 'By God, I'm learning,' he wailed. 'You think this flaming muck's funny. You've got a death-wish, both of you.'

Calum's grin grew grotesque and even Gorme raised a

cackle. 'He doesn't know he's alive; he doesn't know when he's lucky.'

'You call this lucky?' flung Donnie.

Gorme was wrestling the wheel. 'You'd rather be on the *Peg*?' He held the boat's head to sea. 'You don't know you're well off. Man, she'd not last two seconds.'

Calum gave a great laugh, shoulders stretching his oilskins. 'He'd rather be with wee Aggie.'

Water smothered their vision and Donnie fought to stand straight. 'I bet you'd rather be home. You'd rather be with your Mary.'

There was a lull between gusts and Calum's humour had fled. The grin had gone in a trice and when Donnie eyed Gorme the man's features were leery, his knowingness mocking. Through the sea-festooned glass the youth made out a seal rising. Then the next wave had struck and more were queuing to pound them.

An ashen sun showed its face. Tottering on the waves, it was erased by the clouds and the seal could be seen, soaring on the sea's summit. A towering crest racked the boat, slavered monstrously leeward. Slithering down its tail, Wingfoot followed *Goosander*, the wind shrieking round her.

It raged with lunatic cries, its insanity mounting. The sounds were savage and pained, as if a mob was rampaging, loosed from some briny dungeon. The noise concussed, palpitated, dropped to whimpering moans then exploded with rage, deafening in its violence. Of all the winds she had known, none had sounded so evil.

Each rifling gust scalped the waves, tore at her in its wrath. She ducked the worst, bobbing down, yet remained fascinated. Such devilry was mesmeric, its work awe-inspiring. The ocean pulsed in great swells, clifflike ridges of sea rolling rank after rank out of watery space, an inexpressible vastness.

It plucked her up, shot her down, showed her torn sheets of cloud and pits greasy with rancour. *Goosander*'s stern slewed and foamed, a tormented companion. The boat was there by pure chance, the seal not sorry to see her, a fellow storm-traveller to break the sense of aloneness now her friends had gone missing. The boat belonged to the island and bolstered her spirits.

She liked the craft's stubborn gameness. *Goosander*'s decks were awash; the sea pummelled her fiercely. It overwhelmed both her ends, gushed from scuppers, snarled through her. It toppled on her amidships. Massive waves salivated, their drooling tongues rabid. And yet the boat trundled bravely, redoubtably buoyant.

At times *Goosander* was sullen, low-lying and moiling, but then defiance would rise and she would kick up her heels, fearlessly breast the ferment. Crazed, the sea gathered round and the wind cursed her mettle. With witches' oaths the gusts lashed, casting spells of strange light, sinister in the shrouds and on drenched superstructure.

The vessel shrugged it off dourly. She might not have the seal's grace, might be swift in name only, but Wingfoot admired her. The chunky craft was a battler.

Now the wind gave a scream and the ocean's charge quickened, the seal inundated. Swept away from the boat, she turned at length to the depths, wearied by the storm's drubbing. Flippers closed, she sank limply. With several fathoms above, the water's anger declined and she descended in peace, *Goosander*'s churning screw distant. Soon the winds were forgotten, Niamh and Oisin remembered. She went on down, nose alert, in the hope she would find them.

The sandy bed was deserted, oddly calm and withdrawn. Only the faintest of echoes – elfin currents and whirls – of the gale reached the bottom. Where a tiny shell moved, a few grains rose and drifted. For a while the seal searched for her friends then, frustrated, lay resting.

She did not let herself sleep, the gale's nearness disturbing. Once or twice in the murk, massive shapes passed above her. Cruising under the waves they were probably whales, though Wingfoot could not be sure, their resonances storm-scattered. When they had gone she moved off, feeling safer when mobile.

The wilderness showed no friendship. It spread before her unbroken, a realm of bleak sandy plains bare of beast or oasis, and all her searching revealed was continuing desert. Its undulations were barren, its flats without interest. She swam with growing misgivings, the solitude spooky.

At last she spotted the funnel.

It loomed in space like a beacon, familiar decks dim beneath it. She had come back to the wreck.

Wingfoot paused, in two minds, her last rummage unnerving. She felt compelled to explore in case the others were there, returned like her to the vessel. Yet she had strong reservations.

Warily she advanced, her memory flashing warnings. As she closed on the hull she recalled the drowned bridge and the barnacled bulkheads, the eerie maze in the ship, the great tentacled monster. She had bolted the last time. Now it all looked serene, little fish came and went, but Wingfoot was suspicious. The octopus had been huge and its scowling gaze haunted. Besides, as hard as she peered she could see no seals waiting.

For a minute she circled, then, sliding over the wreck, squinted down at the decks. They were as empty as ever. The doors of cabins hung open, cloaked in watery gloaming. Rails and bridge shimmered weirdly. The only creatures apparent were a small school of saith near a waterlogged lifeboat. Turning over the prow, she dived and ran the ship's side, swimming back up the other. Nothing moved, foe or friend.

Where the plates had been torn she gazed into the belly. The great torpedo-hole gaped but it was dark in the ship and the seal wriggled forward. Hesitating a while, she took a fresh look and entered.

It was a furtive incursion, apprehensive and twitchy. Slinking over the coals she nosed the great rusting boilers then stopped, her skin tingling. The stilly water had trembled, stirred by something behind her. In a flash Wingfoot hid, shooting round the first tank, freezing tautly against it. She had been tracked through the opening; she could not see what pursued her but its displacement was bulky. The flow was washing her snout, her long whiskers vibrating.

She did not dare to peep out but her curled lip was ugly. Her fangs were ready to snap as a smooth muzzle ventured, winkling round the corner, as shy as her own. Then she was staring at Treshnish, their startlement mutual. Relieved, the animals paused before showing delight, their past feuding forgotten. Wingfoot tumbled with pleasure. Flippering round the cave, she dashed out through the hole, jigging back to the ocean.

There, she blinked in amazement. Scores of seals were disporting, sliding languidly past her. Pinnipeds banked and climbed, toured the wreck, skimmed the sand, swimming under the tumult, the chaos above them. Suddenly, from the waste, half the herd had appeared, restive as the storm mounted, astir near the bottom. Many of them were strangers but others Wingfoot knew well, as familiar as Treshnish. She spotted Finn and Bragela, several cows from the skerries. A friendly grey female nudged her.

Happily, she swam with them, rejoicing in numbers. She felt secure in the crowd and the joy bubbled in her. Racing up in a loop, she rolled over the top and fell in with some youngsters. The gale had made the group skittish, its pranks aquabatic. The maidens chased down the decks, wheeled in rings round the funnel. The silver seal was entranced. Flinging forward she followed, then in a burst of high spirits zigzagged through the davits. Not far off she saw Cellach. The big old bull reassured her.

All was well in her world – doubly well the next moment, for there was Niamh ahead, Oisin thrusting towards her, their friendly eyes shining. Joining them at a sprint she romped merrily with them, swooping over the flats, rushing back to the shipwreck. Fears allayed, she relaxed. The herd was settling down, forming now in a pack, a long eel-like procession, the older seals leading.

In a leisurely band they set off round the ship, circling its drowned decks, the van catching the stragglers, undulating and twisting. It was a curious ritual. Shadowy, the seals danced, lilting in the green gloom like revellers round a maypole, the dead vessel ghostly. The silent carousel whirled. Phantom shades, the beasts waltzed, their backs rising and falling, their satin thighs slinky. It was trancelike, unhurried – Niamh swayed, Treshnish planed – weightlessly, without effort. A gale dance in the deep. A fling under the tempest.

For some minutes it lasted until the creatures grew bored or their lungs needed charging. Still a few kept on twirling but more reposed on the sand or went up for a breather.

When Wingfoot surfaced to blow, the storm's reality shook her. The rush of air overwhelmed, bludgeoning head and nostrils. It wrenched her snout to one side, screaming past in its rage while the waves roared and hissed, hurling spray as they bounded. They came at her in mad leaps, lunging out of the void, curling over the seal, routing clouds in their fury. Giants, they ruled the sea's roof, spitting lather and hate. Scudding fowl fled in terror.

Wingfoot dived again quickly. Plunging back to the wreck, she gazed at it dumbfounded. The dancing shadows had gone, the graveside was deserted. Only the iron corpse remained, its tall funnel aloft, the surrounding depths vacant. Decks were bare, the sand empty, desolate and uncanny. A slothlike current unfurled. The seal herd had departed.

Aggie clutched at the bike, leaning on it and plodding. Her cycling-cape had ballooned, the hood almost blown off. When she had left on the round she had managed to ride, now the gale made her walk and even that was a fight, the machine tugged about, the wind shoving her all ways.

Breakers boomed like shells bursting, shooting over the rocks, pelting down on the path, trying hard to upend her. Nothing on her was dry, from her head to her socks, these awash in her boots. Hair, escaping the hood, streaked her wet face like seaweed. As she puddled and swayed she kept thinking of Donnie and cursing her temper.

Water spired round the pier in great dirty-white spouts and she prayed for his safety. To send a man off to sea with harsh words was appalling. And for nothing, she anguished. If he was lost in this hell she would always feel guilty. Should he return without harm she would not chide him again, not as long as she knew him. As God was her witness.

She reached the shop numb and dripping. The door was whipped from her grasp, torn away by the wind, and hands reached to help shut it. A little crowd stood inside by Peg Fraser's small switchboard, the atmosphere anxious. Hoarse suggestions were mooted. 'Try the Williamsons, Peggy, see what's happening out that way.'

'Try Flora Macneil, it blows hard on her clifftop.'

'I've been trying her line; I'm not getting an answer.' Mrs Fraser saw Aggie. 'Child, you're back, I'm relieved. No more errands, it's dangerous.'

'Hurricane force in places.' Shawled figures drew closer. 'The radio says so.'

'I'd not care to be fishing.' A wrinkled face viewed the sea. Wafts of spray reached the shop, slamming hard on the window. 'Mind, I've sailed with it worse; aye, I've sailed in worse weather.'

The boatmen's wives took no notice. Someone muttered, 'He would have.'

'Do ye call me a liar?'

Aggie's mother said sharply, 'Be off home with you, man, for you'll not make it later. Have you got what you came for?' Then, turning back to the girl, 'Aggie, take off those clothes; put some warm, dry things on you. Lord, you're dripping with water.'

As if that mattered, thought Aggie, when she was safely on land. What of Donnie out there? What of Donnie the seaman, clinging to the *Goosander*? If the boat was still floating.

She ran upstairs and stripped briskly, furious with herself. She should have held her hot tongue, not gone on at him that way. She did not think half the time, far too quick with her comments. She did not mean to be hurtful but he did aggravate her. She found it hard to be patient, a fault she knew was unpleasant. Donnie did not deserve it. She had sent him off saddened.

She rubbed her hair with a towel and pulled on sweaters and trews.

Her bedroom window was knocking, juddering in the gusts as she stared at the ocean. She had not seen it so high, the wild swell so unruly. Gazing down on the front she saw the rollers careering, splattering on the sea wall, and someone striding along where the path ran beside it. It was Mary, of course; only Mary strode that way. Only Mary would be there.

Aggie sighed as she watched. To think that Mary had mattered, that she had minded them chatting: Donnie and that daft woman. How could she ever have cared? As if Mary might steal him; as if poor Donnie swooned for her. And what the heck if he did, she had no right of possession and less to offend him, to pack him off moping.

Here lies Donnie MacDonald.

She saw his grave by her father's.

Oh, dear God, let him live, keep *Goosander* from sinking.

She turned away from the window. Her wet clothes lay on the floor and she kicked them in anger then, carrying them downstairs, went back into the shop, listening to the others.

'Well,' her mother said calmly, 'there's no report from the coastguard.' She shuffled plugs on the switchboard. 'I'm thinking no news is good news. If there's word then they'll bell us.'

'Wherever else the men land?'

'Wherever they can get in.'

The huddled group murmured quietly.

'They'll not be landing in this,' Mrs Gorme stated bluntly. 'They'd never get into harbour. They'll want a good broad lee coast; that's where Gorme is an expert. Though I say it myself, Gorme's a master of knowledge. It's recognized through the islands.'

Aggie tried to ignore her. Gorme was part of the mess, for if the man was so good he would have known not to sail. Some had foreseen the weather.

'I'm sure they all know their business,' Peggy Fraser said coolly. 'I'll try Flora again, just in case there's a problem.' She shook her head. 'Still no answer.'

A sheet of spume flew outside, hammering the shop window. The sudden noise made them jump and someone said, 'Mind that pane, it could break if this rises.' They stood regarding it dumbly. The glass cleared slowly of water and a pale face could be seen, staring in like a zombie. Seconds later it faded.

'Mary,' Aggie confirmed, not that anyone doubted. 'She's on her way to the quay.'

'Let her go,' said Gorme's wife, 'we can well do without her.'

'Aye,' another exclaimed, 'all she'll bring us is trouble.'

Mrs Fraser objected. She held no brief for the woman but knew she ought to be in. 'Safely out of the wind. Why, a loose slate could kill her, a breaker could snatch her. Call her in, Mrs Johnson.' She reached to answer the phone and Mrs Johnson did nothing. 'It's the Macneils, they're all right. Lost the top of a rick, nothing worse at the moment. Hello, Flora, take care, it's a hurricane warning.'

Mrs Fraser rang off. 'You didn't stop her,' she chided.

'She'd not have heard us, it's howling.'

'She'll be concerned, the poor creature; she'll be concerned about Calum.'

'About herself,' hissed Gorme's spouse. 'In case she loses his earnings, that's Mary's concern. That's why she lives on that quay: she's afraid he'll escape her.'

'The man's as loyal as a dog.'

'More fool him all these years. What's she ever done for him?'

'I wonder,' mused a small woman.

'Well you might,' Mrs Gorme said. By Gorme's account, precious little, and didn't Calum work for him?

'Well you might,' she said louder, the shop door vibrating.

'It's the wee boy I pity,' Mrs Johnson informed them, 'the poor lad MacDonald. Barely shaving,' she fluttered.

Aggie covered her ears.

Mrs Fraser was watching. 'He's not a child any more. Donnie's used to the weather.'

But Aggie ran, her face falling. She was slumped in the kitchen when her mother's arms found her. 'He'll be all right,' said Peg Fraser, 'there's no bad news of the boats. Come on now, they'll have sheltered.'

'Oh God,' sobbed Aggie, 'I blamed him; I snapped at him about nothing.'

'A little tiff, he'll forget it. Make it up when you see him.'

'Mam, it's dreadful, you know it. That sea . . .' She clung fiercely.

'It won't last long, bairn, don't fret. She's a good boat, *Goosander*.'

Aggie shuddered and said, 'And now the *Peg* will be swamped. He's done so much on her, Mam. She'll be battered, they both will.'

'Oh, now, now.'

'It's not fair.'

'He'll be back. Come, he'll soon put things right. This won't help you know, Aggie.'

'Yes, I know.'

'Just hang on.'

'I'm all right, go back, Mother.'

Mrs Fraser smiled firmly. 'I'd better, child, you stay here. Make yourself a warm drink.' She returned to the switchboard. A sudden silence had fallen, the others attentive, and Mrs Gorme broke the spell. 'I've heard a lot about Donnie; I'd watch that one, Peggy.'

Peggy Fraser said grimly, 'A decent hard-working lad.'

'The boy's too thick with Macrae. If your wee Aggie was mine . . .'

Mrs Fraser's lips tightened.

A man came in off the front, lurching as the wind blasted. 'There's someone out on the pier. It's nae healthy, I'll tell you.'

'Mary. Didn't you warn her?'

'Aye, she cursed me,' the man said.

Another hush filled the shop. Mrs Fraser had turned, a hand gripping the headphones. 'Dead.' Her tone was subdued. 'There must be something down somewhere, the line's as dead as a doornail.'

The sea was pounding the *Peg*, inundating the shingle. It rocked the little beached vessel, licking at her new paint, wanton in its attentions. Thundering at her stern, the creamers shot overhead, breaking inboard with violence. The wind had ripped off tarpaulins; they streamed and clapped like torn sails, writhing in the storm's chaos.

Against this vision of wrath a small figure pranced wildly, darting in between gusts, scrambling back as the waves burst. Narrowly, the flood missed it. The ragged demon fell down, paused on hands and thin knees, tottered up and kept moving. Scarecrow arms rose in protest; bandily, the legs jiggled. The hopping freak was demented.

Horrified, Aggie watched.

The gale blew straight at the cliff, shoving her back against it. She had slipped out of the house while the shop was in turmoil, people anxious for news, others testing the phone lines. Once clear of the buildings, where slates and dustbins had hurtled, she had encountered the sand: swirling, billowing densely but less of a danger. There were few trees on the island to crash or shed branches.

Now, a scarf round her face, she looked on as the cove boiled. The dancing madman drew back, gave another lurch forward. He was dwarfed by the foam and she saw the boat deluged, Donnie's dream being battered. Again the futile arms rose, gesturing at the breakers. A mighty roller swept in, towering over the figure.

'Willie . . .'

Aggie rushed to him. Grabbing him by a sleeve the girl tugged at him fiercely. 'You'll be swept out, Willie, leave her.'

'She's winched as high as she'll come.'

'There's nothing we can do, Willie.' They cowed, the wave detonating. 'Please,' she shouted, 'please leave her.'

The man turned slowly, loose-jawed, as if only half-conscious. 'You shouldn't be here,' he mouthed, 'not in this. Does your mam know?'

'Never mind about that. I'll be back before mam knows.'

Another wave roared towards them.

'You're right,' Macrae gasped, retiring, 'nothing we can do, lassie.'

'Not for now,' Aggie shrilled, 'it's not safe on the foreshore.' She steered the man to the path, sand and spume blasting at them. The 'captain's' shoulders had dropped. 'Let's get out of the wind; come on, Willie, I'm freezing.'

She made him sit by the fire and he stared at it, speechless. The sand was piling inside, blowing under the door, and the cottage roof trembled. With every blast the place shook, every shake like an earthquake. She made a blaze with some driftwood. The stuff was piled by the hearth, all three cats huddled near it, their dusty coats bristling.

At last the man said, 'She's doomed. That's the end of her, Aggie.'

'No, it can't be, it mustn't.'

The 'captain' sucked at his flask, grimacing as the wind screeched. The liquor strengthened his tone. 'That's the end of her now, there's no point in pretending. This'll shake her apart; all that effort for nothing.'

Aggie's voice fell. 'Oh, Willie.'

'Aye,' he breathed.

'And the engine?'

'Can't put out on an engine.'

'Let's wait and see – see what happens.' Aggie prayed he was wrong. 'There may not be too much damage.'

'She's finished,' Macrae said.

A fearsome draught swept the hearth and the flames leapt like fiends, leaving sparks on the fire-back. Aggie's glance was despairing. 'Don't say that,' the girl pleaded. 'You're getting stronger, we'll mend her.'

'No, the *Peg* and me's finished.'

Shadows jumped on the walls, making threatening patterns. The cats had fled from the fire into dingy recesses.

'You mustn't talk like that, Willie.'

'To hell with it, I'm through with it.' The man leaned forward and guzzled.

'You've got to fight,' Aggie told him.

'A lot of good fighting's done me.' His eyes were wild, the fire in them. 'You wouldn't know, not at your age. You think it's all there for taking. "Keep it up and you'll win, after that it's smooth sailing." The great delusion, by heaven.'

'Stop it, Willie Macrae.'

'I was fooled. I believed it.'

'It's the whisky that's talking.'

'You cannae win, it's a hoax; the game's rigged, fixed against you. Whoever set the thing up has a sick sense of humour.'

185

'That's not right.'

'You'll find out.'

'I don't like you blaspheming.'

'And I don't like being cheated. To hell with it, take a dram.'

'Willie, stop.' The sea rumbled. 'Donnie's out there,' cried Aggie.

The 'captain' shrugged, leaning back. 'That's not my fault,' he mumbled. 'If he'd asked, I'd've warned him.'

Something bumped on the roof, hurled there in the confusion, and Aggie was frightened. She turned, enraged, on the man. 'Oh, you're always so right, you're so full of your knowledge.'

He blinked and drew on the flask.

'Did I tell you or not? Did I say this was coming?'

'Yes, you might have.'

'I did.' It was gruff but he added, 'The lad'll come to no harm, don't start mewling and wailing. He wouldn't thank you for that.' He peered blearily at her. 'He's young enough to be spared; he'll be saved for the next time. I'd give you nothing for Gorme but he can handle a boat. The devil knows a good skipper.'

'Yes.' The girl tried to smile. It was a straw to hang on to.

Macrae got up, stumbling past her, and flung the heavy door open. The gale came in like a rhino, bringing more sand and debris, the fire-ash sent flying. He leaned a while in the wind, his coat-tails horizontal. The waves still hammered the *Peg* and he watched them, defiant. At length he slammed the door shut and swung back to her grimly.

He said, 'They're having their fun, they'd better make

the most of it for that's the last laugh they're getting. Macrae's no longer in business.'

'It might not be so bad, Willie.'

'I shan't be caring,' he growled. 'I'll be stretched on that bunk with a bottle beside me. There'll be no laughs in that for them.'

'You've had enough of that stuff.'

'I've not started,' he grunted.

'Oh, for God's sake,' said Aggie. She watched him slump on his bed. 'You're like a little boy sulking. You're not alone, damn you, Willie, you've got a partner to think of. Or does your promise mean nothing?'

'Things have changed,' Macrae answered.

The noise outside became frenzied. The wind was mauling the chimney and suddenly the flue rumbled as if a bomb was descending. Flakes of tar fell with soot, half a brick in their midst, the bombarded fire roaring. Aggie jumped like a frog but Macrae scarcely noticed.

'It's not the same now,' he slurred. 'We'll have no assets now, will we?'

'We'll still have *Peg*, she'll not vanish. She started off as a wreck; we'll have to make good the damage. She'll be no worse than I've seen her.'

'No worse? Is that what you think? You've no idea what you're saying.'

'I know what *you* said,' snapped Aggie. 'You said you'd take me out in her.'

'I had a lot of plans, once.'

'You said we'd visit the seals, make a trip round the skerries.' The voyage had stretched in her mind. 'Maybe follow their travels.'

The girl had nurtured the dream, teased it into an epic,

a glowing tour of the isles to the haunts of the heroes, fabled birds, the sea people. In her mind Wingfoot beckoned, the *Peg* obliged like a gull, sailing magical straits towards golden horizons. Islands rose from the mists, tawny eagles flew from them.

The gale was not really happening. She saw herself at the helm, Donnie minding the engine, Niamh's wheaten head bobbing and Oisin beside them. A glossy escort of seals swam in crystal-clear currents, all her favourites assembled. She trailed a hand in bright ripples . . .

'You promised, Willie, you promised.'

He said, 'Stop pestering, will ye?'

'We'll make her good, don't despair.'

'You're like your mam: nag, nag, nag. Did you not see those waves? Don't you know what they're doing? She'd stand a poor chance afloat; on the beach she'll be shattered.' The man lay back with a scowl.

'So you've given up, have you?'

He tipped the flask. 'Let me be. Let it blow, let her smash. Damn the waves, they can have her. I'm done with giving them sport, it can blow until doomsday.'

At the bounds of her vision the seal saw briny eruptions, their lofty peaks flashing, the ocean in ferment. No other gale in her life had so fevered the surface, generated such chaos. No wind had screamed with such spleen or careered so insanely. The universe had gone mad, an anarchic force ranted. From the frontiers of sight maddened giants advanced hissing.

A tracer-line of foam shimmered, lengthening in the murk, and came spitting at Wingfoot, borne along on vast shoulders to roar and spume overhead as she dived in confusion. The roller's drag swept her sideways. She made a shallow descent, then, hanging under the storm, viewed the sea's depths forlornly. There was no sign of her friends; the sea people had vanished.

Below, the wrecked freighter slept, unaware of the frenzy. The flood that cradled it sighed, funereal as a vault, catching whispered reports of the broil it supported. The seal had quartered the deep; its bleak wastes did not tempt her. Submerged, the herd would move quickly, its bearings a mystery. She paused and pondered the gloom, glimpsing bubbles above her.

They were dispersed by the waves, reappearing to windward. Again they bloomed farther off, clustering before drifting, glittering in the swell as *Goosander*'s screw dabbled.

Wingfoot made for the surface. The boat had grown in importance, now her one consolation: not the perfect companion but slow and unswerving. The time for quibbling had past and she was left with *Goosander*. That was all that existed – that and breakers like hills. And the crazed cosmos howling.

A great sea reached from the void and the seal was cascaded. Water streamed down her face; the wind made her eyes tearful. Her ears were drubbed by the din, a combination of sounds from shrill whistles to booms, from low drones to wild roars, like the rumblings of thunder. In the voice of the wind was malign jubilation. It raised belligerent paeans, evil anthems of ruin. It whipped grey squalls overhead, blinding her with chill spray so *Goosander* dissolved, ghosted back, again melted.

In the trough, Wingfoot blinked.

The green walls round her gleamed, slick and gross in the lull, blocking out her storm picture. The tallest teetered above, rolled its crest and collapsed. Seething sea twirled the seal as the dark hollow flooded. With a cart-wheel she climbed, rode the next wave and surfaced. Spindrift whiplashed her cheeks. Then, perched high on the ridge, she could see the boat toiling.

Goosander swam in the pan, her decks fore and aft glistening. She looked small, much reduced, as if shrunk by immersion, like a waterlogged bug struggling for exist-ence. A heaving swell spanned her path and she rose to it slowly. She seemed to strain up its face, levering with her stern, then wait, lost for momentum. Her nose went down in the green and she lurched, boring forward. She reappeared in a while, now tobogganing bravely.

The boat had not lost her spirit. There was thick foam on her planks and her outlets were spouting. She shook the water aside; new seas marched to assail her, bar her way as she trundled. They came in feather-helmed legions, rank on rank, in huge armies. She mounted them one by one, ploughed through those which leapt at her. At every wave she dug in, clung to monstrous escarp-ments. And when she plunged she bounced back, bracing for the next onslaught.

At times she rolled like a sot and her shabby sides vanished. Then, as the sea rushed aboard, she would reel and recover, steadying with an effort, her stubby mast tossing. She was not grandly heroic or supremely athletic but had an oceanwise cheek, riding blows as they struck, cocking snooks at near-misses. Beset by skyscraper waves she would duck along alleys and did not flinch when caught out but went on, bloody-minded.

Had *Goosander* flown flags they might have spelled a lewd message. Enraged, the storm hemmed her in and strove cruelly to swat her. As Wingfoot followed, she slewed, checked on course and held steadfast.

The silver seal closed the gap, now astern of the vessel. A pack of clouds hounded low and in the lessening light the boat's screw broke the surface. The flashing steel dazzled. For several seconds it raced then was gone, the craft's tail-end subsiding. A dusk-like pall had descended, the tempest's glint eerie, devilish on the crests, squinting down the sea's chasms.

It pierced the brine-festooned wheelhouse and Wingfoot saw huddled figures silhouetted in windows. They were as black as the hull. The wind had dropped in the gloom, letting loose a weird hush in which lesser sounds rose, sulky splashes and slaps, growls as vast waves glissaded. The muted interval dragged, ominous and unnerving. Briefly in the grim lull Wingfoot sensed the boat's heart-beat.

Next, the wind had redoubled. At stunning speed it returned, screaming out of the murk, leaping black hills of sea with berserker aggression. Where wind and water enmeshed a boiling mass raged in space, an appalling concoction, the eerie sheen on it. At every side the gusts howled, on every side there was uproar. It was a ship-killing wind. It was a feller of trees, a demented roof-shredder.

Amid the din, vapours swirled, balled like aberrant planets. In the gusts they unfurled, scattering in white fragments. Gobs of spray flew like bullets. A flock of small birds, migrating, was battered and perished. Monsters stalked from the mists, immeasurable in their breadth, composed of volumes of brine too immense to compute. There was no place spared their wrath, the storm's bellowing rampage.

Wide-eyed, Wingfoot looked on, her skull just above water. The boat ahead was convulsed, taking blow after blow. Now she reeled on the crest, now she plunged out of sight, reappearing at planes from which no craft afloat should have properly righted – and yet she did, swamped but battling. Wave on wave struck her decks, their hostility brutal; every hammering shook her. Still she rode the assault, hanging on in the clinches.

And then the seal's focus narrowed. A ray of watery light, filtering from the clouds, made *Goosander*'s deck glimmer. A man stepped into this beam, trying hard to stay upright. Reaching out for supports, clutching stanchions and ropes, he took perilous strides to the gear the boat carried. A net was fluttering loose, one fold blown on the gunwale.

Calum swayed with the swell, stooped and pulled at the tackle. As the sea creamed aboard he worked standing in water. It was a skilful performance. He bent for maybe a minute before the deck tilted steeply, the foam gushing round him. Still he wrestled the net. Then at last he groped back, somehow reaching the wheelhouse.

Wingfoot watched him, intrigued. Scarcely was he inside before a great sea crashed by, surely aimed at his life, and the raking wind blasted. It struck the seal in the ear and she ducked underwater. For a moment she sank, the abrupt silence peaceful, but though a respite appealed the boat's spell remained stronger. Afraid of losing the craft, she soon flippered and surfaced.

She found herself way astern and was forced to move quickly. Swimming into the gale, she dipped shallowly now, sprinting under the mounds, rising briefly to gulp, pressing hastily forward. The chase made her breathless. When she could feel the boat's wake she bobbed up, treading water. *Goosander* slithered and churned, wallowing like a duck, her broad rump somehow friendly.

It had a rusty aplomb no matter which way it tipped, the name yellowing on it, the steering gear wrenching. It might be metal and paint but to Wingfoot it breathed, creaked with effort and stress, throbbed with constant exertion. Like the buoy at the cove the black stern was alive, spirited and enduring. Seal and boat shared the weather. They seesawed madly together, first one up then the other, Wingfoot tossed on the crest then *Goosander* above her.

The wind's intensity grew and enormous seas pounded, the waves driving headlong. In the shuddering wheel-house, Gorme clung to the helm. No one spoke in that place; thoughts were trussed and entombed as completely as mummies. Donnie's eyes bulged with fear, kernel-tight in their sockets. He had been thrown in a corner, shoulders gripped by the walls, where a numb stiffness held him, his teeth grinding quietly.

Calum's feet were apart, his back pressed to the door. As *Goosander* inclined, his legs sagged at the knees, cushioning the man's bulk like immense shock-absorbers. The grin had gone from his face. In its place sea-salt dried so he looked oddly grizzled. Now and then his lips moved but if comment escaped them the uproar expunged it.

Gorme peered forward, hard-visaged. With every jolt of the waves, every fling of the bow, his coarse eyebrows contracted, the gap in them closing. Then his temple-veins bulged and his grimace was darkest. He had dispensed with the pipe, his mouth drawn in a snarl through which broken teeth glared, veneered brown by tobacco. Gorme could swear without words – his expression was filthy.

A vicious blow hit the boat and the shock made them

stagger. She had gone down by the head and Donnie snatched at his breath. The sea she dug was hurled back, landing square on the house, every light in it drenched so they tottered in darkness. As the panes slowly cleared, Gorme reached out for a switch and a radio crackled, plum-voiced with storm warnings.

'Now they tell us,' he spat. His expletives were lurid.

Calum grunted and stared. His thick fingers were spread, his palms flat against wood as he slid to one side. With a jerk he recovered. His weathered face remained set, shadowed in the sou'wester, its gaze enigmatic.

Donnie glowered at the men. Beneath the skin of his fear a sour vengefulness seeped drip by drip, like a plasma. They had mocked him too often. They were not mocking him now; they had given up smirking. He hoped their dread matched his own, for they deserved to be wretched. Gorme at least showed his qualms; he was patently anxious, even rattled, the lad thought.

He did not know about Calum; you could not read Calum's mind. His countenance was a blank. Perhaps the man's head was empty.

Donnie's jaw ached from gritting. He watched a freak gust of wind lash outside, spur a towering wall forward. The boat seemed spellbound before it. She gave a desperate heave and her engine-beat laboured, grew weaker and weaker. For an instant it faltered then, picking up, wailed with rage and he was launched from his niche as a reckless plunge followed.

He was finding his feet when *Goosander* rolled steeply, sluicing water to starboard like a weir in the spate before counter-rotating. She almost lay on beam ends, the youth thrown on a window. Muddled thoughts crossed his mind, scampering in confusion. He thought of being at school, growing up through the war, seeing older lads leave, wishing he could sail with them. Some had never returned.

Had the sea saved this for him?

He thought of Aggie back home and her moods. And of Calum's fey Mary.

A wave enveloped the wheelhouse.

Gorme was wrestling the helm, holding *Goose* to the weather. The skipper's knuckle-bones glimmered. 'We're burning fuel,' he complained, 'burning fuel like pound notes.' It came savagely from him.

The man was mad, thought the youth; he would drown counting money.

'We need some shelter,' he blurted.

'Words of wisdom, by Christ.' Gorme glanced crazily at him.

Spume was rattling on glass, drubbing metal like shrapnel.

Calum braced, his back arched. 'We should be north of the island.' The words were matter-of-fact; he sounded almost indifferent. 'Could find some lee before long.'

'Making this speed?' snarled Gorme.

Donnie groaned as they reeled, shipping sea in green volumes. 'God,' he gasped, 'we'll roll over.'

He raised a hand to his face, blocking out the gale's image. He felt increasingly tired, overwhelmed by the horror. A gull had crashed on the deck and lay fluttering feebly. A second joined it, smashed down, its life instantly over. They were all helpless, he thought, men and birds doomed to perish. There was no hope for the vessel.

The gulls were gone in a moment, either washed to the deep or stuck, he mused, in the scuppers. It was a matter of time and he waited, limbs shaking.

Another sea gleamed and pounced. Somewhere Calum was saying, 'She won't roll over, wee lad; if she goes she'll dive quickly.' The tone was flat, unexcited.

Gorme lurched drunkenly sideways, fists glued to the wheel, his oaths lost in the din, merely petulant whispers. At last he rasped, 'We'll catch fish. When this drops, we'll start fishing.'

He was, thought Donnie, insane. They were mad, he reflected, the wild-eyed man at the helm and the gormless giant with him. As mad as willowy Mary. If only he had worked faster, got the *Peg* ready sooner, he would not be in this mess, facing death in this nightmare.

'You fools,' he wanted to scream, 'can't you see it's all up? Can't you see that we're finished?' Instead he croaked, 'How far is it? How far is the coast?'

If they heard, they ignored him.

A slimy swell caught the bow, an immense greasy ogre, the vessel convulsing. The wheelhouse shook like a reed, then a laden gust hit them. He fought to stay on his legs. He should have listened to Aggie. He might have stopped on the quay and caught mackerel in pails. He could have been with her now, warm indoors, sipping coffee. His mind flashed back to the shop, Mrs Fraser's snug kitchen.

Calum passed him, arms milling. The big man groped to Gorme's side. 'You'll be needing a rest; I'll take over,' he offered.

'You keep off.' Gorme stayed put. There was spit on his whiskers. 'When you're wanted I'll tell you.'

The footing sloped wildly.

Back went Calum askew, making no further comment. He was a bumpkin, thought Donnie; he would go down uncomplaining. Unlike Donnie himself, who would rave, he imagined, cursing Gorme and the devil. His teeth were chattering now and he struggled with panic. A foaming crest was approaching, slithering and corkscrewing. It caught *Goosander* a-glance and she quaked, once more losing her pulse, which picked up very slowly. Flooded decks merged with sea; it was over her bulwarks.

As Donnie watched through the window a mighty mound was framed in it, its green and storm-lit flanks flashing, its polished breast swelling. Atop this surging colossus a tiny nipple appeared, a slick head streaming water. The seal turned, gazing towards him. His mouth was dry; the wind howled. He made no sign to the men, mesmerized by the vision.

It was as if Wingfoot waited, was beckoning to them. He cast the thought from his mind, for he was not Calum's woman. She had obliged him to listen, disturbing him by her closeness, beautiful and tormented. He wished he had not talked to her.

The seal slipped by with the sea and the next wave exploded. He was flung backwards with force and a heavy hand grabbed him. 'Might never happen,' yelled Calum; 'cheer up then, MacDonald.' The fellow's face was intense, the salt powdery on it. It looked suddenly old, humourless, Donnie noticed. Cheerful, Calum was not.

Donnie leeched to the man. They could go down any minute; each sea that crashed could condemn them, send them straight to the depths. Or tear the rudder adrift or put paid to the engine. He lingered morbidly on it. Then *Goosander* would reel, staggering to her end like a hen with its neck wrung. The wind would scream and exult, smashing her as she foundered. He did not want it the slow way; he wished it was over.

Gorme bawled callously, 'Leave him. Leave him, Calum, he's useless.'

In his mind, Donnie killed him; he ran a gutting knife through him. In fact, the lad could not move, still in Calum's embrace, paralysed by his funk.

Something wriggled outside. In the swill of the deck it squirmed aft like an eel, snaking over the planks, its head rearing and flicking. With the next roll it was swamped, then as the flood frothed and drained it crossed the rear portside quarter, climbed the gunwale and flapped, maddened by the wind's violence.

Calum swore, peering out. 'Damn the bitch,' he exclaimed, 'the cow's loose again, damn it.'

Gorme half-turned, his glare ugly. He swung his gaze back ahead, screaming over his shoulder, 'It cost me money, that net. If it's sucked under the stern . . . Man, we'll have to do something.'

'I'll get it,' Calum returned. 'Head her off a shade, will ye?' He bundled Donnie away, wedging him between lockers.

A roaring breaker descended.

'I'll give you what I dare,' Gorme said.

Donnie shivered, appalled. 'You can't open that door.' His voice squeaked in the thunder. 'You can't go out in it, Calum.'

A raging squall swept the boat, beating in from the distance. It came with faraway growls, fustian at first sight, bringing rollers in herds, their hoarse bellows resounding. In rising descant, winds shrilled, drilling, whining, chastising, the furies in war-cry. They threw the boat on her side, picked her up, hurled her down, clawed and plucked at the wheelhouse.

Tensely, Gorme eased the helm.

Donnie saw Calum lunge, breast the door, wrench it open. The gale came in with a shriek and the big man had left them.

Suddenly Donnie followed. He scarcely knew how or why, for he was giddy with fear and all effort seemed pointless. Perhaps he had to prove something, not just to Calum and Gorme – to give the lie to Gorme's sneers – but to Donnie MacDonald. To prove, despite being sane, that he could perish insanely, on deck with a madman.

He paused, repelled by the storm, hanging on in the doorway. The wind carved into his face and the sea swept the bulwarks. It was towering, barbaric, obscene in its vastness. It pawed and poked at the boat, its enjoyment sadistic. On every side the sea seethed like a mob at a gallows.

Through the spray he saw Calum. The man had groped to the stern. A canopy of spume roofed him; the deck streamed with water. For one lingering moment Donnie glanced at the helmsman. Gorme was squinting ahead, judging each coming wave: a great toad, the lad thought, elbows spread, oilskins gleaming. The toad was muttering oaths, noises weirdly inhuman.

Donnie willed himself forward. As he started to move there was a toppling jerk and the craft leaned to port, the sea entering quickly. He was thrown flat, cheek to deck, and saw foam rushing at him. On hands and knees he crabbed sideways, scrambling upwards to starboard.

He could see Calum waist-deep, now below him and splashing. The man was holding on grimly and Donnie, starting to slide, stretched an arm to do likewise.

He was not sure what he touched but he gripped and it held him. Hanging over the sea, he felt the counter-roll start and frothing swill was thrown on him, freezing as it descended, drawn by gravity past him. Drenched and cold he lay prone, the flood level subsiding. Then, the deck again flat, he kneeled up, coughing water.

Calum's voice pierced the uproar.

'You wee damned fool.' The wind broke it. 'Get back in, wee MacDonald.'

The boat kicked up like a mule and the youth remained kneeling. He glimpsed the man's stooping frame, the giant swell ranged above it. The sea changed shape as it reared, shifting mountainous weights, involuted, breath-taking. From its gargantuan peaks the gale swooped and bombarded.

Donnie screamed, 'You need help.'

'Get back in. Leave me to it.'

Donnie rose and swayed aft.

'I'm not a flaming kid, Calum.' He clutched at wires, stanchions, netting. 'Man, I'm not flaming useless. That's where Gorme's got it wrong. You're both wrong, damn you, Calum.'

Calum stared through the spume. Behind the spouts from his hat the blue eyes expressed nothing. He grasped a length of wet rope he had secured to a ring-bolt.

'Grab that net then and pull. Once she's in we can lash her.'

The net was partly adrift, still draped over the gunwale.

Calum lurched and swayed back. 'Don't you say I've not warned you.'

Donnie slipped, struggled up. Behind the boat's tubby stern her wake switchbacked and vanished. The tangled netting was greasy; his hands scrabbled on it. There was a split-second lull, the deck suddenly steady, and the men stooped together. They hauled, not saying a word, then the next mammoth struck them.

It ran in quietly this time, pouncing silently, catlike. Tumbled over in froth, the youth floundered, feet kicking. He did not know where he was. It was black, deathly cold, and he seemed to be turning, very slowly revolving. He was, he thought, overboard. He could feel nothing below him; the big man was nowhere. Donnie held his breath, spinning.

He stretched his arms, searching round, touching something metallic. It was twisted and broken and swam away from him. Perhaps the boat had gone down. She would go swiftly, nose first, or so Calum had reckoned. Something else slithered by and his fingers felt netting. Instinctively he held on, the strands slack, unsupportive. Then they jerked, gave a tug, and his head broke surface.

Some way off, Wingfoot idled.

The silver seal swam submerged.

The beast had seen the men struggling, watched a while from a distance. Inquisitive, she had craned, pressing up on her flippers before the wave forced her down, breaking heavily on her. Now she let the broil pass then bobbed up, once more peering.

She was some way from the boat, abreast the stern and to port. As the craft cleared the sea Wingfoot saw the net dangling, the youth clinging to it. His arms were over his head, his hands almost aboard, near the top of the gunwale. The water rose and fell round him, now up to his neck, now no more than waist level.

There he hung like a puppet.

When the *Goose* took a roll he was seesawed severely, sometimes totally dunked, other times lifted clear, his feet dripping, suspended. It fascinated the seal and she flippered in closer. As she did, two things happened: a further wave shook the boat, wreathing it in dense vapours, and then the second man rose, straightening from the deck, standing groggily upright. Leaning over the side he caught hold of his boatmate.

The seal hauled near, periscoping.

And now the drama was vocal, voices slicing the tumult.

Calum's bawled, 'Don't let go.'

Donnie's screamed out, 'I'm slipping.'

Calum's fist crushed his wrist. 'Can you hold? Hold, I'll get a rope to you.'

The big man's head disappeared and the youth was left swinging.

Donnie's hands had grown numb, his arm-sinews were tearing. As every sea washed and drenched, the weight dragged on his muscles. Making the agony worse, a wedge of water drove in, prising him from the bulwark, twisting him as it did so. A constant spray whipped his face. Shot from barely two yards, where a scupper port spewed, it was icily painful.

He could not hold; he was going.

He yelled hysterically, 'Calum.'

The other fell on the gunwale. He pushed the rope down. 'Grab hold.'

'Can't let go.'

'Get it round you.'

'I can't, for Christ's sake, I can't. I can't loosen hold, Calum.'

He heard the big man cry out, a great oath of frustration.

'I'm going,' Donnie exclaimed. 'I cannae hold any longer.'

The lad could see the wake swerving, bucking over the hummocks. His fingers slipped; he was going. There would be no coming back: he would be sucked round the stern where the boat's screw was churning. It would not take very long – one last gargling breath. He looked up, his eyes rolling, and freezing spume pelted. And then a large leg appeared.

The leg cocked over the side and the man's body followed. Calum straddled the gunwale. He pivoted, slewing round on his thighs, gripped the net and came downwards.

'Hold on, damn you, hold on.' Calum brought the rope with him.

They were both out of the sea, the boat leaning to starboard. Wingfoot watched the man working, somehow hanging one-handed. The seal was close now and bobbing, the wind raging past her. She saw *Goosander* roll back, the two figures descend, water threatening both ways: pouring down from the deck, surging up as the side dipped. They were gone, the sea heaving. The vessel's list seemed unending and then she slowly swung back, the drenched couple still clinging – like crabs attached to a rock as a shore-tide receded.

Donnie felt the rope tighten. It had been drawn round his chest and he could hear Calum bawling, 'Your boots, your boots; kick them off.' They dragged like weights, full of sea, but he was too weak to struggle. An age went by and one budged. Calum's free hand was tugging, wrenching it down his leg, then the other came loose and a great load fell from him.

'I'm going up,' Calum screeched. 'Keep a hold till I haul you.'

Donnie tried to reply. He lacked the strength now to speak, simply gawping askance at the other's wet features. They were grey from exposure. Through the slits that were eyes, two blue shafts drilled back at him.

'If she's worth it, hold, sonnie.'

There was a ghost of a smile, the inane Calum grin, and the fellow was scrambling. He seemed to claw at the net, gain an inch and slide back, water leaping to seize him. The netting slipped, dropping lower; the deck emptied on him. Again he climbed, clawed and slid. The boy had given up hope but the man's efforts doubled.

Wingfoot stared through the spray. The scene pinned her attention.

It could not last for much longer. Another giant sea was mounting, now a maniac roller, bound straight for the vessel. The silver seal watched its gallop. It tossed the boat to the sky, set her down and crashed on her. *Goosander*'s foredeck went under, and then the rest of her length as she paused, beaten back. In vain her screw toiled to thrust. She yawed, ignoring her rudder, sunk to the top of her rails, her decks laden with water.

Still the wave rampaged through. Steaming foam climbed the wheelhouse, shinned the mast to the top where it streamed in white pennons. With a crack, a pane shattered.

Swamped, the silver seal dived, discomposed by the roller.

The youth had not seen it coming. By now his senses had blurred, a red mist filled his vision.

He was picked up by the sea and, only semi-aware, seemed to whirl beside Calum, foetal partners in gloom, in a vast womb of water. Then he was tumbling alone, curled in glittering froth, spinning head over heels until something firm met him. It made him gasp and retch liquid. Dazed, he fisted his eyes, clearing brine from his vision. The sea was draining away, hissing as it retreated. Folds of net draped his head and the rope still embraced him.

He was stretched out on the deck, little streams running from him. He was too cold to feel cold, and too numb to ache badly, but when he tried to sit up every muscle protested. He lay a while to gain strength then contrived to rise slightly, levering on his elbows. His sou-wester was gone and the wind's bellow deafened.

There was no sign of his boatmate.

Bits of gear were strewn round; he saw items of debris. The oily swell glared and glinted. He tried to shout but could not.

Mentally, he screamed, 'Calum.'

But it was futile, he knew. It was no use calling Calum – not now and not ever. His hands fumbled the rope, worrying to discard it, then to cast off the net. He had to get back to Gorme. He dare not linger on deck, for the sea was not finished.

In the storm's final spasm the seal remained underwater. Tired of trailing the boat, she was content to lie low, let the tail-end blow over. Soon the shores would be safe, her homing instinct would guide her. Then the herd would return, her friends haul out on the beach, and she would sleep long and sound, safe again among comrades.

Meanwhile Wingfoot reclined and let the depths gently rock her. Fish were rising once more, drifting darkly in shoals, now and then fluorescent. Dreamily, Wingfoot watched, tranquillized by their languor. Overhead, brightly webbed, the sea's domes caught the sunset.

When next she surfaced for air she was greeted serenely. The wind had dropped, the swell high but now smooth and relaxing. A tail of cloud scurried north while to the west, pale and washy, the sky ran with colours. Strand by strand the hues drained to leave a wall of pure pewter, the light reflected on crests as they aimlessly wandered.

Emptily the sea slopped as if lost for a purpose, abashed by past madness. Normality was returning. Far off, arrowing nightwards, an ocean liner fled sleekly, hardly part of the world by which mortals were bounded. Wingfoot dabbled and splashed, drinking in the day's postscript.

At length she glided back down. Twilit vaults stroked her flanks, smoothed her long muzzle-whiskers. The green-tinged shadows were deep, alive with subtle vibrations that teased her antennae. She paused to note them more clearly: the vibes of creatures approaching. She could not see them as yet but they were speeding towards her.

She turned, her silver snout twitching.

Impatiently the seal waited. The depths were dim in the gloaming and time was arrested. Then they burst from the gloom. The first grey spectre loomed swiftly, snaking out of the void, and another soon followed. They were seals of the Atlantic, big cows on the move. A third appeared and then more, the flow brisk with their bustle.

She recognized one or two, then Bragela shot past her.

It was the herd coming back, the storm fugitives homing. They ghosted by in small groups. Some were near, well-defined, some mere shades in the distance. They were to Wingfoot divine, her grey friends of the sea, and she joined the procession. It surged with common intent, buzzed with mutual elation. The seals were bound for the cove, galloping to their island.

They streamed ahead, undulating, straining forward like huskies. They ribbed the tide in long teams, graceful ribbons of motion, lost a while in the dark then picked out in pale rays, the last fingers of day shimmering through the fathoms. A patch of light flared in front and Wingfoot glanced at the leaders: their humping backs shed the gleams, their wakes glistened and dazzled.

Then something hung in the glare, silhouetted above them. Its arms were spread, its legs splayed, and it sank very slowly. Curious, Wingfoot veered, swirling up to peruse it. The big man wallowed and swayed, obedient to the current. She knew at once he was dead and rejoined the armada.

Donnie said in the dimness, 'It should've been me, not Calum.'

'It wasn't,' Gorme replied harshly.

The couple shivered together. A broken window streamed air and it was cold in the wheelhouse. Neither of them had spoken for maybe nine or ten minutes and in the gathering night the exchange was intrusive.

'It wasn't you,' grunted Gorme. 'It wasn't your number, was it?'

'He tried to save me,' the lad said.

He watched the darkening bow-wave.

Goosander limped for the island, a shard of white moon to guide her. The storm had put out her lamps and she was black in the dusk, creeping now through the swell like some furtive sea creature. There was no glimmer aboard, even Gorme's matches soggy. Only the compass still glowed, luminous in its bracket.

For a time they were quiet then Donnie's voice came again.

'I couldn't help him,' he whispered.

Gorme's emotions exploded. 'By Christ, you're not God Almighty.' He changed the vessel's course slightly. 'We did our best,' he relented. 'We did our utmost, for Christ's sake.'

As soon as ever he dared he had put her about and they had searched while they could, until light and fuel dwindled, but it had been a mere gesture. They had known it was hopeless.

'We might've all gone,' snarled Gorme. 'If I'd been careless we would have.'

The thought returned them to silence.

The boat slunk on, climbing slopes, crossing slack, breathless hollows. The swart brine was smarmy.

Donnie hunched in the gloom, convulsed by spasms of quaking. The shock was still running through him: chill tremors of horror. Like the moon on the sea, his spine wobbled, was icy. Calum's absence was frightening. He was afraid to look round and not see him, no blue eyes staring forward. Or worse, to see the man's ghost, dripping water and grinning.

He counted stars to forget, but the nightmare persisted.

A straggling V spanned the sky, gulls as inky as crows, ragged gaps in their spearhead.

He could not own it had happened, that he and Gorme

were alive, Calum's corpse in the ocean – solid, resolute Calum. *'I'm going up; keep a hold.'* It was a dreadful mistake; the sea had claimed the wrong victim. It had no right to the big man.

At last he blurted, 'Why Calum?'

Gorme eyed the dusk ahead, brooding. 'He was a seaman,' he rasped. 'He knew the risks he was taking. All of us know the risks. Keep your eyes open, damn you.'

A tiny glint pierced the murk and the youth said, 'Light for'ard.'

'Yes, wake up, boy, I've seen it.'

A sound came in on the breeze, the faintest clap of a bell. Distantly, it repeated and where the moon hovered low Donnie thought he glimpsed land, a dark finger that faded. They were approaching the island. It brought the *Peg* to his mind and he imagined her smashed, lying wrecked on the shingle. All he felt was indifference. Only the wheelhouse was real, nothing else was substantial. Nothing mattered but Calum: inscrutable Calum.

'Take it easy,' Gorme told him. The voice was tired, almost kindly. 'You'll get over it, son. It was me knew him longest.'

'Aye.' The youth sobbed abruptly. 'He was a dark one,' he spluttered.

'Kept it bottled,' Gorme grated.

The ocean sighed as it passed. There was a slap in the dark, the black swell fawning round, simulating contrition. The sea was unctuous, oily. It spread its lassitude round them and Donnie found his eyes closing, his feelings exhausted. He caught himself with a jerk and saw that Gorme, too, was drooping, hanging on to the wheel as if he might fall without it.

The man was mumbling now, recalling moments with Calum, less for mawkish relief than to stop himself napping. He spoke of Calum and Mary, of how her beauty had roused him. 'He had to win her,' he wheezed, Donnie drowsily listening. 'He had to win her, did Calum. Every man wanted Mary.' The youth was almost asleep. He stirred and Gorme was proclaiming, 'He soon found out, the poor beggar.'

Gorme swung the wheel, the boat answered. 'He came to sea to forget.'

Windows shone in far houses.

'Kept it bottled,' Gorme grunted.

Donnie gazed at the lights. He said wearily, 'Buildings.'

'Buck up, boy, that's the harbour.'

The gleams traversed, settled forward. The glowing cluster came nearer. 'Yes,' breathed Donnie, 'the houses.' He had not thought it would happen, and now it had he felt nothing. A crushing apathy wrapped him. He had been spared by mistake and brought only guilt with him.

Goosander throbbed quietly. Unlit, she slipped through the night, invisible from the island. It was uncannily still and Donnie might have been dreaming, sleep-walking on water.

Then the pier was ahead and they slewed.

The sea was splashing and squelching. He could make out the grey stones, the moon squirming on wetness, and dark steps approaching. A lamp was raised on the quay, shady figures grouped by it. Gulls were roosting on bollards like shadowy gargoyles, necks drawn into their bodies. Drowsily he heard shouts and Gorme closed down the engine.

'The line, MacDonald, the line.'

'Aye,' he yawned.

'Look smart, damn you, MacDonald.'

Hands reached out as he jumped and he was safe in a puddle, struggling for his land legs. Black outlines swayed round him. The pier was littered with debris and running with water. Upturned boxes loomed dimly, gale-swept lobster pots ambushed. In the murky confusion a pool of lantern-light fell on the men's boots and waders.

Tall and shawled on its fringe stood the drowned seaman's woman.

Donnie froze, his mouth open.

He watched as Gorme staggered forward, the man's sea-roll heavy.

'I know,' the woman said clearly. It penetrated the silence. 'Don't come near me, I know. You had no business to take him; you had no right in seal weather.' She swept him out of her way as if he scarcely existed and Donnie took a step, mumbling. He felt her cold stare transfix him. Then the darkness closed round her.

'Leave her,' Gorme said at last, 'you can't do anything with her.' He spat. 'Calum couldn't.'

PART FOUR

'You're no' so stupid, MacDonald.'

Wingfoot swam round the point and hauled out near the sand dunes. Another three years had passed and she was ready to mate, pestered by the old bulls, Cuchulainn on that morning. He had come over the rocks, snuffling with presumption. His scent was strong, his grunts coarse, his great fight-scarred neck ugly. She had protested and left, seeking somewhere more private. Incipiently receptive, she nonetheless shunned such suitors.

She was by no means submissive. Except in moments of play she had reserved her own ground, defending it with fierce mettle. Thus had it been from the start and she remained on her guard, scorning lustful advances. Beside the dunes it was quiet, the strand warm and deserted, and she tipped her sharp nose with determined aloofness. She had no wish to be wooed by the veteran beachmasters.

Above the tide she lay flat, ogling little white ripples. Far away, rollers cruised, the sun bright on their crowns while, inshore, the sea lazed, casting desultory sparkles. It was as blue as the sky and devoid of intruders. The big old bulls had stayed put, out of sight round the headland. For this the female was thankful, but still the mating urge nagged her.

Now and then she looked up and would grumble at

nothing. She did not want Cuchulainn and yet, alone, she was restive. She did not wish to siesta, nor did she want to be sniffed, hustled round and molested. In short, her mood was perverse: she did not know *what* she wanted, and when a friendly voice called she was unsympathetic.

Oisin rose from the surf, his smooth dark-maned neck craning. He gave a low playful bark, flippers smacking the water. When Wingfoot made no response he upturned, flipped his tail and submerged, bobbing up again closer, his handsome head dripping. Her churlish hiss kept him back but soon, determined to please, he dragged himself to the sand and rolled clownishly for her.

Then, bounding back to the sea, the male splashed and looked waggish, calling on her to follow. It took her back to their calf days. He was no longer a calf but still his antics amused, thawed her petulant humour. At last, cajoled, she dashed in, emulating his pranks, as buffoonish as he in her juvenile prancing. Sloshing spray in his face, she shot off underwater.

Gleefully, Oisin chased her. They ridged the sea with their wash, corrugating the shallows. The twinkling ripples made arcs, little snakes that frothed brightly. Bubbly wakes could be seen where the couple cavorted, their streamlined images plain in the clear, lilting water. With flippers pressed to their sides they dived, banked, soared and zigzagged. Sometimes one was ahead, then the other took over.

Sometimes, brisk and unswerving, they streaked like two arrows. Then they might dip to the floor, churning sand as they skimmed, making shells and stones spiral. Or speed as one to the top, break the surface and porpoise, shedding glittering droplets. Tensions shed, Wingfoot raced, shimmering and gyrating while Oisin whirled with her. It was familiar sport, the old game of the chase, breakneck now and athletic.

The headlong pace intoxicated. Madly, Wingfoot jinked wide, cut back under the male and made tracks for deep water. She was alone for a moment and then the other caught up, their slick flanks almost touching. On they sped neck and neck, the rough headland approaching, the bell-buoy's hull looming. As its chain came towards her, the female hurled herself round it, rolled and kicked for the dunes, Oisin shadowing closely.

On the reverse course they zoomed, skiing over the waves, knifing under white plumes, plunging down through the flow to return trailing fountains. They hurdled drifting green weed, speared the warm azure rollers. They leaped and danced, black and silver; swerved and jostled each other until, once more near the beach, their twin snouts cleft the flood leaving sun-burnished tramlines.

Then they flopped where the tide lapped.

Oisin lay in the froth, Wingfoot out of the water. Both were breathless and limp, their excited eyes staring. Each damp body gleamed sleekly. The only seals on the strand, they made a memorable tableau, maiden cow and young bull, conspicuous from the dune grass.

Aggie parted it gently.

On her knees in the sand, the girl was loath to disturb them. It was her first sight of the seals since coming back from the mainland where she had started at college, resident during term and at home for vacations. The animals were a treat; they might have staged the reunion.

217

Setting out for the cove, she had spotted them playing and, creeping closer, now marvelled.

The silver seal was quite splendid, grown to shining perfection; the male a fine escort. With little doubt, Aggie thought, she was watching their courtship, a stroke of wonderful luck, for after five years of waiting this could be the great moment – the start of Wingfoot's first calf, an historic occasion.

A skirling moan crossed the beach.

Easing back the dune grasses the girl saw Wingfoot's head rise as the second note issued, a strange and uncertain love song, hungering, apprehensive.

Promptly, Oisin approached but now the silver seal gaped, her demeanour defensive, and he held off, gazing at her. For a while he demurred, the female poised to repulse him, and then he turned to the sea, repeating earlier tactics, a flipper splashing the water. As before, Wingfoot followed, reassured by his ploy, though still ready to dodge him.

Aggie stretched herself prone, looking down from the hummock. She saw them circle like dogs and then frisk, Wingfoot's confidence growing. Again the silver seal danced, scurrying in the shallows, stampeding the ripples. She was not wholly relaxed, there was an edginess to it – a tetchy snap and a slap when the male came too close – but she was quickly in form, her adroitness emboldening.

Oisin let her flounce round him. As she did, she grew skittish. Whirling up to his flank, she sped off with a jink then returned to entice him. She flapped a paw in his face, flipped her tail at him drolly, glancing back as she fled, now with mounting composure.

Settling down, Aggie watched her. The seal was

sensuous, teasing, increasingly cheeky. She would surge over the male then loop down, brushing his dusky belly. Or she would bounce off his side, the swift clumsiness wilful.

Patiently, Oisin waited. Once he stretched out a flipper as if to stroke her in passing but she repelled the advance, feigning anger. While she was near he was still, but when she wandered he followed, always dogging her movements.

From the height of the dunes the girl could see through the water. It was like finely stained glass and the seals shimmered in it, never far from each other and yet as shy as first lovers. As Wingfoot turned out to sea Oisin chased, a black shadow. They made the sun-flecked tide toss, casting crinkly mole-ridges which spread out behind them. They surfaced, billowing spray, then were lost in the distance.

Aggie rose, disappointed, moving nearer the water. The soft warm sand filled her sandals, its grains in her clothing. Scrambling the next hummock she held a hand to her brow screening out the sky's glare, and suddenly the seals gleamed, tearing once more towards her.

They came at speed, dancing wildly, and made the swell quiver. The female raced with abandon. She hurtled out of the sea, twisted back, twirled and banked, silvery and elusive. Oisin streaked inches from her, the pair so close as they surged that they seemed joined together. It was a chase in name only, for now the flight was mere whim, Wingfoot's snapping pure love-play. It was a waltz of desire staged with split-second timing.

Frenziedly the seals swirled, Wingfoot leading the male, Oisin prancing with passion. Sometimes now he would break, streaming waywardly from her, and then his partner would veer, brazenly the pursuer. Their turns made Aggie feel dizzy. They made the bright water spin, shimmying in small maelstroms, the blue circles winking.

For the best part of an hour the girl stood watching the creatures. They were oblivious of her, completely enraptured. At intervals, when they tired, they lay and floated together, gently nudging each other, or playfully splashing, their fore-flippers waving. Or else they sank side by side, basking in the clear shallows. Then slowly one would steal off, the other following, dreamlike.

And once again they would dance, swaying under the surface.

The sun moved round, they grew languid.

A silver head bobbed and bowed and a black neck arched by it, the movements unhurried. The girl could see their eyes shining and glossy thighs curving. For one more time Wingfoot dived, her roll slow and inviting. With limbs together they bussed, then Oisin's mouth found her neck and they coupled, descending. At last they lay on the bottom.

The girl walked on up the shore. She was hot but delighted, her sleeveless summer dress crumpled, her sunburnt arms tingling. It was a happy homecoming. She was glad it was Oisin, that she would know the calf's father and not have to wonder. Both the beasts were her favourites: it would be a fine infant.

A man was digging far off, throwing mounds of sand round him. As she drew near he glanced up and she saw it was Donnie. The burly figure was pleasing and somehow surprising. But she was eighteen herself and he was now in his twenties, broad-shouldered and sun-tanned. He had looked down again, forking, and only stopped when she reached him.

He wiped his brow with a wrist and regarded her slowly. 'Got home?' he remarked.

'Last night, Donnie. How are you?'

He drove the fork then leaned on it, and she brushed sand from her front, conscious of his inspection. She wore her hair shorter now and felt safe in her appearance, still slight but less thin; fellow students admired her.

He answered with his own question, 'And how was college?' he grunted.

'Grand,' she said. 'Strange at first.'

He looked awkward, as if he might not have known her, as if the past had been severed. She felt a pang of dismay and kissed him quickly but warmly, a spontaneous gesture, then beamed her affection. It brought no smile of response and she, in turn, was embarrassed, unsure of his feelings.

With Donnie nothing was fast and Aggie wished she had waited, for she had always outpaced him, too bright and too forward. She did not mean to outshine him but it was hard to hold back, to adjust to his nature – at best reserved, at worst dull, now perhaps tinged with shyness.

She watched him rake through the sand with his strong, stubby fingers.

He said without looking up, 'You'll find it strange being back; you'll miss the others you've been with.'

'I've missed the island,' she told him.

He straightened, broad-faced and earnest. 'You'll have made friends at college?'

'One or two.'

She felt vexed. She sensed the young man's resentment but tried to see it as natural. She had a bustling new life while his own had not changed, simply gone on without her – fishing, digging for worms. Little changed on the island. She tried to put him at ease, shifting feet delicately and purring, 'Vibrations . . .'

'What?' said Donnie, perplexed.

'They hear your feet if you clump; they're sensitive to vibrations. You see, I haven't forgotten.'

'Oh,' he said. 'Yes, you're right.'

'Lugs and rags,' she went on, peering into his bait-box. The thick red worms in it wriggled. She made a face and recalled, 'The ragworms kill off the lugworms, or do the lugs kill the rags? I remember you taught me.'

She got no answer to that, the man engaging the fork and pressing down on the prongs before he levered them upwards. He broke the wedge of dark sand and recovered its inmate.

Aggie watched, her lips tight. She must avoid patronizing, or appearing to do so. She did not think that she had, but you could not tell with Donnie.

Presently he glanced up. 'So you like it there, do you?'

'I've missed you, Donnie,' she said. 'And how have you been?' she asked him.

'Not so bad.' Donnie shrugged.

'Good,' she said. 'I thought of you.'

He looked away and she added, 'You don't still fret about Calum? I know the business upset you. That and Mary's behaviour.'

'She went and caught Jimmy Harris, another big fool to keep her.'

'Well, she's still got her looks.'

'Much good that is,' growled Donnie. 'Looking's all she'll allow him. I reckon Calum was wretched.'

'It was a long time ago.'

He shook his head in resignation.

'Still with Gorme?' Aggie coaxed him.

'Not much choice,' he said, digging. He leaned straight-backed on the fork, scrutinizing her frankly. 'You ought to cover those arms, you'll be sore by the evening.'

She grinned. 'They'll soon toughen up. It's the island air, Donnie; it's cleaner here than back there, and the sun comes through stronger. I'm on my way to the cove. I guess the *Peg*'s in small pieces.'

'Not my affair, is it?' He scowled, put out by the subject. 'I've taken care of the engine, the rest's down to Willie.'

'It was a dream,' she replied.

'Aye.' He turned away sulking.

Aggie pondered him sadly. Strong and tested at sea, young, hard-working, good-looking, and yet he looked so resigned, set to work under Gorme for the rest of a lifetime. That, to her, was surrender. Perhaps she *had* moved away, perhaps their worlds *had* been severed. When she looked at him now she could see Calum in him.

She knew her mother had warned her but she refused to despair. He needed shoving, she thought – it was the island blood in him, stoical and accepting, too ready for hardship. That might have done in the past, when there was no getting on, but now you had to shove forward. The war had altered young people; this was life in the 'fifties.

'I'll tell you something,' she cried. 'I'll tell you something tremendous.'

'You will?' he said with a frown.

He looked vaguely suspicious and Aggie laughed at him.

He said, 'Go on, what's so funny?'

'It isn't funny, it's splendid. Wingfoot's taken a mate, she's no longer a maiden. She'll come in calf, barring mishaps.'

The other bent to his task.

'Is that all,' he responded.

'Aren't you pleased? I'm delighted. Better, Oisin's the father. Isn't that a fine match? There'll be a bonnie calf, Donnie.'

'Ach, we've more than enough; we don't need more of them fishing.'

'Come on, you miserable oaf, that's not you, that's Gorme talking. You're a friend of the seals. Remember how we both watched them? Those were good times together; we even planned to sail with them. Another Wingfoot, think of it.'

'Aye.' The grunt was begrudging.

Donnie stretched, moist with sweat, and looked out at the water. He seemed reluctant to speak and when he did it was slowly. 'You know what Gorme thinks,' he drawled, 'he's always threatening the seals. It isn't my business, Aggie, but one of these days he'll do it. He'll get a party together and clear them out, kill them wholesale. I only work for the man, I don't make the decisions.'

'No, you certainly don't.' Aggie turned on him hotly.

'I've my job to consider.'

'Oh, don't you worry,' she snapped, 'I'll stop Gorme if he tries it. I'll have him stopped, believe me. There'll be no killing while I'm here.'

The sun was fierce overhead and the girl's flushed face glistened. Donnie knew her of old and did not doubt that she meant it; she could be fearsome when ruffled. The odds had never scared Aggie. She had been bold as a child; as a young woman she awed him.

At last he said with reproach, 'You won't be here often, will you?'

She sensed the note of regret like a hand stretched towards her.

'Lord,' she said, her mood changing, 'it's not as bad as all that. Much of the time the seals spend here I'll be at home, Donnie. The holidays are quite long. Cheer up, man, I'm just back, don't let's start being gloomy.' She touched his arm. 'Nothing's changed. Let's forget about Gorme, I've got you to depend on. You and Willie Macrae.'

Donnie gave his first smile. It was wry and short-lived. 'Depend on Willie?' he questioned.

'To a point.'

'You know Willie.'

'I'm on my way to him now.' Her smile was prettily teasing. 'Drop by home when you've done, I'll tell you what I've been up to.'

The girl strode on, her hips swinging. Never mind Donnie's shyness, that would quickly wear off; she would soon put him at ease in the weeks now before them. What to make of his life was, however, a problem. She looked on that as a challenge.

But now she simply relaxed. The smells and sounds soothed her soul, the sea views were transporting. On a hazy horizon, warm sister-realms floated, lands of the sea people.

She was back on her island. How different was the *machair* to the streets of the mainland: a bracing, brine-scented difference, the hot gorse-pods crackling. Small birds twittered and dipped, swinging over the grass-heads which hummed very faintly. From a small, stunted tree came the voice of a robin.

She paused to sit on the cliff and gaze out at the headland.

The bell-buoy swam at its tip and there, as if by appointment, the silver seal waited. The creature lay on the platform, alone now and quiet, idly dipping a flipper as drowsy waves passed her.

Aggie hugged her bare knees. The sight completed her pleasure, an unexpected perfection. She could feel Wing-foot's contentment, a blissful oneness with nature.

Neither moved for some time and then the seal left her perch, slipping into the water. There she floated at ease, her flippers splayed, her nose raised, now and then blowing bubbles. The girl recalled her in calfhood, already outstanding but not to this standard: an icon of the blue swell, flashing in the sun's fire as if cast in rare metal.

And then this sea-wonder rolled and swam gracefully round, circling the still float, once more mounting the ledge to show off her sleek glory.

She faced away from the land, contemplating the ocean. Now for months she must voyage, gestation advancing, until her time drawing near she returned to her birthplace.

The girl could understand that: she had herself been away and knew the tug of the island, felt its powerful compulsion. She knew how the seals felt.

A tiny bird chattered near her.

She listened to its 'zak-zak', the sea's glare mesmerizing. The stonechat scurried in rocks, popping up to peek at her. With its black head and red throat it diverted her briefly.

She glanced back at the buoy. The silver seal had departed.

Aggie jumped to her feet. She was dismayed for a trice then saw the animal rise, swimming steadily seawards. Again the seal dipped and rose. In shallow dives she moved off, gliding into the distance, and Aggie wished her good luck. 'Be safe and well,' the girl thought. 'Take good care in the deep. I'll be waiting next summer – for both of you, Wingfoot.'

And then the creature had vanished.

Aggie Fraser walked on, dreaming of that reunion. Down the path to the cove a small breeze stroked her shoulders. A thrush got up as she went and the cliffs were gull-studded. On the pale strand below she could see oyster-catchers, some plovers and turnstones. They marched and paused in short bursts, like militiamen drilling. The heads of seals flecked the bay, many out near the skerries.

The island's peace stole in on her and Aggie stepped lightly. After a term of bombardments – studies, traffic, pubs, parties – it was like being reborn, restored to simple sensation, God-given, transcendent.

A seal patrolled in the foam and as the girl reached the *mul* she recognized Finn's scarred head, his dark eyes turned towards her. Cellach's crag was unclaimed. Not far off on the rocks Cuchulainn slumbered lightly.

The *Peg* invaded the spell and Aggie scrambled towards her, this battered thing on the beach as unwanted as jetsam.

Such dereliction was saddening. There had been so much hard work and it had all come to nothing. The girl thought back to their efforts. They had transformed the old wreck, the two fellows between them, and made her almost seductive. Now again she was rotting.

Now the boat spanned her blocks like a corpse left unburied. Never, Aggie recalled, had the *Peg* looked more plaintive. The sand had blown back inside and tarpaulins were shredded. A strip of planking was loose; several others were bulging. Everywhere, paint had peeled, often down to the primer, to the bare wood in places. What the gale had not done, long neglect had accomplished.

Seaweed littered the seats and gull-droppings abounded, splashed on withering boards and on weather-worn fittings. The vessel's tiller had gone and her rudder was damaged. On pumps, the metal had rusted; debris cluttered the bilge. It pained Aggie to look; much of it was neglect, caused by sheer inattention, the owner's omissions.

The only witness to care was the craft's diesel engine and that had been tended, a cover neatly in place and secured by new fastenings. Trust Donnie, thought Aggie – he had at least kept his word but he had not stirred his partner. That much was beyond him; beyond, she feared, anybody.

'Ahoy. Ye'll find me here, lassie.'

Willie lay by the cliff, sunning on the warm pebbles. He wore a torn and soiled vest and his trousers were threadbare. The old newspaper he read was in pieces and crumpled. He squinted as she drew near, sucked his teeth and reflected, 'It's done you good has away; you look bonnier, Aggie.'

She was not charmed but sat near him. 'I see you haven't reformed.'

He leered and studied her closely. 'You're growing up,' he approved. 'I mind your mother at your age, a fine young woman, I'll tell you. She turned a few heads did Peg and you'll not be so different.'

'You're wanting something, I take it.'

'I'm glad to see you, my beauty.'

'I'd say you want something, Willie; you've missed me running your errands.'

'And what the deuce would I want?' He wedged the paper behind him and leaned on the rock-face. 'I've the sun and a smoke, and time enough to do nothing. I've most I need at my age and there's no interference. Unless you're here to nag at me. Not,' he brooded, eyes hooded, 'that I'd mind your mam calling. She never visits me nowadays.'

'Can you blame her?' asked Aggie.

'I'm not so old,' wheezed the man, 'that the women don't cheer me.'

'You could still get to the shop.'

'Ach, she'd only be busy. I'd meet a lot of old crones.'

'You've given up, tell the truth.' Aggie glanced at him sharply. 'You wouldn't walk half the distance. You haven't walked to that boat since I went away, have you?'

A sea bird screeched overhead and Macrae made a grimace.

'To hell with that, I've retired. I've done looking for trouble; there's no damned profit in toiling, not on this bit of island. You've got to leave to get on. This place is good for one thing and that's putting your feet up.'

'And boozing?' she prompted.

'I've earned a dram, that's my right. You couldnae fetch me a bottle?'

'You don't alter, Macrae. I might, before I go back.' She struck a note of sarcasm. 'There's something else you

229

want first, I can see your impatience. Man, you're agog for my news, you want to hear all about me, about my term at the college.'

'Aye,' the 'captain' said sourly, 'but maybe later on, lassie. The heat's a touch overpowering and I'm a poor one for learning. I'm thinking now's not the time. Unless you've found some new fellows; I'd understand that much.'

'A bit of gossip, eh, Willie? I don't think Donnie would like it.'

'Bah,' the man said, 'forget him.' He closed his eyes and sat brooding.

Aggie looked at the seals and when she turned he was staring, his glare intent on her. He grunted something dismissive about Donnie's slowness. 'You've a future, wee woman. You've a brain, like your mam. Take the chance that you've got, use your life to go places. Don't be getting tied up, for there's nothing here for you. You scoot when you're ready.'

She laughed to hide her surprise. He was a fine one to talk.

'You'd miss me, wouldn't you, Willie? I'd not be here to run errands.'

'You've not been here for a while.'

'Yes, but never again?'

'I'll be away myself soon. You don't deliver to heaven.'

'That's one place you're not going.'

'Maybe, but you listen: you get your learning and scoot. That out there, that's your oyster.' He eyed the horizon.

'Leave my seals?' she said, smiling. 'They've more sense, they come back.'

'Reeking creatures,' he muttered.

Finn had hauled out to bask and they watched him roll over. He stretched a flipper and scratched, the damp sand sticking to him. At length the seal gave a yawn and the girl said, 'You fraud, I bet you'd miss them yourself, if you told the truth, Willie.'

'I'd be well rid of them, lass.'

'So you'd not mind if Gorme killed them?' She knew the answer already.

The 'captain' heaved himself forward. 'Gorme?' he snarled. 'What's Gorme up to?'

'I don't know; how should I know?' Aggie played with a pebble. She let him fret before musing, 'He always said he'd come for them. You wouldn't mind if he came here?'

'By God, he'd reckon with me, girl. I'll have no Gorme in the cove, not while this Macrae's breathing. Damn the seals, I don't care, but I'll stomach no Gorme here.'

Before her holiday ended Aggie went back to the cliffs, dragging Donnie beside her, a reluctant companion. Ever since she got home he had been quiet and withdrawn and now consulted his watch as if the minutes were precious. He had spoilt the weeks for her, often nowhere about and mostly gloomy when present. At the cliff's edge they stopped.

Aggie said, 'What's the matter?'

'Nothing,' Donnie replied.

The seals had gone, the bay empty. She stood and dreamed for a minute, her mind with the creatures.

'He'll have to wait,' she said next and Donnie stared at her blankly.

He sat hunched up on the stone – the stone she found so barbaric, commemorating the sealers.

'Gorme,' she added with bile. 'He can't do anything now until the seals reassemble.' At least for that she was thankful.

'You needn't worry then, need you?' Her escort spoke with disinterest. 'You can go back to school happy.'

'I wish you'd not call it school.'

Donnie shrugged and looked glum.

Aggie said, 'God, you're dull. Must you look so resentful?'

'I can't stay for long, Aggie.'

'You've been avoiding me, Donnie.'

She was both angry and hurt while he sat hunched even deeper without glancing at her. He had been thus all the time, his dour mood unrelenting. Whenever they had gone out he had barely talked to her. And she had let it go on as if she owed the man something. She had tried to be patient; now her patience had ended.

'I've had enough of it, Donnie.'

He hung his head, mumbling something.

She said, 'You've wasted my break.'

'Some of us have to work. I've a job, that's the difference.'

'No it's not, you've had breaks. You've grudged spending them with me. Besides,' she snapped, 'we all work; I work hard through the term. And I'll be glad to get back, away from you and your frown.' She studied him with despair. 'What's got into you, Donnie? This is me, not a stranger.'

'I tell you, Aggie, I'm busy. Gorme keeps us short-handed.'

'Gorme.' The name made her mad. 'You'll have to leave that damned man. You can't go on working for him.'

'Is that an order?'

'It's for the best, you know that.'

'No, you know it,' said Donnie. He rose and kicked the stone roughly. He said irascibly, 'Aye – you always know what's best for me; always did, so you reckoned.'

'It isn't that . . .'

'Yes, it is. You're like your mam, only worse. She's more right, being older. You think I'm some sort of kid. "You must do this; can't do that." You think I'm stupid or something.'

The girl was suddenly quiet. When presently she replied, she was a shade more defensive. She knew she did push him sometimes. 'I'm only trying to help. We both know about Gorme; the man's impossible, Donnie.'

'We rub along, him and me.'

Aggie glowered. 'He's a brute.'

'He's my boss.'

'Damn it, quit then.' It was, she thought, just that simple. 'You don't *have* to work for him.'

'You don't,' Donnie said harshly. He turned his gaze to the sea, lumpy hands in his pockets. He had a stubborn expression. 'You can join your new friends and discuss higher matters.'

His clumsy irony stung her.

'But *you're* my friend,' she protested.

He kept his eyes on the water.

'Heavens, man,' she went on, 'we've been friends since for ever.'

'Yes, well, now you've got others.'

'You see,' flung Aggie with scorn, 'you've a chip on your shoulder.' She paused, regretting her candour. 'I'm sorry, Donnie, it's true. I can't help it, you've got it. Nothing's altered for me; if it's altered, you've done it.'

He looked ruefully at her. 'Things change,' he said slowly. 'I mean . . .' The meaning was lost. 'I'd best be pushing along. He'll want to know where I've got to.'

'Donnie . . .' Aggie broke off.

'Time I went.'

'Yes,' she answered.

She had her packing to do but let him leave before she did. When he was lost to her sight she watched the ocean a while and tried to order her feelings. She had matured, she supposed, for he seemed suddenly childish and draining of effort. She had, she thought, done her best to show tact, snap him out of his mood, but perseverance had limits and hers had been tested. If he was hurt it would pass; it was no rift of her making.

She took the longer way home, past the Macneils' modest holding, to give her mind time to settle. There would be other vacations and if he threw off the chip — for he most certainly had one — they might again be companions. Whatever Donnie might think, she was still the same Aggie: she did not dump her old friends. She was loyal and forbearing.

All the same, she had doubts, for some resentments went deep and if it turned out like that, why then, no one could help him.

Near a little stone homestead she waved to Mrs Macneil, who waved back from a window. There were some ricks in a yard, and a couple of trees which gave shade to the livestock, a few sheep and heifers. Beyond them, half in the shadows, their backs turned towards her, two figures were resting, their arms on a farm gate.

One was the Macneils' eldest child, a pleasant girl her own age who now worked on the croft. She had left school at sixteen, never bright as a scholar but homely and jolly. She was chuckling loudly; Aggie heard her quick giggle.

The other figure was Donnie's. His shoulders rocked, loose and supple, actuated by laughter.

Aggie stopped, then strode on, for a time disbelieving. The scene remained in her mind: the trees, the gate, the young couple. It was as if, being blind, she had been granted a vision, one stunning perception. It left her dazed and then chastened. What a fool she had been, what a blind little dunce, self-engrossed, self-deluded.

The short walk home took a lifetime.

Later, stuffing her bags, she found her mother behind her. The woman stood in the doorway, one eyebrow cocked slightly. 'My,' the soft voice exclaimed, 'but your packing's got quicker. I'll make some tea if you've done. Come on down, child, and chat; a wee chat can work wonders.'

The cow seals mined the Atlantic. Wingfoot swam with the pack, thrustful, pregnant and hungry. They hunted now to gain weight, amass the fatty reserves they would draw on when nursing. It took them far out to sea beneath the great northern current, the broad stream that rolled east from the New to the Old World.

It took them far from the islands, beyond the range of *Goosander*, to wild domains of the deep where their quarry abounded. Here they prowled the green lump, stalked and chased, ate and slept, seldom restful for long on their twilit safari. The realms they plundered were cold, sometimes bottomless to them. From the turbulent swell jutted snowy ice-molars.

The 'bergs slid southwards like ghosts. Some of the small ones were flat and the seals would lie on them, then slipping back to the depths scout the watery gullies, fly alongside drowned mountains, bounce like hounds across plains as the fleeing game scudded.

On the surface for air, they saw little but cloud, the endless shoaling grey throng of a sky thick with winter. Occasionally whales spouted and Wingfoot once saw a black one, and later a humpback, neither of the beasts harmful. An even larger sea monster passed the seal with a whirr, fins unnaturally rigid. Curious, she took stock, watching as the giant faded.

Melting into the flow, the submarine headed east, its base somewhere in Scotland.

It was the last ship she sighted.

Above, the weather grew colder, a change less marked in the depths where the big fish were waiting. Wingfoot did not much care, too well covered by blubber to find the chill daunting. Blizzards smothered the waves, hurling snow at the rollers. It flecked her head when she rose and made blobs on her whiskers. She did not surface for long; she had one urge now, to hunt, to raid the sea's teeming larder.

A freezing dawn brought excitement. Strange seals had been glimpsed, beasts from alien islands, their urgent movements a sign that the feast was impending. The silver seal grew alert. Fish were not far away and her keen senses tingled. With several eager companions – she could see Niamh and Treshnish – she dived into action.

Gaining speed as she plunged, she passed two of the strangers, eager now for a lead when the quarry was sighted.

On either side seals were streaking, tearing hungrily downwards. Wingfoot matched them for speed, quick as most when aroused, her eyes wide in the flow and her long body thrusting. Soon she swam to the front, a sleek phalanx behind her. Every nerve strained ahead, probed a tinted opaqueness, the teasing veil of the deep, never fully revealing.

The long descent seemed unending. For fathom after green fathom the water was empty. And yet the scent-taste was strong, growing stronger, pervasive. Hounding down, the seals surged, Wingfoot holding her place, sure that bounty was close and in no mean proportion. Its aura flooded her nose, spurred the predator in her. Treshnish flashed alongside and the other went faster.

Then suddenly the prize showed, its munificence princely.

The fish were large, vast in number, a shoal that stretched beyond view: fleshy cod, quietly browsing. At first they looked dull in colour, like muddy torpedoes, but as the seals bounded up they could see glossy spots and the white, curving line on each flank from the gill back to tail-fin. Beneath each bulky-lipped mouth hung a sizeable barbel.

Fleetingly Wingfoot gazed, then the distance had narrowed. It was too late to deploy, the seals in headlong advance, and she could only rush on, whirling down willy-nilly. Still the shoal held its ground; cod were slow to take fright and the host remained static. It seemed bemused by the charge until, with one massive lurch, it fled into the gloaming.

Its startled sprint hauled it clear but did not lose the hunters. Accelerating at speed, the seals came up at the rear, hastening finny stragglers. Across the flood they took off in alarm, like an army in panic, the mass soon extended. In two wild, swerving processions fish and mammals careered, the chase flowing in earnest.

Wingfoot raced beside Treshnish. Ahead, the shoal snaked and jinked, lengthening as it sped, its van deep in the murk, trailing fish in their hundreds. Mindlessly they stampeded, drawn on by the foremost. Behind, the seals strove for place, for the best striking stations. They were now close to the floor, dodging rocks and dim crags, skimming over dark scree to a watery plateau.

Wingfoot veered with the cod, harrying the rear markers.

As she banked they changed course, causing her to twist quickly. The flashing tails drew away. She saw the feast slipping from her, becoming small in the distance. From her lengthening viewpoint the fish appeared to rise gently then as gracefully fall, as if glimpsed in slow-motion, their efforts deceptive. And all the time the gap widened, her hunger frustrated.

No matter how hard she toiled, still the quarry fled faster, their dim shapes departing. With little hope she held on: she could not sprint any more and her staying power dwindled. Then, near the end of endurance, she watched the shoal veer and swoop, vanishing in a chasm. At last the swimmers had erred and a new strength suffused her.

Seconds later, she followed, entering the deep gully. Inside, the sea became darker and confining walls flanked her. Between their dim interfaces the flooded throat narrowed. The cod had streaked to their doom, milling now to her front as the pass grew congested. The thwarted mass churned and swirled, individuals reversing, their slick green backs glinting. Racing up from the rear, the seals fell on them, ravening.

Wingfoot, picking a victim, sank her teeth in it quickly. Niamh passed, jaws agape; everywhere fish were threshing. With her fangs into flesh, the silver seal spiralled upwards. As she surfaced to gorge, a vaporous sky scudded south, arctic air currents biting. She gave no thought to the cold, busy now on the swell, gulping steak after steak in a trance of contentment.

The coming months brought fresh kills and the pregnant seals fattened. In time, as winter ran out, their unborn infants grew faster and soon the cows thought of home, hankering for the nurseries. They were now tired of the deep; each new dawn brought a call, signalled summer's bright promise.

Warming rays brightened troughs; in the glare the cows wallowed. Lazily they took air, one or two drowsing off, soothed by what had become a reposeful Atlantic. Friendly groups basked together, ripening and benign, set at last to begin their return to the islands. Wind and current were fair; they relaxed before starting.

Lowing calls crossed the swell, boon companions drew closer. Finally, without a fuss, a veteran seal dipped her head and struck out underwater. It was the doughty Bragela, a calf by Cuchulainn in her. Another animal followed and presently more were moving, heading under the waves for the isles of the sunrise. A few stayed on for a while but by dusk most were travelling.

Wingfoot swam with Niamh, later picking up Treshnish. Navigation was easy: they simply went with the rollers, assured of land to the east and the chance to take bearings. By now they knew the coasts well and would recognize landmarks. There would be sights, smells and sounds, many welcoming pointers.

At intervals the three slept, the sea's drift in their favour; otherwise they cruised calmly, sagely pacing their efforts. They had no need to waste strength, all the signs were auspicious. They had done well while away, unmolested by foes, the sea's harvest a rich one. Nor had the weather been bad by the ocean's rude standards.

It kept fine for the trip and they swam in good spirits. By and by they saw gulls, some of them on the waves, and when a heron lazed past they knew the main haul was ending. They glimpsed the first crags at Malin, the northernmost tip of Ireland, veered for Inishtrahull then ploughed on towards Islay.

A heavy mist was descending. It limited surface vision but amplified a sweet sound, the island ferry in passage, its steady throb heartening. It was a sound of home waters, a sound of the summer. Nostalgically the seals listened; they could hear noises aboard, passengers on deck talking.

'We'll be running in late, unless this clears beyond Islay.'

'Oh, the sun will shine soon; it always shines for Seal Island.'

'I wish I had your vacations.'

'Not you, too, Mr Muir.' Aggie's voice was reproving.

'Ach, I know you deserve them.'

'You don't do badly yourself, travelling round for a living.'

'Can't complain, can't complain. Meeting pretty young students.'

A mocking hoot pierced the mist. 'Now then, mam'll be jealous.'

A hearty male laugh succeeded. 'And if she is, she'll be wrong – my favourite customer, bless her. How's your boyfriend then, Aggie?'

'It's getting damp, Mr Muir; a cup of tea would be nice.'

'Let's go in. You shall have one.'

'Wait, I thought I heard seals.'

'You won't see anything, Aggie.'

'Maybe not . . .'

It was quiet.

'With sugar please, Mr Muir, if you're getting it for me.'

Wingfoot flippered and dived, swimming wearily forward. Eager now for a rest, she wished a beach would turn up, anywhere to haul out, take a break from the water. There was no need to rush on, the last lap would be easy.

She surfaced, missing the others, peering into the fog. Ahead, a soft 'hooo-oo' skirled – Niamh's call – and she followed. The murk was thicker than ever. Again, the call lured her on, though to where she knew not, save that countryside beckoned. Scents of growth crossed the tide, moist and pungently earthy, and next the sea bed had shelved and she was into the shallows. Here were rocks, a few stones and then a slope up to grass, a small field in the vapour.

Niamh and Treshnish were there, already sprawled on the turf. The world beyond was a blank, lost in smothering whiteness: not that Wingfoot much cared, far too tired for inspections. Crawling into the field, she dozed off within seconds.

When finally she aroused, the mist was fast disappearing. The sun was warm on her back and the others were bathing, swimming round by the rocks inside Islay's Loch Indaal. It was a pastoral scene. Through the field where she lay a small beck ran to sea over short mossy grazing. Wingfoot listened, still yawning. Above the spring's cheerful song came the sound of beasts chomping.

With a stretch, the seal viewed them.

The steers had long curving horns and were shaggily coated. She did not like the look of them. At first they watched her, unmoved, then, on friskier impulse, upped their tails and romped forward. Charging down to the seal, they encircled her, puffing. Their heads were low, nostrils flared, and as their noses came close she could feel their breath on her.

Niamh was flippering wildly, treading water and splashing.

In the field, Wingfoot froze. The shaggy cordon drew tighter. Shoulders jostled each other. A great rough tongue was pushed out as one blebbed snout advanced and she inched away stiffly. Other noses were poking. She gave a hiss; the steers flinched, backing off for a moment.

There was a gap to her front and she could see Treshnish through it, clear water inviting. Wingfoot gave a quick heave, levering from the turf with all the pent-up disgust of her new-found aversion – pasture might do for some, it was not for sea creatures.

Breaking out through the ruck, she hit the beach and humped on, crashing into the shallows. Smooth round stones passed beneath her, the large ones luggers took on when such craft needed ballast. Suddenly she was safe and, towering up from the tide, flung a snort at the cattle. The gesture, pleasing her friends, set all three seals cavorting.

More like calves than calf-bearers, they raced, pirouetted. They played for almost an hour before, in spirited humour, they stood to sea and swam on, journey's end their next landing.

Donnie swilled down the deck, scrubbing where the grease lingered. Beyond the pier a seal bobbed as his broom scoured and chivvied. He was hot and bad-tempered, the chore for Gorme doubly riling when he thought of his pay: a boy's pittance, he brooded. He planned to ask Gorme for more; he was resolved to demand it.

Or he would quit, he would threaten. He had the speech in his head and rehearsed it while scrubbing.

'So there you are, Mr Gorme – either that or I'm quitting.'

From time to time he looked up, glancing furtively landwards. Across the quay from *Goosander* the shop door was jangling. People went in and out: old MacPhee, Mrs Edwards. Every jangle disturbed him. It might or might not be *her* and his feelings confused him, for while he hankered for Aggie part of him feared to see her.

He had no confidence with her; somehow she made him feel smaller. Girls, he thought, did that to you, they weakened you by their presence, especially bright girls like Aggie. He never felt at ease with them.

'So there you are, Mr Gorme . . .'

Donnie tried to forget her. He dipped a pail for more water and glanced again, the door chiming. It was only Wee Hughie, a casual labouring man, coming out with tobacco. The bucket slopped, brimming over.

It made him think of the mackerel when they had swarmed by the quay and been collected in pails, before that last trip with Calum, before the fateful storm hit them. He shot the water out quickly, the thought of Calum upsetting. Donnie still suffered nightmares and now scrubbed hard at the deck as if to banish the memory, erase the ghost from the vessel.

He had a terror of spectres, half afraid to look up in case Calum was watching, a grinning shade at the stern or ensconced in the wheelhouse. Instead, he bent to his task, his gaze fixed on the broom-head. When someone's hand touched his back he whirled round, his eyes bulging.

At first he thought it *was* Calum. The man was almost as large though somewhat older and coarser, the lumpy face grinning. The grin, more twisted than Calum's, fell on a soiled sealskin pouch in which rough fingers were delving. They rolled a thin cigarette and, when the paper was licked, raised the thing to dry lips.

'Is Gorme here?' asked Wee Hughie.

'No,' said Donnie, disgruntled.

He glared and toiled with fresh vigour.

'Expecting him?'

'By and by.'

The man watched, his lips curling, the cigarette dangling. He said, 'You'll wear out those planks; save your strength for the lassies.'

'Damn them,' Donnie responded.

Hughie leered, squinting round, weighing up boat and tackle. At length he drawled, 'I can't stop. Tell him I'll be back, will ye?'

Donnie grunted, uncaring. He had no time for the man, other matters more pressing. 'So there you are, Mr Gorme . . .' He ran it through once again. 'Either that or I'm quitting.' It was the umpteenth rehearsal and still, when Gorme climbed on deck, the performance was ragged. He stumbled through it red-faced, urged by dogged conviction. The speech was stammered but stubborn.

'If I'm not worth it I'll go, but I'd say I'm deserving. If you can find someone better . . .'

Gorme's small eyes had contracted. 'Maybe I can.'

Donnie stared.

Gorme was searching for weakness. 'Maybe I can,' he repeated. He saw resolve, obstinacy, and trimmed his sails to them. 'But I've got used to your ways so I'll say nothing hasty. Don't mistake me, my lad, you're not perfect, far from it. You're no' God's gift, son, I'll tell you. Indispensable you're not.'

'I'm a worker, you know it.'

'You're a worker, I'll gi' you. You try, I'll be truthful.'

'If you're not satisfied with me . . .'

Gorme eyed the gulls on the gunwale. Their cold orbs were neutral. When he looked back he said slyly, 'Let's not be rushing it now; you'll do yourself no good that way. You have to think these things over.'

'I've thought a lot, Mr Gorme.'

'Then you'll mind all I've taught you. I brought you on from a boy; you've had the finest tuition. It's worth a lot is good training. You'll not have overlooked that? Ye've obligations, MacDonald.'

'My training's done, Mr Gorme. I've a right to my value.'

'Ah, a right?' Gorme looked doubtful.

A hand was stroking the beard, the broad jowls gently massaged. 'You'll need to study the market; you cannae buck the facts, laddie. You'll know there's little work going, for it's tight on the island. Verra little work going. And self-employment, oh dear, friend Macrae got you nowhere. Man, the world's awful hard and a billet's a billet.'

Gorme stuck his thumbs in his belt. 'Rights?' He shook his head gravely. 'They'll no' buy porridge, young fellow.'

Donnie wavered a moment. He rallied, thinking of Aggie. She would have stood up to Gorme.

'I'll take the chance,' he observed. 'I've got no future on my pay.'

'Ach, you're young,' the man told him, 'you'll be in no tearing hurry. I'm only saying,' he coaxed, 'that you'd do well to consider. I've got your interests at heart; take my tip and sleep on it. Take a while to think, Donnie.'

Donnie's brow wrinkled deeply. 'Well, if you will,' he muttered.

'Yes, yes, we'll see. There's work waiting.' Gorme restrained his impatience. 'We'll come back to it later; we'll not fall out, young MacDonald.' The bad teeth showed through his beard, the lop-sided smile grudging. He faced the sea for a minute and swore at the seal there. 'That's quite enough about that – I've got a wee job to give you. Drop that brush and come with me.'

He clambered back to the quay and the younger man followed.

A tranquil swell sucked the wall, periodically slapping. Donnie glanced at the buildings. The shop was quiet, the door closed; there was no sign of Aggie. Most probably, he supposed, she would be down at the cove, for soon the cows would be calving. By the sheds, Hughie lurked, hovering like a footpad.

Gorme strode on up the pier, his gait rolling and powerful. The man's movements were bull-like. 'There,' he growled when he stopped, 'there she is, still a dandy.'

Steps descended to moorings, the felspar sun-loaded. At their meet with the brine a long, open boat joggled, its empty seats tilting. 'She's no *Peg*,' Gorme said, gloating, 'she's been cared for has that one. They don't build her kind nowadays. I've had her round at my place since the old man was buried. Still shipshape, MacDonald.'

'Built roomy,' mused Donnie. Built for oars then converted.

'Aye, she'll carry a coachload. I want her motor tuned up, she was coughing this morning.'

A shadow fell on the pier. 'Bonnie craft,' said Wee Hughie. 'About those men, Mr Gorme, I've had a word in quiet places. I've raised the gang that you wanted.'

Wingfoot swam through the day, sighting land in the early evening. Treading water, she craned, pressing up to see better. The air was clear and at peace and there they were, the old landmarks: strands and dunes, the tall cliffs, the small pier, huddled buildings. She was back at Seal Island, safely home from her travels. Niamh and Treshnish sped on; for a moment she lingered.

She viewed the bulwarks of stone, the long stretch of *machair*, the low sun on the crofts and the shadowy hummocks. No more ocean for now, or snatching sleep in the fathoms; she would lie on warm sand, dunk in snug little rock-pools. She would be where she belonged, among her own at her birthplace. She would be restful, secure, complete with all the herd round her.

Satisfied, she swam on, turning in by the headland.

Now the cove was in sight with its summery bluffs, its steep path through the rocks winding down where birds nested. Smears of colour stood out, hazy patches of wild flowers. At the bottom, unchanged, stood the old seaman's cottage, the battered boat near it. The tide was out, the beach shining, moistly crankled and worm-pocked. She could see the seals on it, some drawn up to the *mul*, others nearer the water.

A gull flew low with a screech, peering beadily at her: a gull with one red leg missing.

Wingfoot savoured the setting. She passed the buoy and the point, its crags straggling seawards; she viewed their plateaux and shelves, the blue channels between them. Seals lay out on the rocks, somnolent or just gazing, some inclined on one side, flippers limp in the sun's rays. Others dotted the bay, their wet, wide-eyed masks beaming. Seagulls bobbed on the brine with white tail-feathers hoisted.

As the skerries came close she could smell the bulls waiting. Cellach, back on his throne, watched her, huffing and grunting, his wrinkled face ageless. Cuchulainn hit the swell, breasting forward to meet her. He made an arc round the cow, his great grizzled snout snuffling, but merely counted her in then returned to his platform. Not until she had calved would the males show more interest.

A warmer welcome was waiting as she came to the shallows. Niamh, already beached, galumphed up to embrace her. They shared their joy to be home, nuzzling with affection. There was a flurry of kissing before they playfully wrestled, the tide frothing round them. Then side by side they stretched out, contemplating the beach scene.

Almost nothing had altered; the rocks and pools were still there and the shingle still glittered. It still held seashells, bleached bones, bits of tide-polished glass, shrivelled pods of dry seaweed. There was the same line of jetsam, the same old cracks in the cliff, the same smells she had known as a three-weeks-old moulter – salt, iodine, seal scents.

Pregnant cows had hauled out and were spaced up the

foreshore. They scratched and fussed at their claws for a short while at leisure. Now and then one would stir and hump in for a bathe, content to lie at the edge as if weary of swimming. Where the wavelets effused, the large creatures rocked gently.

Here and there the males slept or disputed their boundaries. Finn and Oisin were sparring, the younger bull so far landless. Across Finn's frontier they roared, the beachmaster aggressive. His pitted neck was cranked up and his features were ugly, the toothy snarl threatening. As they grimaced and swore, nearby females ignored them.

The contest flared, soon resolved. There was a short, blasting hiss and Finn grappled the other. Oisin struggled in vain, no match for the veteran, then broke and ran, his mane bloodied. His tail was tweaked for his pains as he scurried to safety.

Yawning, Wingfoot looked on as her erstwhile mate suffered, last year's loving a whim in the annals of nature. Maternal instincts would rule before she sought a new partner. Meanwhile she pondered the *mul* where Macrae was approaching, staggering towards home with an armful of driftwood. He stopped to reach for his flask, took a swig and looked round.

'Aye, you reeking great beasts, you'll be breeding,' he muttered, 'dropping bawling wee brats to disturb me at night-time. Go on, roll your damned eyes, you'll not soften me wi' them.' He stumbled on with the wood. 'Inconsiderate vermin.'

The seals were used to the man; few of them moved far from him.

Oisin, skirting Finn's ground, had seen Wingfoot and joined her. All he got was a glare and a snap for encroaching. Since these failed in their aim, the cow slipped to the sea, swimming languidly from him. He tried once more to get close, cruising up to her flank, but the silver seal shunned him. At last she floated unruffled, the atmosphere dreamy.

The sun had set, the sky flushed, and Wingfoot lazed to the bell-buoy. She flopped aboard, deeply pleased, as serene as the evening. Immense contentment engulfed her. Birds were heading for land, seals were settling. Soon the first calves would mewl, until when it was quiet, the dark shapes of the rocks touched with pink as day ended. Like an old, long-missed friend the cove snuggled beside her.

She heard Bragela's low song, lullabying the skerries. There was a throb in her womb, a small kick of assertion.

Through the window Mrs Fraser watched Donnie and anguished for him. He had passed slowly three times, once peering in so intently a patch of glass had been misted, and now he paced for the fourth time. It was a shame about the youngsters but Peg had guessed it would happen.

Already weary, she sighed. The store was empty of people and she was ready to close but she had feared he would enter, and when he did, with feigned calmness, she beamed her own drummed-up pleasure.

'Why now, Donnie MacDonald, you're quite a stranger.'

'Yes,' he blurted, 'it's been the work, Mrs Fraser. Dreadful busy this summer, a lot of fishing.'

'Out of mischief, eh, Donnie? Well, better working than not. There'll be others less lucky.'

'Aye,' he answered.

'You're keeping fit?'

'Aye, I'm fit, Mrs Fraser.'

The woman studied him wisely. 'Uh-huh,' she said with approval, 'you don't look bad on it, Donnie. Maybe you'll find some time later and drop in more often. You know you mustn't neglect us, I miss you calling.'

Donnie blushed and said nothing. He was as tongue-tied as ever, Peggy Fraser reflected, and when the silence persisted, 'Have you come to buy something?' she prompted pleasantly.

'Oh – no, Mrs Fraser, not really.'

'Then I'll close up,' she responded. Her feet were aching. 'If it's a social call, Donnie, you won't mind waiting a minute?'

'Actually, it was Aggie . . .'

'My dear, she's been out since lunchtime.'

His face had fallen.

'What a shame. Perhaps later?'

He seemed unsure. 'Would it matter?'

'Matter, Donnie, why should it?'

'You think she'd see me?' he dithered.

'See you?' Peggy clucked briskly. 'Lord, I'd hope so, young man, you're not infectious, for God's sake.'

'No,' he said without humour. 'I really do need to see her.'

'Well, there you are, don't be daft.' The woman bustled about putting things in their places. At last she took off her apron and ran a hand down her skirt. He was pathetically anxious. 'Heavens, Donnie MacDonald, you call back, don't be silly.'

'You're right,' he said. 'It's important.'

'Then I'll make sure she stays in.' The other folded the apron. When she had slipped it away she shut the drawer and glanced up. Her voice had grown a shade sharper. 'You're not afraid of her, are you?'

Donnie faked a hoarse laugh.

Mrs Fraser ignored it. 'You wouldn't be alone, Donnie; a fellow could be, you know.' She regarded him shrewdly. 'Those young fellows at college – I'll bet they hop when she tells them. Her personality's forceful; she's very strong-willed is Aggie. If you lie down she'll walk on you.'

'Aye, well, yes . . .'

'It's none of my business, Donnie, but if you asked I'd be frank. She's got a lot of good points and she'll not lack for admirers, but they'll get nowhere with meekness. The child needs handling firmly. She's never known her own father and wants a man to look up to, someone not in awe of her, someone who can take charge.'

Peggy Fraser smiled quickly. 'That's just a mother's opinion – just in case you had asked me. You mustn't get in the dumps, not because of our Aggie. There's plenty more nice wee lassies. Cheer up then, young fellow.'

Donnie turned to the door. 'I've got to see her, Mrs Fraser.'

'Uh-huh,' said the woman.

'I need to see her, I'm worried.'

'Perhaps you'd best stay to tea. You could always wait, Donnie.'

'Thanks.' He shook his head slowly and paused outside, the gulls screaming.

He could not talk to the woman, he must confess to her daughter. More than a week had gone by since he had spoken to Gorme, and Gorme had made no decision, or if he had, had kept silent, not mentioning money. That in itself was a worry but only part of the crisis.

He looked across to the quay and saw the open boat swaying, as low and raked as shark, as if waiting to plunder.

'A cough' was how Gorme had put it and when the motor had started there had indeed been a splutter – a loose connection to tighten. It had been done in a minute. Gorme had vanished with Hughie, leaving Donnie to rummage. He had already been anxious, for Hughie's 'gang' boded ill, and when he opened the locker it had confirmed his suspicions.

It had been packed tight with cudgels, some old, dark with stains, and some fresh, cut from green wood. He should have gone straight to Aggie; she would have known what to do. But he had thought of his pay, kept on thinking about it, the ways he might spend an increase. And what would happen with nothing, just the dole, if Gorme fired him.

He lingered now, feeling guilty.

'Hey, MacDonald, come here.'

The voice was Gorme's from the *Goosander* and Donnie trudged across, grumbling. The skipper leaned from the wheelhouse. 'Come on in, make some tea. On second thoughts, fetch the bottle; that tea you make is foul poison. We'll take something better.' The man half-filled two chipped cups, peering up through thick eyebrows. 'Get that into your teeth and don't say I neglect you. We're celebrating – least, you are.'

Donnie frowned.

'Well, look lively.'

'Celebrating?' said Donnie.

'Right,' cried Gorme with a glint, 'so wipe that scowl

off, you monkey. By God, you're awkward to please, I've seen corpses more cheerful. If you can't shine, we'll forget it.'

'What?' asked Donnie, confounded.

'Your bloody rise, man, that's what. You're like a flaming wet Sunday. I ought to dock you instead; I'm wasting good liquor on you.'

Donnie stared at him dumbly.

The man was wiping his whiskers. He grunted, 'Bloody good liquor.'

'You're going to give me the rise?'

'I'm telling you,' Gorme said, cackling. 'You've not the wit to catch on. Wake up, laddie, it's payday.'

'I thought . . .'

'I know what you thought. I had my doubts, I can tell you. I still ha' doubts that you're worth it but I'll make certain you earn it; you ken there's nothing for nothing. I'll see I'm not out of pocket.' The man looked out to the pier, to where the open boat joggled. 'You've got your uses,' he growled, 'you've got a way with a motor; she's running sweet since you fixed her. You'll get your bob or two extra.'

Donnie sipped from the cup. He choked and felt his gut burning.

The skipper grinned. 'You'll be handy. I'll want you with me tomorrow.'

'I didn't know we were working.'

'Don't know you're born, do you, sonnie? Call it work if you want to.'

'Tomorrow?' Donnie despaired.

'Aye, MacDonald, tomorrow. Crack o' dawn at the boat. Hughie's friends will be waiting.' Gorme slammed his cup down and left, calling, 'No sleeping over.'

A gloomy hush filled the wheelhouse and Donnie's fears turned to panic. He threw the drink back and blinked, staring seawards a moment. Then, clambering from the boat, he made a rush for the shop, found it shut and knocked loudly.

'Oh, you're back,' Peggy sighed.

'I'll not be stopping,' puffed Donnie. 'Has Aggie taken the bike?'

'She took mine. What's the matter?'

'To the cove?'

'I don't know.'

'Mrs Fraser, it's urgent. The other bike – could I use it?'

The heavy trade machine rattled as Donnie's boots pumped the pedals. He raced it over the bumps, climbed the sandy track, sweating, until he came to the cliff and could hear the calves bleating. Plunging on down the slope, he saw them scattered below, small white shapes on the strand, some alone, some with adults. The fishy odour was strong and the bleats had grown louder.

Braking, Donnie dismounted, left the bike and ran forward. The infants showed no fear of him, their trusting eyes soulful. One lay flat on its back, paws upraised like a puppy. Donnie shouted to Aggie, 'It's Gorme, he's coming tomorrow.' He took a couple more steps. 'At dawn. He's going to kill them.'

When he had gabbled the story, she turned on him fiercely.

'You hopeless dimwit, how could you? You knew it wouldn't be long; you saw the boat and that man and could've spoken a week back. We could've got someone over, somebody official. Dawn tomorrow, dear God. There's no time, you fool, Donnie.'

'You needn't spell it out, Aggie.'

'Spell it?' Aggie assailed him. 'You'd need it in pictures. I can't believe this,' she told him, 'I don't believe this is happening.'

It was uncannily still, the sea flat, the view glazed, drained of passion and weather. Seals apart, it was lonely, the girl and Donnie bleak figures, the sky's vastness darkening. Their sense of helplessness grew, became spatial, unbounded, emphasized, by the bleats — bleats like lost spirits pleading.

'We can't get help, it's too late.' Aggie groaned, then stared dumbly.

The seals lay round them in droves, lovely indolent creatures at rest now or nursing, some floating nearby, motionless as the water. Whatever else the beasts dreamed, it was not of their danger. Wingfoot gleamed at the tide-line. Her calf had yet to be born, probably before morning.

The girl despaired, her fists clenching. 'It can't be true, I can't bear it.' Her desperation scared Donnie.

'We'll think of something,' he muttered. If she could not, he must do so. 'Suppose we drive the beasts off? They'd be all right in the water. At least they'd be safer.'

'No,' hissed Aggie, 'for God's sake.' She held her head for a moment then dropped her arms, shoulders slumping. 'The newborn calves wouldn't go, nor would plenty of others. They'd only swim to the rocks then come ashore in the night and be suckling by daybreak. Try to make some sense, Donnie.'

A white-faced mite wriggled near them and mewled for its mother.

'We'll have to beg,' said the girl. 'We'll have to make the men leave them.'

'You don't know Gorme and his cronies.'

'We'll have to tackle them, Donnie. I'll take the louts on if you won't.'

'Now who's daft?' the man grunted. He punched an open palm, scowling. 'There'll be a dozen or more; you and me won't deter them.'

'There's Willie, too.'

'A big help.'

'And so are you, you've been *brilliant*. Oh God, you're right,' Aggie gulped, 'I don't suppose the fool's sober.' She viewed the cottage through tears. 'I'm stuck with fools,' she bewailed, 'and Wingfoot's going to be murdered. They'll all be murdered,' she gritted.

There was a shout from the dusk; Macrae came lurching towards them. His bloodshot eyes were inquiring. 'You're both here, are you?' he spluttered. 'Like old times. So what's happening?'

'What's happening?' Aggie flared up. 'I'll tell you, Willie Macrae – Gorme's coming sealing tomorrow, a crew of riffraff behind him, a gang of murderers with him. At dawn you'll meet your friend Gorme. That's what's happening, you drunkard.'

'Gorme?' Macrae slurred. 'I'll have him.'

'By then, you fool, you'll be legless.'

'If Gorme sets foot here, I'll have him.'

'You're disgusting,' snarled Aggie.

'I'll show you, lassie, you'll see. You gi' me Gorme and I'll show ye.'

'You damned old drunkard, you're useless.'

Donnie's voice interrupted. 'Have you finished?' he

barked, and they broke off in surprise, as if a stranger had spoken. The tone was brusquely commanding. 'We're getting nowhere like this, blathering at each other. I'll tell you what's going to happen. We've got one chance against Gorme and I've been too dull to see it. We're going to stop him at sea; put the fear of God in him.'

He half-turned, facing the *Peg*. 'There's our hope. Pray she helps us.'

'You're right, by God,' cried Macrae. He swayed and almost fell over. 'You're no' so stupid, MacDonald. We'll fight the devil like seamen.'

'It's worth a try,' declared Donnie.

Macrae was dancing and chuckling. 'We'll see how good he is, laddie. He thinks himself a fine skipper.'

The younger man nodded grimly. 'I'd say we'd turn him, eh, Willie? I'd say he'd run if we pressed him.'

The girl had whirled, her glare scornful. 'You're off your heads, the pair of you. You're helping nobody, Donnie.'

'Have you a better idea?' He waited calmly a moment. 'Well, when you have, let us know. Meanwhile shut up and listen.'

'That wreck will sink like a stone.'

'Maybe she will,' he returned, 'maybe she won't, I don't know. She's got two pumps, if they'll work, and she can carry some water. I said a chance – it's a chance. If she sinks, we'll have tried.'

'And if the engine won't start?'

'Ach, she'll start,' wheezed Macrae. 'It's me who gave up the ghost; the wee lad's kept his end up.'

'And shamed you, Willie,' the girl said.

'We needn't bicker,' snapped Donnie. 'She'll start all right and there's fuel, enough for what we'll be asking.

I'll have to rig up a tiller – we might make do with an axe-helve; I've seen one back in the store. And I'll need lubricant, too, to ease those pumps where they've rusted. And lamps to work by when night falls.'

The 'captain' lurched. 'I'm right wi' you.'

'Then light a fire by her, Willie, it's not so warm after dark. And, Willie – keep off the bottle.'

The young man rolled up his sleeves, his air of competence mounting.

'Donnie,' Aggie said quietly, 'I'll cycle back for those things.' Her glance was newly respectful. 'And fetch some food, you'll be hungry.'

Wingfoot moved up the beach. It was dark, her time close, and she was seeking the seaweed. The stuff was thick near the *mul* and she reclined on it, blowing. One distant night, in a storm, she had come into the world there; now a tranquil sea pulsed and her own calf was coming.

She had seen much in between, cruising depths and far coasts, touching islands of legend: Iona, Islay and Mull, and many more rugged outposts. At last, her maiden years gone, each with its bounties and perils, she faced the future a matron, her breeding life just beginning. She could go on to reach twenty, even thirty, fate willing.

Her eyes were wide in the gloom and the stars glittered in them. The seal was listening acutely. The herd was quiet, no night music; even the young had stopped bawling. Along the strand by the boat, a fire's glow pricked and flared and men's voices buzzed faintly, as insects churred sometimes. Every now and again she heard knocking and banging.

In the glare of the flames the boat's beam had turned

ruddy. Presently there was scraping, the sound of shovels on shingle, and then small figures were shoving, straining at the craft's stern, and again there was digging. Gradually the boat shifted, emptiness in the firelight. Slowly silence returned and the embers grew dimmer.

A sea-bird squawked on the cliff, disturbed at roost, quickly settling.

A deep repose lulled the cove and the skerries were peaceful. Only the breaking sea stirred, its tongues drowsy and muffled. Wingfoot lay on her belly, aware of movement inside her. On her seaweedy bed she eased herself to one side then resumed her position, the dark litter flattening. A little later, unrestful, she repeated the action.

There was a pause of some minutes before her motions continued, their frequency quickening. Beneath the gaze of the stars she tipped a little one way, swinging back to the other, her back raising slightly. From time to time she rocked, the sleek creature moaned softly. For twenty minutes or so the seal rolled in this fashion.

And then, beginning to labour, she arched with more agitation and blew as she did so. As a reward for her efforts a small white head soon appeared, shimmering in the starshine. The rest was rapidly over. It took a few more contractions to slip the calf to the kelp – a silky, glistening bundle – then Wingfoot rested a moment.

For a while neither moved, parent still beside newborn, the tide's murmur soothing. At length, extending a flipper, the silver seal touched her babe and, drawing it to her breast, nuzzled it as it grizzled.

As first light wreathed the point the *Peg* emerged from the greyness, now lying close to the sea, her shabby bows in the breakers. She was a lump in the murk, a dead thing resurrected. From her stern, up the beach, ran the tracks of rollers and, where her hull had ploughed in, deeper furrows were clearer. There was a pit in the shingle, the grave from which she had risen.

Macrae was staring to sea, fidgeting with impatience, the waves round his waders. 'Come on, Gorme, show your snout.' The man splashed, legs unsteady. 'Just show your nose round that head; you'll get more than you've planned for.'

He took a drag at his flask and tucked it out of sight quickly.

'Thinks he can handle a boat? We'll see, the son o' the devil.' He swigged again, squinting sideways, his glance finding Donnie. 'We'll teach the beggars a lesson. It's time we launched her, I reckon.'

There was a mist on the bay, hanging over the skerries, curled in skeins round the rocks and embroiling the bell-buoy. It thinned and rose very slowly to show a spectral horizon. Lighter seams streaked the sky but the land was still dusky, the seals largely hidden.

The younger man viewed the inlet. 'Hang on, Willie, we'll wait. She'd only start to let water. They could be half an hour coming.'

Aggie shivered beside them. She said, 'They'll likely be waiting; they'll still expect you to join them.' She felt afraid but concealed it.

'Aye, let them stew,' Donnie muttered.

The 'captain' slapped a thigh, cackling. 'They'll see the lad soon enough, and he'll have Will Macrae wi' him – that's a partnership for you. We'll settle Gorme, son, between us; we'll singe his beard, the marauder.'

Donnie scowled, his arms folded. 'You've not stopped

tippling, Willie. You mess things up and I'll choke you.'

'Oh God,' breathed Aggie, 'let's pray – pray she doesn't sink quickly.'

'She'll be all right for a while.' Donnie's smile reassured her. She had a new respect for him. He had toiled like a Trojan, working into the night, patching up and repairing, directing their efforts. His confidence had sustained her; he had been strong and commanding.

He said, 'We'll have to keep pumping; if we keep at it, she'll float – at any rate, long enough.' He put an arm round her shoulders. 'Don't worry, I'll be there, Aggie. Do as I say and we'll manage. I won't let anything harm you.'

'I'm not afraid for myself, it's the seals,' she responded.

'We're going to see there's no landing.'

'Let's hope so,' Aggie exclaimed. She squeezed his hand, staring seawards. 'I trust you, Donnie, I do. It's that old man – the fool's sozzled.'

Macrae was knee-deep in foam, propped against the *Peg*'s timber. 'Let's have ye, Gorme, bring your dogs on.' As each long wave rocked the prow he cut loose with a war dance, his worn jacket flapping.

Donnie frowned but said calmly, 'He's handled boats all his life. He'll bear up, it's instinctive.'

Unconvinced, Aggie shuddered. A gleam had spread to the cliffs and she could see the calves feeding, mouths clamped to their mothers. The little groups remained dim; she could not pick out favourites. Somewhere Wingfoot was there, as was golden Niamh, clad in baffling greyness.

At Aggie's feet the sand oozed, footprints filling with water. She thought of long-ago mornings and Donnie

264

digging for bait, teaching her about lugworms. 'Lugs' and 'rags', she remembered, and how he had thrilled her. There had been nothing since then quite to match Donnie's wisdom. And now she clung to his strength, his stern-faced resolution.

'It's going to be all right, Aggie.'

'You'll lose your job,' she replied.

'I'm through with Gorme; he can stick it.'

'I'm sorry, Donnie . . .'

'What for?'

'I've been a bitch to you lately; we've been like strangers, I'm sorry.'

'Ach, that was my fault,' he growled. He watched the headland, eyes narrow. 'I'm no' much good with the girls. I'm no Romeo, Aggie.'

Macrae glanced down at his watch.

'They've called it off,' he complained. He tugged his cap in annoyance. 'They've funked it, hell rot in their guts; they've got wind that we're waiting.'

'Not Gorme and Wee Hughie. You don't think that would alarm them?'

'Don't know, laddie – don't know.'

'I'm telling you they'll be coming.' Donnie stared ahead fiercely. 'They've got a loaded boat, Willie, and they'll be taking it easy. It's not a speedboat they've got; the *Peg*'ll clip along faster.' Fingers crossed, he reflected.

He stood regarding the craft in all her many short-comings. She looked a fair to good hen-house. Her paint was gone, her wood cracked; he put no faith in her caulking. She had an improvised tiller, a gap in her rudder. Only her motor consoled him. On form, the diesel was fine; it packed a walloping thump. It just remained to be seen if it would shake her to pieces.

265

Macrae declared with a grin, 'We'll sweep them off the sea, laddie.'

'If you're not pie-eyed, Macrae.'

'Donnie . . .' Aggie's voice shook. 'Look out there, past the rocks.'

'What?' said Donnie.

'The long-boat.'

'Aye, that's her. See her, Willie?'

'See her, man? I can smell her.'

'Time we got this thing floated.'

All three were pushing the stern and when the *Peg* became buoyant Aggie scrambled aboard, the two men wading deeper. Donnie gave a last shove then swung over to join her. As they stood in the boat, Macrae threw up his arms, still awash in the breakers. They grabbed a scrawny wrist each, shipping him like a trawl-net.

He snatched the tiller and gasped, his cap crazily tilted.

'Are you all right?' Donnie asked.

The craft rocked, losing headway.

'I'm not a child.'

'You've less sense.'

'Just get her started,' the girl begged, regarding the bilge-boards. Already, water was seeping.

'She'll start, don't fret,' replied Donnie. He turned and bent to the engine. It gave a low, grinding moan and then a long expiration. 'Next time,' he grunted, 'no sweat.'

'*Please*,' prayed Aggie.

'Don't worry.' There was a minor explosion and blue-grey fumes smudged the waves. The old diesel vibrated. As Donnie straightened, relieved, he looked round, smiling grimly. 'There she roars; take her Willie.'

'Like a lion,' cried Macrae. He teased open the throttle.

The *Peg* responded unsurely, as if surprised to be sea-borne. At first she shied at the swell then her wide bows grew lively. The 'captain' staggered, eyes gleaming. 'Man, she's a lion,' he exulted.

'Just take her easy,' warned Donnie, 'she'll only bear so much shaking.'

He stood to one of the pumps, the girl manning the other. His large fists were greasy. Peering out through the spume, he was blinded by brightness. The sun had started to rise, the bay quickly alight, as glossy now in the dawn as their vessel was shabby. He looked ahead to the point and could see Gorme progressing, his long-boat low in the swell, fully loaded with sealers. The craft had yet to stand in, still far out from the skerries.

Donnie's gaze slewed to Aggie. She was wrenching the pump and his meagre grin found her. It was intended to cheer but she was not reassured, her responding smile fearful.

'There are a lot of them, Donnie.'

'That won't help them at sea.'

'They'll wish they never came, lassie.' The helmsman cackled his glee. 'Half of them are landlubbers.'

'But they're not leaking,' snapped Aggie. The girl glanced down at her feet. She was standing in brine, the swill submerging the slats, creeping over her sandals. 'It's rising, Donnie,' she breathed. 'I can't pump any faster.'

'It's not so bad, keep it going. We'll have to stick at it, Aggie.'

The 'captain' spat. 'Ach, that's nothing.'

'It's not *your* arms that are aching.'

'I'm navigating, wee lass, these are mischievous waters. You need a fellow who knows them.'

'Yes, all right,' Donnie grated.

'The rocks, ye ken, and the depths . . .'

'Keep your eye on them, Willie.'

The *Peg* rolled on with a growl, as if finding her spirit. They skirted east of the skerries, the sealers still not diverting, running due east to west across the gape of the inlet. 'They're going wide round the reef.' Donnie's voice had grown anxious. 'You'll have to turn her back, Willie, they've got too much of a start. They'll beach before we can catch them.'

'Turn her back?' wheezed Macrae. 'What kind of blather is that?'

'There's no way through the skerries.'

'You've no more knowledge than Gorme.' Will Macrae's scorn was gleeful. 'You've got a wee bit to learn; I'm not so simple, young fellow.' He gave the tiller a heave and the *Peg* answered slowly. Her battered prow faced the rocks, ploughing headlong towards them.

A great stone slab loomed ahead and another beside it. The swell was breaking on crags; seals were ogling from them. A creamy fountain of spray spouted up from the fastness.

'Oh, God,' screeched Aggie, 'he's mad. Take the helm from him, Donnie.'

The young man reeled to the stern but the 'captain' repelled him. 'Have you no faith? Let me be.'

'Hand over, Willie, you'll smash us.'

'You think Macrae's suicidal?'

'You've had a dram or two, Willie.'

'Bah, you've seen nothing yet. Take a peep for'ard, laddie.'

'The skerries,' Donnie proclaimed. 'Man, you're running us on them.'

'D'you see the wee tidal channel? It cuts clean through,'

cried Macrae. He gave a chuckle of triumph. 'We'll be across when Gorme gets there. We'll have him scuppered, the beggar.'

'Don't listen,' Aggie protested.

The water came to her ankles. She watched the rocks drawing nearer, craggy seal-bearing platforms. A hoary bull raised his head, peering down from his keep, and she recognized Cellach, his glazed eyes inquiring. 'God,' she moaned, staring back, mesmerized by the Abbot.

Donnie said, 'You're sure, Willie? You're sure you know the way through?'

'Unless I've wasted a lifetime.'

'We'll have the depth all the way and not be tearing her bottom?'

'You couldnae pray for it better; the tide's nigh perfect, I tell ye.'

Donnie shrugged and turned back. 'Take us through, then, but steady.' He grasped the pump and yanked fiercely, rebuffing Aggie's, 'God help us.'

'You want to save the seals, don't you?'

'I'm not so trusting as you are.'

'We've *got* to trust him,' snarled Donnie.

The girl scowled sullenly, pumping.

'Ach,' the 'captain' enjoined, 'stop your moaning and mumbling.' He pushed his cap back, eyes twinkling. 'I'd steer her blindfold,' he boasted.

Ugly rocks shut them in and the *Peg*'s rumble echoed. They were advancing in shadow, the narrow waterway gurgling, bowled in scurrying waves up ahead of the vessel. Where the light filtered through, the flow's jagged floor glinted. Walls of stone flanked the boat; her broad beams flirted with them. Macrae's expression was mean, his wild throttling capricious.

Donnie issued sharp warnings; quietly, seals hit the water. Some dived into the channel, their skulls bobbing darkly. Above them, towering to starboard, Cuchulainn held his ground, a black, barnacled eyrie. Bragela humped away, startled.

The helmsman shouted to Aggie, 'I said you'd sail with us one day. I said we'd show you the skerries.'

She held her breath, staring dumbly.

She could have touched the wet crags, plucked the weed from their sides, or the tiny crabs from them. Whelks and winkles abounded. She could have scrambled the slopes to their peaks had the boat stopped a moment, and jumped the little blue streams which criss-crossed the bleak refuge. The bay had vanished from view and the engine's thump deafened, a monstrous growl in the cleft where the *Peg*'s exhaust gathered.

Suddenly the rock shelved, a low sill of stone passing, and Aggie spotted the sealers, their faces turned to her. They dropped away in a trough, rose again, eyes still watchful. Their closeness was eerie. She could make out Gorme's thick beard, Hughie's leer, strangers glaring. And then a large crag obscured them.

'They're getting near,' she exclaimed.

'Aye,' said Donnie, 'keep pumping.'

'I told you,' gloated Macrae, 'I said we'd outwit the beggars. We're going to run out ahead, then let Gorme try to pass us.' He crouched, the weathered face fiendish. 'You watch me turn them, the beauties.' He jerked the throttle wide open. 'A mite more speed,' he delighted.

The heaving surge almost felled him. The *Peg* took off

271

with a leap, her ungainly prow tossing. Bellowing through the chasm, she scraped one side then the next, the bumps rasping and jarring. Her helmsman wobbled and bounced, muttering like a demon.

'Stop him, Donnie, he'll wreck us.'

'Aye, you fool, Willie, ease it.'

The 'captain' whooped, his legs splayed, his fists glued to the tiller.

'We're almost clear,' he rejoiced. 'Now we'll show them some action.'

They burst at speed from the rocks and pitched into wide water. It rolled and shone on each beam and the *Peg* bounded on it. The other boat came on smoothly, the sealers packed side by side, most of them sitting down so that Gorme rose above them. Men were craning, mouths opening. Their oaths were less than admiring – the *Peg* did not evoke envy.

Her battered stem ploughed and spumed, fresh scars flared on flaked paint, from her stern burnt oil billowed. Her engine drummed like a road drill. She plunged and bucked as she charged and her course was alarming.

Gorme was waving an arm. 'Pull her off,' he was shouting. 'You'll take my water, Macrae.'

'Turn yourself,' Macrae taunted.

'You imbecile, we'll collide.'

Donnie bawled, 'Go back, Gorme, you've no right to be sealing.'

'You're fired,' screamed Gorme, 'do you hear? You're fired, MacDonald, you're finished.'

'I quit already.'

Gorme fumed, 'Stop that madman Macrae; we'll end up in the water.' He swung his vessel aside and the *Peg* thundered past her. Macrae's expression was blissful.

'None too soon,' he sang hoarsely.

The other reeled in the wash. 'I'm beaching, damn you,' roared Gorme. 'You won't stop us, you cretin.' The long-boat veered back on course and her passengers muttered. Wee Hughie was swearing.

Macrae was sucking his flask, leaning hard on the tiller. There was a glint in his eye, a resolve that scared Donnie.

'Take it steady now, Willie, you cut it close enough that time.'

'And he's nae learned, so we'll teach him. He's had the warning, my friend, now we'll see what he's made of.' The *Peg* slewed round on the swell. She pointed straight at Gorme's vessel and Will Macrae gunned her.

'For God's sake, man,' Donnie rasped.

'He'll not hear reason, yon pig, you've to show him some muscle.'

They bulldozed back at the sealers. Every board was vibrating, the engine-housing was rattling, and as they pitched in the troughs wings of foam rose beside them. Donnie stared, his jaw dropping. If someone did not give way they would ram Gorme amidships.

Aggie's hands grasped the gunwale. She watched the sealers in terror. They seemed to leap at the *Peg*, flashing closer each moment. As hardened faces distorted, she saw her own horror mirrored. The charging 'wreck' sloshed and lunged, her drab bulwarks convulsing, and like a gnome at her stern the old 'captain' was prancing.

Just then, Gorme's nerve departed; he turned his boat on full rudder. 'Keep him off us, MacDonald, keep that lunatic off us.'

'I can't swim,' howled Wee Hughie.

'Quit the cove, Mr Gorme.'

'I'm leaving, damn you, MacDonald.' The bearded skipper swore loudly.

'And mind your tongue, Mr Gorme, there's a lady among us.'

The loaded craft was retreating, its human cargo still frightened. Men were urging more speed, some haranguing the skipper. Some were wanting their money, more were too sick to worry.

Macrae had let the *Peg* idle. The sun was full now and warm and he basked in it, chuckling, his tactics triumphant. Aggie hugged Donnie limply, drained by all the excitement. 'They've gone,' the young man assured her. 'You can relax and forget them.'

'I hope they never return.'

'They'll not return,' grinned the 'captain'. 'We've put the fear of God in them.'

' "We" frightened me,' confessed Aggie.

'Ach, you were safe in the *Peg* – a bit wet, that's all, lassie.'

'He could be right,' Donnie laughed. 'The boat's not leaking too much; she's not as bad as I thought. Maybe it tightened her up, knowing which fool was driving.'

Wingfoot's baby was hungry. Sucking eagerly at her, it drank from one teat a while and then tugged at the other, the first still dribbling milk, soon reclaiming attention. At times the infant's nose strayed, losing track of objectives, and the adult gave guidance. Redirected to source, the young seal resumed guzzling.

At the edge of the sea a dark guardian hovered, Finn's vigilance constant. A week or two would elapse before the cow left the calf, her maternal urge waning, and she showed interest in mating. The bull was ready to wait. Meanwhile, watchful for rivals, he prowled the waves as they broke, covetous but respectful.

Up the beach, nearer Wingfoot, the girl and Donnie had halted. The infant's tail-end was wriggling. 'The wee white lamb,' Aggie cooed, 'have you seen one so lovely? I knew Wingfoot would do it; I knew she'd bring us a fine one, as strong and greedy as she was. It's going to be a real winner.'

'Is it a boy or girl?'

'Take a peek,' Aggie challenged.

'And lose a finger? No thanks.'

She took the man's arm and laughed. 'It's all right, coward, I've looked. It's the superior sex. She'll grow up just like Wingfoot.'

The calf stopped feeding and belched, peering up at the couple. It flopped out, chin to the sand, like a satisfied puppy, its moist eyes expressive. Nothing looked more appealing, quite so cuddly, mused Aggie, although she knew it could spit, already snap if upset, and discharge mucus at them.

Wingfoot fussed her babe gently then settled to slumber.

Donnie said, 'We're not certain – I mean, that they'll be alike. You can't be sure until it moults that the calf will be silver.'

'It's got to be,' Aggie cried. 'The mite's special, it must be.'

'I wouldn't raise too much hope.'

'Let it dare disappoint me.'

A little pool bubbled quietly, making strange gurgling noises. Niamh's calf surfaced slowly, its snowy coat

275

streaming. Wingfoot's infant had stirred, grizzling for attention. It scratched its mother's sleek flank then, ignored, nibbled at her. Drowsily the cow roused and fondly cuffed the babe's head. Cow and calf nestled snugly.

Donnie strolled to the boat, leaving Aggie entranced. When at length the girl followed, he said, 'I hope they were grateful, they owe their lives to the *Peg*. She did us proud, this old tub. She's still game for a tussle.'

He looked amused, gazing seawards.

'Penny for them,' said Aggie.

'Ach, Gorme's face – did you see it?'

'I saw them all; they were green.'

'I'd not have missed it,' grinned Donnie.

The other smiled warmly. 'Nor me. You were splendid,' she murmured. She viewed the boat, looking thoughtful. 'You could still put her to rights. You'll need a livelihood now. She could still take you fishing.'

'Aye, I suppose,' he replied. 'Willie said I could have her. He wouldn't work with me, though, he's grown too fond of his leisure.'

'Is that what he calls it?'

Donnie said, 'I've been thinking,' and stuffed his hands in his pockets.

'You've got plans?'

He said, 'Sort of.'

'Well, come on, are they secret?'

He shuffled, looking embarrassed. At last he said, 'Jimmy Harris – he had the right idea, Jimmy.'

Aggie frowned. 'Mary's fellow.'

'He soon rumbled her, Aggie. He wasn't trapped like poor Calum. Jimmy's off round the world, joined the Mercantile Service. Last thing I heard, he'd made Cape

Town, full of it, they reckon. Thought I might try the service.'

'Join a ship?'

'Yes, why not?'

'Oh,' said Aggie, upset. She felt unreasonably hurt, as if she had a claim to him. She watched a seagull descend, its acerbic cry piercing.

'You've got the college,' said Donnie, 'all the bright ones are leaving. I've been thinking about it: you've got to travel for knowledge. I could get on, win promotion; I'd earn and save while I learned. I shan't get anywhere, staying.'

'I see,' she said.

'Don't you think so?' He searched her face for approval.

'Perhaps,' she said with an effort. It was, she knew, the right thing. She knew her feelings were selfish; she had no right to feel injured. 'I'm sure you'd do very well. It's just, I thought . . .'

'Mind, I'd miss you.'

'Would you, Donnie? How much?'

'A lot,' he said, drawing closer.

'Yes,' she said, 'I'd miss you.' Not only on her vacations, perhaps the whole time, she anguished, since she had found the true Donnie. The irony was not kind – a man of bold new decisions. 'You'll have to make your own mind up.'

'I have,' he said.

'Then that's that.'

'You know I'm fond of you, Aggie.' He kissed her slowly and gravely, then stopped, his eyes troubled. 'I'm awful fond of you, Aggie, but I've my doubts I deserve you. You need a canny high-flier. One day, maybe, I'll be that, when I've rank to pull on you. If you're not hitched . . .'

'Hitched?' She gave a wry smile. 'I've no plans. Hold me, Donnie.'

The steamer stood at the pier, the usual small crowd beside it: three or four hardy tourists, a few mainland-bound locals, a farmer shipping some boxes, the ferry's captain and crew gossiping by a bollard.

Donnie wore his blue suit. It was, thought Aggie, too small, so he looked like a bruiser. His single suitcase was sad, packed with all he possessed save his rods and sea tackle, these lent to a neighbour.

Mrs Fraser had said, when she had wished him good-bye, that he should keep himself warm and not stint on his eating. 'Lord,' she told Mr Muir, who had come in on the steamer, 'the poor bairn's got nothing.'

'He's got his youth,' laughed the traveller, and when they looked from the shop Donnie and Aggie were kiss-ing, oblivious on the quay of the people about them. 'Would you not swap with them, Peg, be in their shoes for a moment?'

'That I would not,' huffed the woman, attending briskly to business.

'Ah, well,' exclaimed Mr Muir, the colour in her cheeks noted.

There was a stir on the pier as passengers began board-ing and spreading out by the rails to call back as they waited. The captain, now on the bridge, leaned over, casually chatting. Donnie picked up his case; it might have had nothing in it. 'I'd best be moving,' he muttered.

'Yes, take care then,' said Aggie. She held his sleeve for a moment. 'It'll be lonely till term starts.' She did not wish to stop talking. 'The seals are leaving,' she breathed, 'I didn't tell you that, Donnie. The nursery's getting empty. Wingfoot's gone, and Niamh; I haven't seen Cellach lately.'

'You'll have the calves for a while.'

'And Willie,' Aggie pronounced, trying hard to sound cheerful.

'Tell the man to behave.'

'I'll tell him, Donnie,' she blurted. He eased away and she added, 'I'll think of you,' her voice husky. 'Will you think of me sometimes?'

'Even better,' he promised, 'I'll write you when I get settled.'

'I bet,' she answered him, tearful.

'I can,' he jollied her, grinning. 'I'm not a bad one at letters.'

'All right then, post them in port, batches of them together from all those faraway places. Don't forget, I'll expect them. And, Donnie – mind yourself, Donnie. We'll both be home again one day.'

'Aye,' he said, 'like the seals.'

He paused then swung up the gangway as confidently, thought Aggie, as if the ship was his own, as if already an admiral.

'Wave to me from the bay, before you reach the point, Donnie.'

She watched him go, her eyes misty, and as the steamer stood out, raced her bike up the coast, her hair blowing, legs straining. The breeze was sharp on her face as the harbour receded.

It was turning autumnal. Most of the wild flowers had died and small birds fluttered quietly, no longer in song. On the strands, waders dozed, heads drawn in, their backs mousey. Only dunlin were feeding and some of those paused to rest, tucking legs in pale bellies. She saw no seals on the rocks, glimpsed no heads in the water.

Turning down to the cove, she flew swiftly, free-wheeling. She could still make out the vessel, the bay her last chance to view it, and near the *mul* she braked hard, dropped the bike and ran forward. She heard Macrae call her name.

'Has he gone?' the man shouted.

She ran ahead.

'Has he left?'

Dumbly, Aggie sped faster. At the end of the stones she kicked her shoes from her feet, pattering on the wet sand, spattering through the rills to the edge of the tide where her toes met the ripples. Wading two or three steps, she stood breathless, arms waving. A tiny figure waved back, then the headland obscured it.

She stared a while, her eyes stinging, then turned in the water.

The calf was gazing up at her, its round face inquiring. The great dark orbs were intense, the young body a barrel. Where a new coat was growing, the short hair was silver.

AUTHOR'S NOTE

There are many seal islands but the Seal Island of these pages does not, to my knowledge, exist on any chart. Perhaps, in certain conditions, it can be glimpsed in the sea mist – I do not know.

The 'sea people' themselves are less elusive.

Of an estimated world population of fifty thousand grey seals, the largest concentration, about thirty thousand exists round Scotland and its islands, with upwards of another ten thousand round England, Wales and Ireland.

The animals can also be found in Iceland, Norway, North America (in the Newfoundland area) and in the Baltic. Readers familiar with grey seals in America and the Baltic region will know that the breeding there takes place in late winter and early spring rather than autumn, and that the seals involved form smaller groups than those of the Eastern Atlantic.

They vary, too, in that the bulls and cows of the Western Atlantic and the Baltic are more equal in numbers than are the sexes in the Eastern Atlantic, where the cows outnumber the bulls by at least five to one.

In 1914, due to fears of their impending extinction,

Britain's grey seals were protected by an Act of Parliament prohibiting killing during the breeding period. This 'close season' was extended in 1932 to cover the four months from 1 September to 31 December. Since then the animals have flourished in their British haunts.

While a good deal remains to be learnt about seal behaviour, especially in its pelagic or sea-going aspects, I have tried to depict the lives and adventures of Wingfoot and her companions without taking too many fanciful liberties. To the extent that I have succeeded, I am indebted to the accounts of many enthusiastic seal-watchers and to the existing works of reference.

For engrossing as well as scholarly expositions of the natural history of the grey seal, interested readers should seek in particular the works of H. R. Hewer, Grace Hickling and R. M. Lockley. For wider reference, William B. Scheffer's book on seals, sea lions and walruses is invaluable.

Along with the rest, these authorities have my gratitude for a wealth of fact and my apologies for the failings of a simple story.

A. R. Lloyd
Kent
1991